Praise for

"In her debut novel, George brings forward the home-educated Cornish daughter of a prominent Land's End mining family. Elizabeth C.T. Carne emerges as an unforgettable and challenging character in 19th century social history. How surprising that most of the main issues of her time still ring true, presenting us with the path from Mary Wollstonecraft to roles for the 'new woman.' An excellent and inspiring read!"

**- Melissa Hardie, Director, The Hypathia Trust and
  Women in Words**

"We welcome this book which throws a new and extremely well researched, though fictionalised, light on the life of Elizabeth Carne, who was an important civic and social scientist in the Victorian life of Penzance. As a mineralogist, she was the first woman to be elected to the Royal Geological Society of Cornwall and to present learned papers, as told in this intriguing novel."

**- Loveday Jenkin, V.P., The Royal Geological Society
  of Cornwall**

The Light Among Us

The Story of Elizabeth Carne, Cornwall

Jill George

With John Dirring

atmosphere press

When I was small, I would "time travel," using my bedroom closet as a time machine. It took me back to life in colonial Williamsburg and Boston, as well as Victorian London, because I was fascinated by how they lived, what they did, and how they spoke. My imagination made it seem as real as it could be. Now, in the midst of a pandemic, I do not have to use my imagination, as I feel I am *actually* living for real amid the crises of those worlds, as we experience first-hand what must have also been their struggles, suffering, terror, and loss. I feel the ambiguity I know they must have felt. I admire our predecessors' courage and grit even more as a result.

> *Suffering becomes beautiful when anyone*
> *bears great calamities with cheerfulness not*
> *through insensibility but through greatness*
> *of mind.*
>
> *- Aristotle*

To my brilliant father, James Richard George, who was one of those who recently struggled, suffered, and is now free.

Table of Contents

Preface ·· iii

Part One: Becoming (1832-1838)

Chapter One: Discovery ······································· 5

Chapter Two: Mockery ·· 21

Chapter Three: Remedy ······································· 37

Chapter Four: Treachery ······································ 44

Chapter Five: Country ··· 70

Chapter Six: Poverty ··· 82

Chapter Seven: Empathy ····································· 91

Chapter Eight: Journey ······································· 110

Chapter Nine: Promissory ··································· 119

Chapter Ten: Integrity ·· 133

Part 2: Being (1858–1873)

Chapter Eleven: The Youngest Successor··················· 157

Chapter Twelve: Modernist ······························· 173

Chapter Thirteen: Geologist & Preservationist ········· 179

Chapter Fourteen: Capitalist ···························· 201

Chapter Fifteen: Philanthropist and
Political Scientist···219

Chapter Sixteen: Bravest···································239

Chapter Seventeen: Futurist ······························247

Epilogue ··263

Character List and Chapter Notes ·························269

Reading Guide ···291

Elizabeth Catherine Thomas Carne

Preface

We must look back in time to see how far we have come, and how much further we need to go. Looking back to inspiring people gives us a sense of our common historic grit and determination, things we need to move forward and cope with the challenges of tomorrow.

Looking back, we have only one known image of a subject of true inspiration: Elizabeth Carne, who first grew her family, then her region, her nation, and the world. Without that one photo, this brilliant, "modern day Hypatia (i.e., a prominent Greek think-er who taught philosophy and science)" might have vanished from earth completely, her inspiring works and messages forgotten. Elizabeth Catherine Thomas Carne (1817–1873) was a published geologist, ecologist, first thinker industrial psychologist, mathematician, industrialist, philanthropist, poet, artist, and friend to many luminary thinkers. Yet, we know very little about her. Why? Because she was a modest woman, overshadowed by the males of her own family and even her literary friends, who were also scientists and authors.

Comparatively little has been written about Elizabeth and it is my privilege to be the author of this, the first novel about her. The few pieces that have been written mention more details of her family and friends than they mention of her. The most prominent observation is of her having inherited her father's mineral collection. It seems unfair to remember such an incredible person only as the recipient of an assemblage of rocks. In fact, she was one of the two very successful women bankers in Cornwall in her time. She increased her personal wealth by sixty per cent as the senior partner in the family's bank, which no other woman banker did in Cornwall. We would acknowledge that level of growth as incredible today. Between 1752 and 1906, there were over seventy women partners in the private, family-run banks of the United Kingdom. Of all these, Elizabeth was one of the twenty who ran their banks successfully for fifteen years or more. Even so, she is hardly known.

A famous Black American author, Walter Mosley, once said, "If your people don't appear in literature, then they don't exist in history." That seems to be the case for Elizabeth Carne. Besides running a bank, which in later years would have several branches, she built schools where there were none, preserved ancient stone circles, created museum quality sketches, and wrote and published books, articles and pamphlets that still resonate with the diversity issues of today, which were, in my opinion, her greatest accomplishments.

Gifted and modest, this woman achieved what very few women did during her lifetime. My aim is to include Elizabeth as one of "my people" and write this tribute to her, an extraordinary individual who paved the way for other women and the less fortunate around the world. If she could use her voice in 1868, when it was unheard of and very socially discouraged for women to even write books, perhaps we can use some of her wisdom about inclusion in this day and age. It takes all of us.

So, how did Elizabeth become this brilliant person, living in Cornwall nearly at Land's End? How did she become so insightful about diversity and inclusion? We do not know. All we have of her are scraps of history, culture, family, friends, and geography. We know much of her grandfather William's accomplishments. We know even more about her father Joseph and his path to fame. But what path did Elizabeth have, being a woman, from a small, remote fishing town and port? In this tribute, we piece together these scraps of information.

Using an analytic method linking scraps of fact, dates, towns, and people, we expand upon what little we know using reasonable possibilities contained in the meagre evidence. For example, do we know for a fact that Elizabeth was at her grandfather's funeral? No, we do not. Is it probable that she was there? Yes. We offer you a work of historical fiction that is a construction of genuine Cornish history and people, their roles, geography, family, friends, and religion, to tell the story of how Elizabeth Carne most likely became one of the most influential women of her time in England, perhaps the world.

All the locations in this novel are real, existing locations that Elizabeth did visit or inhabit or very likely visited. The context of the rise and fall of the mining industry is legendary and spelled out with historical accuracy here, as is the rise of private family banking in Cornwall. To find out more about the characters and places in the book, please refer to the List of Characters and More Information in the back of the book, which will tell you who was a real person and who is fiction. But be careful, it contains spoilers!

I write this novel because I am afraid the historic scraps we have about her and her foresight on diversity will be blown away by the winds of time, and she will be forgotten completely. To me, to forget this outstanding woman would be like demolishing a masterpiece painting or a world heritage site. So, we give you a story where most of the characters existed and some I invented, to represent what Elizabeth learned and how she learned it so that we may all benefit from her wisdom and foresight.

You will notice that all the chapter titles rhyme and describe her. By doing so, I hoped to acknowledge Elizabeth's keen ability as a poet in a small way and you will see a little poetry appear in the novel as well.

As I wrote this book, I had a constant image of the standing stones, which were so important to her (she inherited and continued to preserve the land at Boscawen Un, upon which a stone circle still stands). In my mind, the characters in the book represent a stone circle around Elizabeth, as if they too are standing stones, where each stone is a person, real or fictitious, while she occupies the centre, the earth that grounds and joins her friends and family together. I hope that by reading this tribute to Elizabeth, the youngest, but perhaps the mightiest Carne, you will be able to add her as an immovable pillar of strength to those you would call upon in times of need.

In honour of Elizabeth Carne, a portion of the proceeds of the sale of this novel will be donated to children's educational needs in Penzance and surrounding areas.

Part One

Becoming

(1832-1838)

Chapter One

Discovery

October 1832

I stood nervously in the doorway of our large stone home on lower Chapel Street as our house loomed over me. I waited for Father to explain the sweeping landscape and seascape before us to our esteemed visitor, Mr John Mill, and I felt even smaller than usual in comparison to it all. The seagulls, so familiar and commonplace in Penzance, screeched to each other overhead in the early morning light. *Why do I have this bothersome lump in my throat?* I asked myself, ignoring the raucous seagulls and looking off towards the harbour. Despite my efforts to swallow hard, the pressure in my throat persisted. *I have met with many of Father's dignified acquaintances before when they have come to Penzance, so no need to be timid,* I told myself, as I tried to wait patiently, but to no avail, as I could not quell my fears. *But this time, I am to be the one to do the talking, with Mr Mill no less, on behalf of all of Cornwall!* I thought, anxiously.

If she were here, my mother would say to me something about the influences of women on the world from the scriptures, such as, "Remember, it was a woman who delivered righteous Mordecai and saved a whole people from their utter desolation." She would also say, "You are my youngest of eight but also my bravest," *If only you were here now, Mother, and not buried in the family vault in Phillack. You would be here in person, and I could soak up your strength. But now, I must summon it for myself.* I sighed, my stomach clenching.

Shifting my weight from one foot to the next, holding my writing box, ready to start our journey, I tried to remain as calm on the inside as I appeared on the outside. I tried to see things through Mr Mill's eyes. *What would he, one of the most educated, brilliant people I am likely to ever encounter, think of all this?* I thought as I looked around me. All the houses around us, ours included, are over one hundred years old, and mostly built from large, heavy, dressed granite stones with tile or slate roofs. Some, like our home, overlooked the harbour below with their gables facing the street, while others were aligned with the contours of the hillside. The tower of St Mary's, the Anglican church directly across the street from our front door, was a prominent landmark for mariners as well as townspeople. In fact, everywhere one looked, one saw greyish brown stone. Except for the painted windows and doors, everything was stone, with an occasional spray of flowers. *I wonder if what he sees will make Mr Mill think of us as a sombre-looking stone village, or whether he will see a bustling, sprawling castle-like town, covering a broad steeply sloping hill by the seaside. I hope he will come to see Penzance as the latter, as I do, after his visit with us.*

After a few more minutes of waiting, Father led us brusquely off on our morning's walk to St Michael's Mount with our distinguished guest. *Father is my guide and my true anchor,* I said to myself as we trekked down the hill. *Whatever happens with Mr Mill today, Father will not let me run aground or make a fool of myself, or him,* I thought, more reassuringly.

"Mr Mill, you have met my daughter, Elizabeth," Father said, hand outstretched in my direction as we walked. "She will accompany us today and be proof of one of your premises about society." Father had one hand on my shoulder as we walked down the steep lane towards the harbour.

"Oh, and which premise would that be?" Mr Mill asked, with one eyebrow raised.

Oh, please be an open-minded man who actually lives and believes in what he writes. I inwardly begged.

"She will prove today that education for women will improve civilisation," Father confidently said with a smooth tone in his voice, arms swinging lightly at his sides, holding his walking stick with a firm grip.

It is not like Father to exaggerate, but I fear he has over-stepped himself this time, I thought with dread. I raised my chin with difficulty as my eyes felt as heavy as the boulders around us, wanting to stare at the ground rather than at my companions.

"Well, I shall look forward to that most certainly!" He responded eagerly, looking at me as if I could pull something magical out from behind my back.

Knowing that I had to establish myself in the ongoing conversation, I jumped in. "It is said that Cornwall is a land of uncommon discovery, valuable treasure, and daring legends."

Mr Mill smiled and nodded eagerly. "I do hope you will show me all of that and more!"

I looked at our esteemed guest appreciatively and wondered to myself, *Will Mr Mill – Mr John Stuart Mill, no less – an author from London, who is becoming better known and whom, perhaps, thousands of people around the world will come to read – really find us to be uncommon discoveries and as exciting as a daring legend? Will he find anything I have to say, on behalf of Cornwall, of any value?* Being a widely studied man, he was obviously used to conversing with prominent thinkers of the day: industrialists, philosophers like himself, and those interested in science. I had begun to read some of his work, and I was keen on his thoughts on women's education.

While the two men talked, I thought about the significance of this meeting. *He has come three hundred miles, arriving by mail coach, visiting us to discuss his positions in philosophy and religion, as part of what he calls "a walking tour" today, the outcomes of which he will likely publish. No, this is no ordinary walk or tour. This is a meeting of titans in their fields; two famous men of science who are among the foremost thinkers of our time. What might look like a scenic walk to others could turn out to be a discussion of a revolutionary new theory in geology, biology, or philosophy. Casual discussions of politics could have untoward effects that could indirectly advance, diminish or even end a politician's career. And I would be part of the conversation! Me, a fifteen-year-old girl conversing with the luminaries of our time! I would have to draw carefully from my education on many different subjects as Father recommended in preparation for Mr Mill's visit. I am excited for the opportunity, but my heart is racing, and I feel my voice trying to waver with nervousness as if it has a mind of its own.*

At any rate, I aim to delight Mr Mill by pointing out our fascinating geological and historical treasures along the way, I said to myself as we walked down steep, sloping Abbey Street to the harbour. The two men discussed recent meetings and their outcomes in Parliament while we walked. I glanced at my father, with his thinning hair, hooded eyes, clean-shaven face, and full bottom lip, who wore his typical stern facial expression. Politics always interested him even though his face did not seem to show it.

The sunshine had made it look like a perfect day for walking. *But will the weather hold?* I asked myself, looking out to sea with the dark, solid-looking clouds looming on the horizon, which threatened to curtail our walk to St Michael's Mount, an island nearly three miles away around the curve of Mount's Bay from Penzance, which we would reach by walking along the long pebbled and sandy beach. *Thick clouds are no matter for Father and me. I hope Mr Mill agrees,* I thought anxiously.

As we went down the several flights of stairs to reach the waterfront, we could see that a few small boats were moored in the shallow water, close inshore. Larger vessels were moored along the old pier, towards the white lighthouse at its outer end. Many fishermen had gone to sea earlier in the morning, their berths empty. The sea air was heavy with the odor of seaweed and fish and smelled the way oysters smoked over a fire taste. We passed small brown stone houses at the edge of the harbour where many of the fishermen lived, and the chandlers who sold nets, lines, baskets, and other maritime necessities lined the street. A few older women also sold fish here.

"I understand that Cornwall is well to the fore in mining, as copper production has been growing significantly for the last thirty years," Mr Mill said to my father, agilely sidestepping a muddy puddle with his long legs.

"Yes, copper, tin and shipping have all been expanding," Father replied as we walked.

Being a banker and an industrialist like my grandfather, who had joined in the partnership which established the Penzance Bank, Father knows more about local business and commerce than just about anyone else here, I commented to myself. Gulls called to each other overhead, their clamour a constant sound, especially here at the harbor where fish scraps are a ready supply of food.

"That must be why the area is so plentiful with industrialists and philosophers who are so interested in scientific matters. I believe there is much to learn from discussing my hypotheses with you and others here, so that I may extend my theories," Mr Mill offered, turning to my father, whose eyes seemed fixed on our destination.

Mr Mill was lanky and sinewy, twenty-six years old, and seemingly in strong physical health, so it occurred to me that his regular walking tours all over the country suited his natural abilities. He had a very large head with protruding eye sockets and cheekbones. His long mutton chop side whiskers that looked like sheep tails curled amply around both sides of his face. His hair was thick and wavy, and it also protruded from the sides of his head. His bony features conveyed determination to me. He was poised, confident, and stood erect as he walked. *Charming, even*, I thought.

My father walked on vigorously without comment, so Mr Mill continued:

"Not having much to go on, I expected Penzance to be rural and unsophisticated. I knew about vast rocky cliffs and spectacular views of the English Channel on this side of the Penwith peninsula and the Atlantic Ocean on the other side, of course. I will admit that I relish the stories of the frequent shipwrecks, and secretly hope to see one while I am here." We all laughed at this. "About how many people live in the Penzance area, would you say, and what are their occupations?"

"At most I would say we have fewer than three thousand inhabitants. Most are farmers harvesting their produce from the soil, fishermen harvesting the sea, and miners harvesting rock underground – people who work the earth and rock," Father said, tapping his wooden walking stick on the ground. "You could say they are unsophisticated, but you can find no better miners or fishermen, for that matter, in the world," Father responded with genteel pride. He did not care for outsiders who often demeaned the hard-working people of Penwith, and I also held that opinion, as he had taught me for years. My father was a taciturn, opinionated man, but he was generous and kind, and I hoped Mr Mill understood his comments in relation to how proud we both are of our homeland and the people here.

Mr Mill continued, full of questions, and I liked that. I had many questions too but knew I should wait to ask when Father prompted me to do so because polite women were quiet in public.

"How did the town of Penzance originate?" he asked, loping along beside Father as we walked onwards to the Mount.

Father gave me a look that said I should answer the question.

"In March of 1512, Henry VIII gave the town the right to collect harbour dues from ships for the benefit of the town and, thus, our small harbour became as large as or larger than others nearby, such as Newlyn or Mousehole," I said, hoping not to sound like I was simply reading from a book.

"I see. And I have heard that Cornishmen are all one – that they are all one in sentiment and tradition, in customs, and dislike of outsiders, even of other people in Britain. Do you find that true?" he asked. His eyebrows were knitted together in concentration as he looked directly at Father.

"Yes, for the most part. Many folks here are nonconformists who follow the Wesleyan Methodist religion, which binds us in integrity and Christian values," Father said as we reached the flat beach path that would take us around the bay. The geography of the region also contributes to our unified culture, is that not true, Bess?" he asked me, looking straight ahead, unexpectedly.

"Yes," I said. I knew that the proper way to answer my father was to add insight to my comments as he had taught me so that I would not sound as if I was simply reading from a book. "Since Penwith, which is a peninsula, is connected to the rest of the country on only one small side, the land and rocky cliffs tend to isolate us, causing us to draw to each other more. One can think of Penwith as the hand and the fingers as our headlands, all connected at the wrist to the rest of the body, or the rest of the country," I said, with a clear voice, looking him in the eye to show confidence and demonstrating the wrist and hand analogy in my response as we continued walking. I added, "In addition, the dramatic cliffs, beautiful ocean, and sea vistas and panoramas, as well as the bounty they afford, create a deep sense of pride in our land, a point upon which we can all agree, and which binds us in shared opinions and values across many generations."

"Well said," commented Mr Mill, with a nod.

Father also gave a slight nod of approval, in his stiff way.

Mr Mill, of course, knew that our family had been in Penwith for generations. My father, Joseph Carne, followed our forefathers, who had been adventurers, pursers, agents and experts in everything mining in Penwith for a very long time. He was now a partner in the first bank in Penzance which had been started by my grandfather, William Carne, with Mr Batten and Mr Oxnam; and he also owned much of the surrounding land.

Father is a valuable guide for Mr Mill because he is not only accredited and well written in geology, but he has also been influential in wider philosophic thinking and in the practice and observance of Christian principles. He is a leader in our Methodist Chapel as well as the treasurer of the Royal Geological Society of Cornwall, the second oldest of its kind in the country. This must be why Mr Mill chose Father for his walking tour, I thought to myself, stepping over a dung pile near the path. *Father, however, can also be a brutally driven, competitive, and hard charging man. It will be interesting to see if that side of Father comes out on our walk today. I doubt if it will, since Mr Mill is not in competition with my father for anything,* I mused.

"Mr Carne, I am interested in your thoughts about my theories linking human behaviour and spirit to Christianity, the perils of the subjection of women, and my political vision based on more liberal principles," Mr Mill said, just as we reached the small crest and the beach path at the shoreline, where the sea in all its magnificent dark rolling glory awaited us. From here, with the sea directly in front of us, and our backs to Penzance, the entire expanse of Mount's Bay spread as far as we could see, from Penlee Point on our right in the west to the Mount itself on our left in the east, with Cudden Point in the hazy distance beyond. The Mount, an island with a lovely stone castle and matching tower of its chapel perched on top, was now about two miles away in the distance.

Before Father could reply, Mr Mills gasped, his hands on his hips, the wind whisking away his words as soon as he spoke and his long whiskers bobbing.

"I see I was not wrong in venturing to Penzance!" he exclaimed, his face full of joyous discovery. "The sandy beaches and the views of the bay are staggeringly beautiful and on a scale that is difficult to describe! It is a splendid view!" he proclaimed, looking out over the crescent-shaped Mount Bay, nodding his head. We all stared out to sea, taking in its magnitude.

I thought to myself, *The sheer size of the sea always staggers me. Standing before the open sea like this is humbling. I wonder if it also humbles these powerful and influential men. Or maybe it emboldens them in some way. Perhaps I will ask Father later.*

"It is truly vast, both in size and in the dangers of the unknown," Father commented darkly, his face expressionless. The sea had been flat and calm earlier, but the swell was now beginning to rise with the strengthening wind. We continued walking along the beach path, and Father pointed to St Michael's Mount, slowly becoming closer and now straight ahead of us.

"That is the Mount ahead. We will use the causeway to walk from the beach to the cottages below the castle and then walk up the hill on the island to the castle itself," Father said, plainly.

Father was mainly interested in discussing politics, Methodism, and geology, and was amiable enough with Mr Mill, although he could be very sullen at times. Father was not known to be a friendly sort. He had a shrewd eye and tongue and was a keen observer. I knew he certainly had wisdom to impart, and with Mr Mill as our distinguished guest, I knew Father would be more conversant today with Mr Mill than he usually would be with someone else.

"One of my interests is erosion of granite, which originated in the Earth's crust. This red and black colouring is an example of the results of weathering and something that we study." He pointed to an example of this under the Mount, and Mr Mill seemed to take note.

We followed the sandy and pebbled path down to the water's edge, backed with sheltering sand dunes. Our boots made a crunching sound on the sand and stones. We walked the two miles in pleasant and pithy conversation. We came upon the flat, large stone-paved causeway leading across to St Michael's Mount, which is only passable at low tide. Otherwise, it is only reachable by boat. Mr Mill was careful not to step in any of the water that was still lapping over the sides of the causeway as the tide was ebbing. I concluded that he did not want to have to continue the tour with wet feet. Father and I both had on our thick walking boots. We often walked calf-deep in the water and sand, not caring if we became wet or sandy.

"The granite setts laid to make the causeway, Mr Mill," I explained, waving my hand down to the large, flat stones at our feet, "are only passable between mid and low tide. The castle and chapel on the Mount have been the home of the St Aubyn family since 1650." I continued with a complete historical description of the Mount dating back to the twelfth century, and then I described the layered granite foundation upon which the Mount was formed as we walked across. Several cottages dotted the bottom of the rocky island, with green grass surrounding them. It was as if we had travelled back in time to the seventeenth century, gazing at the history before us.

"Your detailed knowledge is uncanny, and your discourse equal to any of my male colleagues," Mr Mill said with quiet intensity and piercing eyes. "It is a shame that there are very few opportunities for women to attend college in this country, or anywhere else, do you not agree?" He directed his question to Father. Father simply nodded.

"The rock exposures at St Michael's Mount, Mr Mill," I continued, "allow us to see many features of Cornwall's geology in a single location. The Mount itself is made of the uppermost part of a granite intrusion into metamorphosed Devonian mudstones. The granite is mineralized with a well-developed and sheeted vein system." Pointing, I said, "As you can see there, the Mount has two types of granite visible. Most of the Mount is tourmaline-muscovite granite which is poly-phyritic. By that, I mean that it has crystals of varying sizes. The other type of granite is biotitic muscovite graphite sepa-rated by pegmatites, all igneous rocks found in the veins, as you can see. Next, we will make the climb up to visit the chapel on the Mount if you like," I continued without hesitation. "Please have a care with this rocky path. It can be slippery and unsteady."

My demeanour was sturdy and unwavering. I did not expect any amount of thanks or encouragement for my minia-ture tutorial on the geology and history of the Mount. I tried to make sure my tone was confident but not overbearing, and that I appeared to be a calm, reflective person with a steadfast demeanour but very pleasant at the same time. I wanted to show Mr Mill that I was not intimidated by him and that, in fact, I was used to discourse with my father's distinguished friends.

After some time spent touring the chapel and its welcoming chambers, we descended the loose rocky hill back down to the causeway and crossed it just before it began to be covered again by the incoming tide. We stopped to take in a last review of both the cliffs behind us and the Mount, with its profound beauty. I climbed a nearby small rock that was almost a miniature version of the Mount and sat down on a dry slab of granite a short distance away from the men. I took a small paper tablet and a piece of charcoal out of the slim writing box I carried and started sketching the scene before us. The wind threatened to blow my paper away, so I held it down with two small round white stones, which were plentiful here on the beach, as I sketched in my lap. I was pleased that none of my thick dark-brown hair, which was parted neatly down the middle and pulled back tightly, escaped from my black bonnet in the persistent wind. The wind made my eyes water, but I blinked the tears away to continue my work, mindful of the still-rising tide. *I think that I have done well so far,* I said to myself, taking in what seemed like my first full breath in several hours. *No need for any silly nervousness. I am fully prepared and can answer any questions Mr Mill may have,* I told myself confidently.

I was dressed in a modestly made, plain black frock with a brown knitted shawl and wore no jewellery. *I imagine Mr Mill thinks me plain looking, but my mother told me I had beautiful large blue eyes in a lovely, creamy-looking face.* Father and I were both modestly dressed in mourning clothes in remembrance of my brother's still-recent death the previous year. I glanced at Mr Mill, his feet moving away from the lapping waves that dared approach his fine leather shoes and his black tailored trouser hems. Father and I were perfectly at ease on the beach, not only getting our boots wet and sandy but our hems and hands dirty as well. *We truly are naturalists, he and*

I, perfectly at home out of doors and in the elements. We get along well and are happy to spend a lot of useful time together. I understand Father's disposition and interests, and he understands mine. I know how and when to engage him, I thought happily to myself as they discussed politics.

Mr Mill spoke loudly to Father so that he could be heard over the wind. "Your daughter is very knowledgeable in geology, sir," he said, eyebrows arched, looking a bit surprised.

"Yes, she has studied with me over the years, assisting me in writing my papers and has helped me identify and assemble over eight thousand minerals in our collection from the area so far. In fact, this week we were able to procure a fine specimen of orange calcite crystal on iron-stained quartz from a mine in St Agnes. Bess is equally conversant in mathematics and has learned two additional languages as well," he said, matter of factly.

"Impressive. And how has she attained this education?" Mr Mill asked. He bent down and picked up several round pieces of trap rock, tossing them in the air and catching them.

"At home, in her study, with her mother and I, as well as tutors, of course," Father replied rather curtly.

Hearing this, I thought to myself, *Careful, Mr Mill. Do not tread on Father's toes!*

"I see. It is similar to my own educational experience. And, has her gender hindered the pursuit of an education?" Mr Mill asked, curiously. "The reason I ask is that one of my areas of study is the subjugation of women and their underutilization in society, as you know. I hypothesize that educated women will lead to increases in the education of future generations, leading in turn to a growing and superior society."

I glanced over from under my eyelashes, as I was very interested in this part of the conversation but did not want to appear to be listening. Father studied Mr Mill.

"Yes, she is only fifteen, but as you can see, she is already making a superior impact on society, thus proving your point as I suggested earlier this morning," Father replied, his posture stiff and upright.

"Oh yes, I do see that," he replied quickly.

"To my way of thinking, Elizabeth is my most intelligent child, and I mean for her to continue her education to the highest level. My other children do not seem to share my interests the way Elizabeth does. I have it in mind that she will take over my work as I grow older." Father coughed, almost convulsively, struggling to regain his breath. He had come down with a lung ailment, which was now evident from the cough's intensity. Mr Mill looked away, I noticed, out of politeness to his host.

"By your work, you mean your mineral collection, I assume?" He held his hand over his eyes to shade them from the glaring sun that still shone between the bands of heavy grey clouds. Seagulls screeched loudly and swooped down at us, hoping for food. The waves in the background were in constant motion, their thick foamy fringes creeping ever further up the beach.

"Yes, and I also plan for her to take a position in my bank. Now, I think it's time for us to get back to the house as we have more to look at nearby in Madron after lunch," Father said, rather abruptly.

Surely, I have not heard Father correctly, I thought, startled. I was shocked by his announcement of some type of bank position. *Surely not! Women do not hold positions in banks. Women are silent in public places. Women are, at most, governesses or perhaps a teacher. What was he talking about?* His words frightened me, but I tried not to panic. I felt my arms shaking. I grasped my hands together in front of me to steady myself. My confidence was rapidly evaporating.

"That trap rock you hold, Mr Mill, is equally as hard as granite and has a hornblende, a mineral, composition – that is brown mixed with black, if you look closely," I offered, hoping he would be interested.

"They resemble lumps of coal, lining the boundary of the earth and sea," Mr Mill replied. He gave me a slight smile as we turned to trudge up the sandy beach towards the path. Father waved me over and indicated that we were to walk back to the house. I nodded obediently. I knew when to challenge him and when to abide by his requests. I turned as we walked and gently handed Mr Mill the piece of paper I had been working on. It was a detailed charcoal drawing of St Michael's Mount, complete with the castle, granite, and gulls. I covered it with a slip of rice paper so that the drawing would not smear.

"A keepsake from our walk today, sir," I said, smiling up at him. He nodded faintly in return and slid the drawing into the breast pocket of his jacket.

As Father and I strode back up the beach to the path, Mr Mill trailed after and asked Father, "I would like to correspond with you and your daughter in the future, as part of my work, to discuss philosophy, as well as other topics. Would that be acceptable to you, sir?"

"Yes, quite. I think she will be quite challenging for you, professionally," he replied with a tight-lipped, wry smile. We walked back along the long sandy path by the seashore, and later on past the harbour to our grey stone and red brick family home, with its wide stone quoins and great ornamental chimney pots that had seemed to reach the clouds. The house was situated at the bottom of the hill leading up to the market area of Penzance, occupying a prime and rare flat plot, and it seemed like a cat that had found the perfect place to curl up in the middle of a shelf full of houses that resembled curio items. I walked stride by stride with Father despite my heavy wet hem, my bonnet ribbons flapping in the wind.

I did not dare to ask Father what he meant by a position at

the bank at this moment, but I was glad to get a brief moment with him to discuss something that had been on my mind.

I asked, "Father, what do you think about the rising business of selling arsenic as a byproduct of copper for commercial use? To me the risks are unsavoury. Do you think the risks outweigh the reward?"

"She's even more remarkable than her father," I heard Mr Mill mutter under his breath behind us as we walked along the path flanked by grass and randomly strewn stones. He raised his voice slightly to be heard above the wind. "A future woman geologist and banker? Completely unheard of! You have a rare treasure indeed, sir."

Father and Mr Mill both looked quite pleased as we entered our house, and Mr Mill a little more than surprised. *He seemed to be altogether astonished by us, the locals of this remote and rocky fishing and mining town. It appears that I have achieved my goal for the day and have made Father proud as well, despite being the youngest Carne. But me, a banker? A geologist? He has never mentioned any of this before. What could Father have meant by that*? I wondered, troubled, as the two men walked through our entryway, adorned overhead with elegant glass panes that resembled the sun and its rays during sunrise, and into the parlour.

Father walked towards the parlour door and turned to me, and said, "Bess, you are dismissed."

I gave a slight nod.

"You did well today. Thank you," he added, with a small, quick smile, as if an afterthought.

"The pleasure was mine. Thank you, Father." I gave a slight smile in return.

Dismissed, I was allowed to seek the solace of my studies, so I gladly mounted the main stairway that led directly to the women's small study on the second floor as well as my bedroom. The curving handrail was smooth and cool to the touch, soothing my hand as it glided along the banister, which guided me up the stairs as I contemplated what sounded like an ominous future.

Chapter Two

Muckery

1835

"I wish I had got out of the entire dismal business back in '19! Are the mines you have invested in not producing as planned?" I could hear Father's voice, grouchy and lamenting, booming up the stairwell from the parlour by the garden door to my study on the second floor, where I was listing our new minerals in the mineral collection book. Father was meeting with two senior men from the Cornish Copper Company, of which he had been the managing partner many years before, a position from which he had resigned the year after I was born.

I had become used to his black moods and lengthy discussions in our plain-looking parlour where he conducted some of his meetings, sometimes along with Grandfather William. When paying calls to friends, I had noticed that many parlours in Penzance's more stately houses were decorated with hues of pink, blue and yellow on the walls, often with lovely swirls of plaster moulding, usually painted white and adorning the dado rails and ceiling cornices. Our Chapel Street home, however, had little adornment and, therefore, was considered plain and even drab. It had our personality; it seemed: studious, serious, modest, and plain.

Since my older brother, Joseph Junior, had died in 1831 in Madeira, that Portuguese island far out in the Atlantic, Father had been uneasy and dour. *Who could blame him?* I thought. Mother had then contracted the same consumptive illness and had been in such pain with coughing convulsions. The doctors had tried the usual rest, cod liver oil, vinegar massages, and inhalation of hemlock and turpentine, but to no avail. She had died of the consumption not so very long after. Then there had also been my sisters' weddings, Mary and Anna, all in such a short time. I could plainly see that Father was worn down.

I know what he is referring to, of course, when he says he wished he had gotten out of the entire miserable business. He means mine merchanting in general and the harbour at Hayle in particular. As I recall, Hayle had been the best and most accessible port on the north coast of Cornwall from which merchants could ship the copper from the mines and bring in the coal for the engines and the materials that the mines needed for their work. Harveys of Hayle, and the Cornish Copper Company, where Father had been in charge, both wanted to expand their activities at opposite ends of the harbour. They had been in fierce competition ever since John Harvey had established his first foundry at Carnsew, along the south-western inlet of the harbour.

Each side had boundary disputes leading to physical altercations. Violent conflicts over boundaries erupted and divided the whole town of Hayle. Currently, Father is mentioned politely as having been the driver of his firm's attempt at a monopoly, as if that could be polite. No one ever discusses the Hayle riots of 1818. I had heard that legal actions continued long after that, after Father had resigned and we moved to Penzance. It is my belief that his reputation has a shadow following him to this day from those frightening events, and that the shadow hovers over all of us as well.

For years, Father had wished he was out of the mining and copper trades altogether. He was always generous and kind to family, friends, and people at the chapel. But I have heard a few things here and there and read accounts in the papers over the years about how he was also a hard-driven industrialist. I wondered how much of the fighting and legal action had been on Father's initiative. In the papers, he had protested inno- cence, protecting the Company's property and rights. Still, I wonder if I would ever hear the true story of Father's role in the battles that left Hayle bitterly divided into two camps between the Copper Company and Harvey, and if the lurking shadow would ever be removed.

Grandfather, on the other hand, is a different story alto- gether. I smiled as I remembered how Grandfather had always been warm and outgoing, despite looking rather formidable with his long white beard, straight nose, and beautifully intense eyes. People have always loved Grandfather William and his generosity and often said there are none better. He and Father are still shareholders in the Copper Company and often discuss the company's new business strategies, still competing with Harvey. I can still remember Grandfather's boisterous walking tours around town with Grandmother, handing out thick clothes and food from a trolley pulled by a servant. I wonder if Grandfather had been pleased at the Hayle contro- versy. He surely was not, considering the results.

Because I was seated in the small study at the top of the stairs and the parlour door was open, I could hear everything the men were saying. I often spent time in this room, which was the main area for my studies, and which contained the most interesting minerals from our collection. Father would occasionally show his guests some of our top mineral speci- mens at the end of a meeting. He would call to me to bring down specific pieces to show, and I would place them on a polished board that brought out the colours and shine of the minerals. The remaining pieces and the bulk of our collection were on shelves stored in black metal trunks, which we kept in the basement of this house and the house next door, which we also owned. The houses were connected by a door on each of three floors. About twenty of the trunks resided here and about thirty resided in the basement next door. My sisters and I had the job of cleaning, identifying the minerals, and writing the notation of where the mineral was found on a small tag tied with white string to each piece. Then, my job was to list the information for each piece in the catalogue book that we kept for documenting the collection.

The catalogue of our eight thousand finds is almost as much of a treasure as the mineral collection itself. It is portable and tells the story like a book of all the natural treasures in Penwith, I noted as I laboured over the entries. The information in each entry had to be perfect in content and legibility. I bent my head down to examine our latest mineral find from a visit to the Wheal Alfred mine, near Hayle, earlier in the week. This was one of the mines in which the Copper Company held shares. I put the mineral closer to a candle flame so that I could see it in better light. I fingered and admired the bright orange spheres of calcite crystal on the iron-stained quartz. "Now, I will put you in the case to be admired with the amethyst, iron pyrite, clinoclase and the other best specimens in the collection," I said to the stone lightheartedly, showing the orange-dotted stone its new home. *How is nature capable of creating a colour of stone that is brighter than the sun? More deeply coloured than gold?* I wondered.

I remembered asking that exact question of the mine's purser, Henry Pearce. At twenty-one years of age, he was very knowledgeable about minerals in his own right. In fact, it was he who had found this specimen in the mine and given it to me that day. Henry had grown up living on a small orchard halfway up one of the hills above Penzance, with his parents and sisters, and first had gone to work at the count house, or office, of the Levant Mine near St Just. I was surprised to see him at Wheal Alfred, where he had only recently taken the purser position.

"Only God can produce something as pure and fine as these unique minerals. And it seems like only He knows what they are for!" he said, with a brief but broad smile showing his straight, white teeth. "But He gives us the power to figure out how to use them." He seemed to me to be a positive, strong-minded person in his own education, which was limited – a consequence of his station in life.

"I hope this brings you knowledge and happiness. I myself have learned to survey and plan to offer my services for new ventures around the Penwith mines," he said, confidently. "Well, good day to ye, miss." He put it in my hand with a warm smile and tipped his dusty hat. Mr Pearce was a tall, strapping and strong young man in worn brown breeches and a white cotton shirt. Even his brown hair looked strong, the way it curled up, trimming the back of his hat. I noticed his thick brown leather boots had recently been cleaned and polished. He seemed without an ounce of malice and was known to be hard-working; he had a reputation amongst the men and women who frequented the Methodist book room in our base-ment, which also contained our kitchen and storage rooms, for being kind and fair to all. *I admire his strength, both physically and mentally. Henry is different from my brothers, who had been scholarly types when they were at home. Did his warm green eyes linger on mine? Well, no matter. He is just a friendly man who is also interested in minerals,* I told myself.

"Thank you very kindly," I had said lightly.

He said, eyes twinkling, "Until next time."

I sat in my study and wondered how such a bright young man could work underground in the mine for hours on end.

Then I realised with a short laugh that we had something in common: the love of stones, minerals, and rock formations. Geology was a part of us, just like mining.

The mine! My mind now leapt back to the mines. *I had visited many mines before, thinking that their activity was very much like a large anthill. The miners hacked away at solid stone with their shovels and picks, making me pity their poor aching arms and backs. So many women, and children too, worked at the mines! Father had said that as many as two thousand women worked in the mines of Cornwall, although they did not go underground. While we were at Wheal Alfred, I watched the bal maidens, as they are always known in Cornwall, crack open the ore with their hammers on the dressing floors at the heads of the mine shafts. What strength and skill they needed to do that all day! While young men broke up the biggest rocks with the heaviest hammers, it was the bal maidens who performed the subsequent stages. Riddling was done by girls of about my age with sieves. Spalling hammers of about seven pounds in weight were used by more of my contemporaries to reduce the rocks further. Younger girls would then use smaller cobbing hammers to separate the metal-bearing parts from the useless and unwanted gangue mineral in which they were embedded. The best-paid job was the last stage, called bucking, done by experienced women skillful in the use of another and specially-shaped kind of hammer, manipulating it with a grinding action against an anvil to produce a fine granular material ready for the further stages of the process.*

Thinking of that visit in my study, I knew from previous visits to mines that the bal maidens were a tough sort, often cursing and yelling obscene things in loud voices. *Do not be intimidated by them,* I had told myself. *After all, some of them do go to chapel regularly.*

"Why don't ye come over and have a go?" One of the hard-looking, older bal maidens had asked me, with a bit of a sneer, prompting the exchange of furtive glances from three other women seated around a plank table.

"I would like to give it a try!" I had said enthusiastically. I went over to their working tables on the dressing floor and sat down, spalling hammer in hand, while Father talked to the Mine Captain, Richard Rowe. They watched my hammering with interest and smirked at my wobbly attempts to break the ore. My hands developed the beginnings of blisters within the first thirty minutes, though, so I put the hammer down, rubbing my sore hands together.

"I lack sufficient hand strength," I recalled telling them, smiling. The women and I laughed. I enjoyed sitting with them, and we chatted about how cold the upcoming winter might be. I tried not to grimace at the acrid smell of the women's bodies at work in the scorching late summer sun. I hope I was discreet.

I also asked them, "How do you protect your hands in all this hard work?"

"Oh, we don't," was their response. "Our hands soon got used to the pain and the open sores hardened quickly enough." I recalled looking at one of the women's hands, who could not have been much older than me. Her hands were like toughened leather, thick, cracked and calloused. *I have seen hands like that before. I know the bal maidens' job is comparatively well paid and even enjoyable. Yet, I feel the difficulties they face in their adequate but often ragged clothes and communal water basin. All through every shift, an endless supply of newly hewn rock demanding their attention, waiting for tough hands and minds to break it up and sort it. How is it that these women carry on given these conditions?* I wondered in admiration.

I sat in my study and continued thinking. I could hear the men below me arguing about supply problems. I returned to my thoughts.

What a contrast these women are to the girls of my age that are the daughters of the landed gentry. On the way back down Chapel Street after the mine visit, I recalled that Father and I had seen two girls around my age who were walking down Chapel Street as we were walking up towards our house. They were wallowing in their own finery and wealth, in my opinion. Last summer, these same two girls annoyed me at a summer party. "Miner's daughter!" one blonde girl named Delen had hissed at me at the party under her embroidered fan and "book worm," Carenza, the taller girl, had laughed, her nose in the air. Fortunately, my best friends, Caroline Fox and Emily Bolitho had come up behind them at the party and encircled me.

"Pay those who are jealous of you no mind at all, Bess," Caroline had said. Outside of my own family, Emily and Caroline were my best friends. We attended discussions and presentations together and dined together when we could. Caroline's intelligence was greater than my own, I thought, and we often shared opinions on recent novels through our letters. This reminded me that I needed to write to Caroline that week. She would be interested in the new minerals we had found.

"I doubt if those girls you saw have one brain between them, Bess," Father had chuckled as we passed them, their noses still in the air, as we entered our front door on the way back from the mine trip.

When compared to the bal maidens, the way of life of the wealthy seems shameful to excess, especially given the vulgar display of wealth that Delen and Carenza had no part in making. I doubt either of them knows of the conditions women and girls of their age worked under at the mines. Life could be cruel in its harsh juxtapositions. What I learned at an early age is that what matters is inward polish and refinement, not outward show as a braggart.

My wandering thoughts were broken as I heard Father shout to Charity Hosking, our head parlour maid, "Find Elizabeth and tell her she is needed in the parlour!" Although I was eighteen, I still knew that I had to do as Father bid me; *but why? Why is he regularly inviting me into the parlour meetings while he debates this investment or that?* I gingerly laid the mineral in its new glass case, shut the beveled glass lid gently and walked steadily and calmly down the stairs.

As I came down the stairs to the landing, Charity was there to meet me, hands on hips. "You have been officially summoned," she said, with a smile.

"So I heard," I replied, returning the smile. Charity Hosking was a light-hearted soul and always brought a positive outlook to our days. She came from Phillack, as did my family and I, and we regarded her as a blessing, especially after the loss of my mother. She had become like family to us, as indeed had most of our servants.

"Good day, gentlemen," I said as I entered the room, trying to make my steps as silent as possible on the hardwood floors. The pocket doors to the dining room were closed, I noticed. I sat down, slowly, on the dark-green brocade sofa with carved wooden scrolling on the back and armrests, hands folded in my lap, ankles crossed underneath the sofa. I noticed the intricate swirls on the scrolls on the arms of the sofa were perfectly dusted and polished. The room was large and dark, even with the morning sun shining through the large windows facing the harbour, and sparsely decorated. The small stone fireplace was softly glowing, adding only a small orange light. It smelled of freshly cleaned hardwood floor with a mix of the smell of men's suits that had been worn a bit too much.

Father sat in his black jacket, grey tweed waistcoat with small black buttons, and white stock, neat and tidy but with a curmudgeonly expression on his face. I knew what Father thought of the intelligence of these two men from the Cornish

Copper Company. "Short-sighted at best" were his words. Mr Richards and Mr Alexander, both closer to Father's age than mine, were seasoned men and knew all there was to know about mine merchanting.

I could sense their discomfort with my presence, as they stared at the floor immediately after greeting me. Mr Richards was a very tall, thin man with a deep, resounding voice. He was handsome enough, but I knew he was a man of slippery integrity. Mr Alexander was a portly gentleman with long brown hair that draped down either side of his head. He was fastidious in his apparel, as if trying to dress in a way that would elevate his station. I pitied him as he seemed to be a slower wit than Father had patience for. In cases like this, Father could be quite curt.

"Elizabeth, we are discussing the considerable benefits of selling the Copper Company's stores of arsenic to make up for the loss in revenue from the copper that they cannot seem to acquire for the life of them. I thought that your ideas on this would benefit our discussion. What are your particular thoughts on this matter?"

To hesitate now would be opening the door to being ignored, dismissed as a woman with no value to add. I quickly brought to my remembrance what Father and I had discussed of the extraction of arsenic in Cornwall, which had only begun in recent years. I know that it is an obnoxious and toxic substance to handle, with the fumes from the calciner flues causing considerable damage to the countryside around. Most of the production came from the Carnon Valley area between Redruth and Devoran. Arsenic, I was aware, was not merely a poison, but was now being used more and more as a paint pigment, and in glass manufacture and tanning. Although the demand for it is increasing, there have been times when it is difficult to sell to the established users; and this it seemed is when the Copper Company, as merchants, is able to buy it speculatively at a cheap price.

I began. "I imagine the decision to sell arsenic seems simple. You need to sell enough of it to meet the wages bill, and arsenic is plentiful and available."

The men nodded. I knew Mr Richards, with his heartless reputation of pushing to make money no matter what the cost to human health and life, would be in favour of selling arsenic.

"You have been searching for working mines which may have new copper lodes on their setts. That is the future of the Cornish Copper Company's prosperity, is it not? And, as a prime investor in the Company, and your banker, you are asking my father for his advice on how to proceed. Am I correct?"

"Yes, yes," and "quite right," the men both said, nodding and now looking at me, reluctantly.

"Yet, with arsenic as a product, even as a partial side product, come issues that can impair the overall company's reputation, its revenues, and the reputation of the Penzance Bank."

I paused. I knew full well that the men knew the risks of arsenic. For the uneducated public, it was a lethal poison. In no way did I consider selling a poison indiscriminately to all and sundry, as well as to the established manufacturers of glass and paint and dye pigments, to be a wise or prudent means of doing business.

"You *could* flood the market with arsenic, which would lower the price, and you may be able to sell large quantities for a short while. *Or,*" I continued, "you *could* limit and control the amount of arsenic you sell over a much longer period, selling at a higher price, which would keep it out of reach of irresponsible and even criminal users, and therefore demonstrate concern for the public's safety and well-being, which would prop up your image in the community as well as making more money. You could do it in a rising market."

Mr Alexander rubbed his whiskers with his chubby fingers, considering my proposal. He wore a gold signet ring on his right hand.

I continued. "While simultaneously spending more time and money on what is the reason you are in business in the first place: the search for more and cheaper sources of fine copper that the world is demanding for plating ships' bottoms, brassware, and so many other uses. Perhaps you should look to your most promising supplying mines and push them to do more prospecting and surveying work."

"Surveying work ..." Mr Alexander said, mumbling.

"Yes, exactly right," I said, illuminating each word with a smile. "Why, Father and I visited Wheal Alfred earlier this week, and didn't we hear someone mention additional surveying work starting there?"

"I don't recall that, daughter. Who said that?" Father asked in his usual, abrupt tone.

I responded, "I believe it was either the Mine Captain, Richard Rowe, or maybe it was the purser. What is his name? Oh yes, Henry Pearce. Would you not be able to help them, seeing that the Copper Company is an investor in the mine, to employ some competent prospectors and surveyors, perhaps led by this Mr Pearce – who seems to have abilities beyond those needed by a purser? You could take out a small loan from Father at a favourable rate and help them find whatever copper is there more quickly. Selling arsenic is only an interim measure."

"Splendid idea, Elizabeth. Yes, give me a plan of action, and we can provide a short-term loan!" Father bellowed. "Meet me at the bank next week and we will discuss your plan."

I nodded. "I now have family matters to attend to. I must take my leave, sirs."

"G'day to you, miss," they both said quickly, seeming

happy to be rid of me.

"Elizabeth, you are not dismissed," Father said quietly. "We have additional matters to discuss that could use your fresh insights. Please remain and we will continue with our next piece of business."

I nodded, returned to my seat, and tried to look happy, rather than surprised, about my extended time in the meeting. Our discussion continued with assessments of the prospects for several additional mines in the area. For the most part, I sat and listened. *I am surprised to find that these assessments are, in fact, interesting in terms of the increases and the implications for shipping and employment that arises from them.*

At the close of the meeting, I swiftly bid them good day and slipped out the garden door, down the steps and into the garden, where we had a small fruit orchard, to breathe some fresh air, collect my thoughts and reflect upon the things that had just transpired. I walked to the side of the garden, out of sight, as the heavy stone garden wall towered over my head. I leaned on the wall and let my body drink in its cool exterior. After the men walked out the front door, they stopped briefly on Chapel Street, and I heard the sound of flint striking as they lit their pipes. I heard Mr Alexander comment.

"The market – what does an eighteen-year-old girl, a female, know about the copper market, I ask you? Humph. Damn that Carne, bringing her into our discussion."

"Don't be daft," I heard Mr Richards say, coolly, taking a puff of his pipe.

"I don't take your meaning?" asked Mr Alexander, quizzically.

"Why do you think he's bringing her into the discussions?" Mr Richards asked in a conniving tone.

"I don't rightly know," replied Mr Alexander, sarcastically.

Mr Richards responded snidely, "He's bringing her up to be his heir apparent, you fool."

"Her?" Mr Alexander exclaimed. "A woman? That's impossible. What of her older brothers? What about the other men at the bank who could replace him?"

"They aren't his family, now, are they?" sneered Mr Richards. "Carne has two sons left and then this girl. The older girl still at home has the household responsibilities. The other older girls are married off. Carne has told me that none of the other children seem to have any interest in his affairs."

I stood completely still, hoping my skirts would not make a rustling noise in the wind and give away my presence. I could scarcely breathe, and the large lump in my throat returned as I leaned on the wall, listening, hands clenched. *What? No, it's not possible! Me?*

"Now that you mention it, I've been thinking it is time for me to court a new wife!" Mr Alexander chuckled, various body parts no doubt wobbling.

"Now, there is an idea!" Mr Richards said, with the sound of a smirk. "You would be a little old for her, but she would keep you young enough, I daresay."

With that, they guffawed, and I heard some backslapping as they ambled down the street. I crept over to the gate and watched the two men disappear from a crack between the garden wall and the iron gate.

I re-entered the back of the house, dazed, and my stomach sour. *I assume they were joking, of course, especially about that courting suggestion. But were they?* My stomach lurched, disgusted at the thought. *What gives men the right to speak like that about an eighteen-year-old girl? How could they be so heinous in their thinking? Men think themselves all-knowing and all-powerful, while we women must bear the results of their ideas, their decisions, and remain silent. What they think is right and proper becomes the reality for all. I am not angry at their comments, more astounded at their ignorance and insolence*, I thought as I walked to the backdoor of the house.

My older sister by two years, Caroline, glided up to me in the doorway in a lovely fitting, dark-green day gown with a black silk jacket. Not quite appropriate for the state of mourning we were still in, but I understood how tiresome black clothing could be. She was the picture of grace, etiquette, and grooming. Her shiny brown hair was immaculate, twisted into a tight coil at the nape of her sturdy neck. We were both of "sturdy" builds, as Father would say. We were trim but had muscular legs and arms from our love of walking, horseback riding, and our work about the house. I glanced down at my own black wool mourning dress with shiny black buttons from waist to chin. *I am rather drab in comparison, I think,* I noted to myself.

"Elizabeth, dear, your hair is untidy," she said, her high voice shaking. She grasped my hands, which was very unusual for her to do. "We have received some terrible news!" Caroline said dramatically, shaking her head, eyes cast downward.

"What sort of terrible news? I asked distantly, slowly disengaging my thoughts from the two horrid men.

"We have just received word that our dear uncle James and his dear wife, Charlotte, have died in the cholera epidemic in Plymouth. They were helping the sick and caught it themselves. They died within four days of each other. The poor darlings. Such horrible deaths!" she wailed.

"Oh, dear, no!" I said, my thoughts shattered in pain. "How horrible indeed. What will become of their five children?" I asked her slowly.

"They will be moving in with us, here on Chapel Street, in the house next door, as soon as the arrangements can be made," Caroline sobbed. "So, no more dawdling. We must make ready. You will have to move your study down to the basement room next to the mineral storage room, and Father will have to move from his large study next door into your small study. We will set up a girls' and boys' room next door, as well as a room for at least one governess there. We will need more chairs and a table in the kitchen. Miss Ann will have to be notified that she will need to cook for five to seven more now if you count in two governesses. You may be called in to help with meal preparation or assist in the garden." She then called out, "Ann, bring me the burning feathers, as I think I will faint." This was Ann Bodinner, the maid, not Miss Ann Morris, who was our cook. We called her "Miss" to clarify which Ann we were referring to, Miss Ann the cook or Ann the maid.

All of the Carnes have a certain cold disposition, as has been told to me by my friends, which is our misfortune, especially in times like these, I said to myself, miserably, suddenly missing my mother. *We cannot help it, but it causes us to be indifferent in showing affection,* I thought, sadly, rather than taking offence at Caroline's bluntness.

I had the most peculiar feeling of my heart sinking and soaring at the same time. *Poor Uncle James and Aunt Charlotte! Father, already heartbroken over our previous bereavements, will be devastated. Then there is the shock to their five children, aged from six to twelve. What must they be going through?* I wondered, piteously. I whispered, hands clasped, "Dear Lord, please bless James and Charlotte as you take them into your care and please see that they are reunited with Mother."

I must make diversions to ease the children's suffering, I thought. *I must comfort them, but how?*

Chapter Three

Remedy

1835

"As lady of the house, without our dear mother, I will be required to receive callers and make calls on behalf of Father and the family. Therefore, the children will be Elizabeth's main charge," Caroline announced at breakfast the following morning, her hands folded in her lap, seated at the dining room table. "In addition, I have my regular meetings with the antiquities society, which I intend to continue to attend. As a matter of fact, there is one this very evening," she said casually, sipping her tea.

Father was in no mood to hear about any conflict between us and was in no mood to be entertaining ideas or schedules of meetings. He stared down at his newspaper, his eyes fixed.

"Elizabeth must finish her education without disruption, Caroline," he said sternly, one hand holding the newspaper and the other his fork. "I suggest you find suitable tutors and nannies for the children, depending on age, and install them immediately, despite your busy schedule of meetings."

"Yes, Father," Caroline answered demurely, with a sharp look in my direction.

Excusing myself, I said, "I am going out riding to Boscawen Un." I typically rode there when I wanted to find solace, and the stones were the perfect place. *I definitely need solace today and I cannot wait to return to the stones! Standing as they had done since time immemorial, I feel like they were waiting for me in their perfectly concentric circle. We all love them, but especially Father and me. Somehow, we rely on them to renew our energy during times of loss.*

"Excellent idea. One of John Wesley's tenets is the benefit of walking or riding. You must take a manservant with you, as I have heard there are ruffians wandering about," Father warned.

"Of course, Father," I replied as I leapt out of my chair.

Boscawen Un is my favourite ancient stone circle, I thought, *because it is lesser known in Penwith; it has more solitude. And that solitude at the stones is like a salve for the rawness my heart and mind are feeling at the moment, given our tragic family news. That is where I shall go this morning,* I said to myself determinedly.

The nineteen granite stones in the circle at Boscawen Un, each about four feet tall, surrounding the grassy area in the middle and the larger angled centre stone pointing upwards towards the eastern sky, have always been trying to tell us something, and had given me solace as far back as I could remember. The area, called St Buryan, is surrounded by the farms out towards Crows An Wra, which were quite quaint, and the stones and farms provided the right change of scenery I needed to recover and collect myself.

I flew out the back door, into the garden and then around to the stable and considered my options. Usually, I rode or walked and included several companions, or our maid Ann, and a manservant. Earlier today, I had seen William Lock, our coachman, whom we called "Jacka," looking tired and leaning against a tree near the stables. I had also seen Ann earlier looking tired as well, sweeping the floor halfheartedly. Ann was not much of a rider, though she was willing to mount a horse if needs must. But it did not seem fair to make others ride just because I, as a young person, wanted to. I ran back into the house and found Ann in the parlour, now sweeping the floor.

"I would love to accompany you, miss. Let me drop this in the broom closet, and I will be right there after I grab me hat," she replied with a toothy smile, happy to accept my invite instead of sweeping the floors.

Ann and I climbed in the carriage and took our seats. *Usually, I admire the interior of the carriage when first seated. But today, I am in a raw mood, I feel anxious and distracted.* The carriage rounded the stables and curved around to the right through our entrance by Dock Lane and the bottom of the hill on Chapel Street.

As we went along the street, I looked out the window at the diverse morning activity which began to buoy my spirits. I saw the tailor nearest to us opening his shop door for business. Next door to him, in his fine-cut granite house, was the dental surgeon, a good man to have nearby with all Grandfather William's problems with his teeth. Next in line on Chapel Street was the chemist, Charles Brown. As we drove slowly up the hill on the cobblestones, I admired the style of his shop. As his door was also open, I could just make out the fine mahogany counter tops and Corinthian pillars inside. I also saw the print and stationery shop, which reminded me to ask Charity to retrieve the latest *Royal Geological Society Transactions* for Father. I tried not to go there myself, as it would be unseemly. Just lately it had become a centre of gossip in town for news about the latest scandal. I also admired James Tonkin's grocery shop and flour merchanting business, not so much for its dusty trade as such, but more for the miniatures he painted of the town and boating scenes, and for his genius in tuning our pianoforte.

I recalled there had formerly been in the line of shops on Chapel Street a tailor who had fitted out many young ladies – bal maidens among them – with suits of clothes and a parasol for a guinea, but he had gone out of business. *Father said that he was a man not satisfied with having the good fortune of a lucrative shop and had heard of a new and supposedly promising mining venture that was starting up just outside Penzance. Captain Trepen had convinced him to take a stake in it, as there was no better time, Father had said. Ah, the evils and perils of mining. The tailor was ruined after the mine had not hit paying ground, and he had quite simply been speculating, along with all his neighbours. It was sad to reflect that many persons made money from his ruin, according to Father. After his debts were settled following his bankruptcy, the creditors used their dividends, such as they were, to buy shares in a new venture which sought to revive the unprofitable workings, which then made a valuable discovery in a crosscut at the thirty-fathom level, south of where the former expected lode was supposed to have been. The fortunes of mining indeed! I am glad Father is only a small investor in mining now and not in the thick of the business any longer. Good riddance!* I thought to myself as we turned the corner to head west to the stones.

"Thankfully, today is not mule train day," I observed to Ann.

"What an unpleasant business that is," she replied. "Running eighty mules, each loaded on both sides with panniers of copper ore from St Just down the middle of Chapel Street, making pedestrians jump out of the way to let them pass. And then that smell!" She pinched her nose for effect.

It is so disgusting and inconvenient here in the middle of town, I thought, *I must urge Father to ask the mayor to find another way for these mules to go. But why do they come to*

Penzance at all? Most of the ore, and the incoming coal for the
mines, passes through Hayle. Perhaps they dislike dealing with
Harvey or the Copper Company. The mines mostly use mules
– there are thousands of them in Cornwall – because the roads
are so bad. Up in Portreath, they use the Poldice Tramway
instead. But I had other, far more pressing matters to think
about today.

I could not help but think of Mother and missed the days
when she was alive, and we would go to the stones. I smiled
as I remembered Mother, and how we favoured what we
called the "Quartz Stone." *Together, we often wondered about
where it was found, what its particular purpose was – and how
the stones came to be placed there, and so meticulously spaced.
We also speculated about why the largest stone in the middle
of the circle was slanted and leaning. It had always been like
that, Father had told us, possibly so that the sun would strike
it at a precise time in the year, marking the date of a ceremony
or a battle, most likely. It must have been a grand meeting
place thousands of years ago, and the Quartz Stone must have
been sacred.*

As Ann and I swayed back and forth and jolted in the
carriage, given that the road was more like a rutted path.
Memories flooded my mind of how we would walk around the
stones, touching them and imagining the clans of primitive
people, men, women, and children, with the same needs we
have today: food, shelter, family, and safety. *Did they go to the
stones to honour the sun and moon or perhaps to receive
healing powers? Father told us when we were last there that a
person believes, naturally, that we as humans always have
more time than we actually do. That is, there will always be
more time to work, time to be with family, and more time for
study. It is in our nature, I remember him saying, to assume
we will live beyond tomorrow. But he admonished us to live
our lives always keeping in mind that time is promised or*

entitled to no one, and death seeks out its victims regardless of social status, age, or even previous good health.

As the trees flashed by, his words now stung me with their bitter truth. *All his work and interests seem now to be an annoyance to him. His loving wife, Mary, is gone. His brother and sister-in-law are dead from the cholera epidemic in Plymouth. Four years ago, my brother Joseph died of tuberculosis. And we had had a baby brother who only lived a very short while. Death looms around us all. What will become of Father and Grandfather? Will they also die soon? I worried. How much more time do we have with them? Where will Mary, Anna, Caroline, and our older brother William and his wife Fanny and I be without them?"* I asked myself, anxiously.

I thought about last night, when I went in to say goodnight to Grandfather and he reminded me at his bedside that Caroline and I must continue our parents' and grandparents' philanthropic missions in and around Penzance and continue to uphold the Methodist faith in our family and community. Holding his cold, bony hand, I promised him that we would. That helped me feel closer to Mother. *I am so very tired of the agony of loss and do not want to think about life without Father and Grandfather. They are my rocks of stability and faith.*

As I sat there in the carriage, ambling along the muddy, bumpy road to the stones, more questions started to fill my mind. *Why would Grandfather say that to me last night? Why has Father been including me in his discussions at the bank? It all seems strange. Am I really being prepared to receive another and greater legacy, the financial prosperity of the family, as Mr Richards said?* I sat and thought about this legacy of the bank and the family properties – for the prosperity of future generations and for new philanthropic efforts. *Mr Richards was right in saying that it is clear that none of my siblings are interested in Father's affairs. None of them have ever mentioned any wish*

to step into Father's shoes. Not even William. He has been
enjoying France, perhaps a bit too much, with no known
intentions of coming home to Penzance soon. Not Caroline. She
does not have the disposition and determination required.
Mary, our oldest sister? Not with a growing family far away
in Madeira, I supposed. One of her sons, if and when they come
into the world, might; but that is in the as yet unknowable
future. Then, who is left, as Anna had also married and moved
away?* The carriage hit a rock, heaving me around in the
carriage and making my insides feel like they were coming
loose. I said to myself, *I believe Father will need someone to
take his share in the bank, and continue with the shipping
interests, and his residual involvement in the Cornish Copper
Company. I could certainly look after the mineral collection.
But, if it is true that I would be responsible for the entire
legacy, how will I take Father's place after all the years he has
spent in all his demanding activities? How will I step into his
shoes as a young woman with no college degree and no
experience? The resistance I would face would be considerable
– heated, even. I would not be surprised if lawsuits appeared –
maybe even from my own family. How would I ever command
enough respect?* I stared out the window at the old, ivy-
covered stone farmhouses and the chicken coops we passed.
So many complicated and painful questions ran through my
head. The carriage slowed to a stop. We had arrived at the gate
to the stones. I had lost track of time, deep in my troubled
thoughts. *How is it that I will be the remedy for the lack of a
family heir? What will become of me?*

Chapter Four

Treachery

1835

I sat down, letting the bag of food I was carrying drop, happy to be out of the lumbering carriage, and leaned against the Quartz Stone, admiring its grizzled texture. I opened the writing box that Grandfather had given me on my thirteenth birthday – the same one that I had used at the Mount on our excursion with Mr Mill. It had several compartments. One for paper, one for the nib pen, and another was an inkwell compartment with a little hinged top to prevent ink spills. The box was also useful for holding flowers to press.

Grandfather always believed that writing is the expression of education and therefore should be pursued whenever possible. The contents of the box allow me to do exactly that by drawing and writing letters on walking tours and trips. I immensely enjoy the time I can commit to writing. The next time I see him, I must thank him for helping me to gain a worthy habit.

I leaned my back on the Quartz Stone. Parts of it glistened in the sunlight, which was oddly reassuring. I began to write, telling Caroline Fox about our grievous news regarding Uncle

James and Aunt Charlotte, as well as to ask for her best thoughts on how to support five grieving children. Games at the Boscawen Un stones would be at the top of any list of amusements. I wrote that the bramble thickets lining the path to the stones would yield an excellent reward of blackberries when they were in season. They were already in flower.

One of our horses whinnied suddenly and stomped a hoof on the ground. I heard a faint sound of running water across the stone circle from me, by the gap which formed the entrance. *That is strange.* Before I could turn to look, large hands and arms swung around me, knocking my writing box askew and taking my breath away. I winced and writhed to see who had grabbed me.

"Hold on there, missy. Quit yer squirmin'." Another man appeared in front of me, adjusting his dirty, patched trousers after urinating on one of the stones. "Well, look ye 'ere, Jake," he said, eyeing me from top to bottom, his hands on his hips. "Who do ye s'pose this is?" I could smell him as he put his face near mine. His foul breath reeked of liquor and pipe. His ragged trousers were streaked with small lines of blood, and I also detected the smell of fish.

"Don't know. Wha's yer name, gurl?" asked the man named Jake from behind me. The man in front of me had a grimy, tanned face and very greasy long black hair. His hands were filthy and his fingers were gnarled. His eyes were flashing and desperate. His yellow teeth looked like kernels of corn. He was thin, giving him an angular, bony appearance. I could not see the man behind me, but he was strong. I tried to get out of his grip but I was powerless against him.

"She's a migh' pretty lit'l thang, ain't she, John?" Jake reached around from behind me stroked the shiny small curls of brown hair on either side of my black silk bonnet lined with lace coils. I was stunned but tried not to be afraid, as I knew Jacka and Ann were close by. Surely, they could hear what was happening.

"Give us yer valuables! Yer jewels! Now!" The man in front of me named John barked in my face.

"I have nothing of value," I said, as clearly and calmly as I could manage. *Be calm and do not act afraid. Be strong.* Father had taught me what to do in a situation like this, since he and I were often at the mines or remote cliffs in areas where minerals could be found and, therefore, we were vulnerable to ruffians.

"Reduce yourself as a target," he warned. He drove it into me to never say our name, never get on a horse or in a carriage with someone, slap my own horse as soon as I could, and scream out as loudly as possible. *I am nowhere near the horses and the carriage, nor can I even breathe, much less inhale to scream with the man's arms locked around me. I am in trouble! Be calm. Be calm.*

"Oi 'av notin' o' value," John said, mimicking my tone, chortling, and mocking my manner of speech. "She sounds high and migh'y. Don' she?" he sneered, rubbing his gnarled hands together.

"You will take your hands off her – now!" Jacka said quietly and sternly as he circled around the men to appear behind me. I had never heard him sound so angry before. I heard the cocking mechanism of the shotgun Father asked him to carry.

Thank heavens. Jacka did hear. I will be fine. Be calm. Remain still.

"Don't ye know it's dangerous out 'ere?" John, the man in front, said, reaching into his pocket and producing a long bladed, sharp fish knife. My eyes widened. Clearly, a knife like that was capable of terrible things.

"Yes, and if ye want to live, drop the knife, back away, and be gone!" Jacka yelled loudly. Ann ran up beside Jacka with the black horsewhip raised over her head, her teeth showing. Ann was not someone anyone would want to cross. She was the size of an average man, stout and muscular, in her muslin dress and apron. Sweat rolled down one side of her red face. Her appearance surprised the attackers. The whip, most likely the most surprising part.

At the sight of her, John dropped the knife, Jake released me, and the two men backed up, quickly. I stumbled to Jacka and Ann, gratefully.

"Aw, we don't mean nothin.' We best be on our way, Pixley."

Without thinking, I bent down to pick up the bag of food nearby and walked up to the two men. "You appear to have encountered hard times. Here, take this bread," I said, tossing them the bag of bread and cheese. "All is forgiven."

"Ye thinks ye is smart. Well, ye ain't!" John spat on the ground, his body jerking forward. He looked like he was considering his chances. His eyes darted back and forth. He bent down and snatched up the bag with a dirty hand.

"Do like the lady said," a low voice said coldly. Click. "I got a shotgun here too, so we have one for each o' ya. I'm a good shot. Best round 'ere."

It is a farmer. Praise the Lord. A young, strong-looking farmer, in his late twenties or thereabouts, had come by on horseback from a field near the Quartz Stone and heard the argument. Jacka bent down quickly and, with a swift movement, grabbed the knife by the shoddy wooden handle.

I shook the entire ride home in the carriage. I washed my face with a cold cloth, but I could not stop seeing the desperation in the men's eyes, almost turned into sinful crime. I asked Jacka to allow me to explain the situation to Father later that evening. *What would make a man wield a knife on an innocent girl?* I thought to myself. *I have never known hunger like these men must face daily. Hunger and poverty will make a man, or woman, do anything they can to survive. It becomes a test of wills to survive in this world. Do the churches and chapels not see these ragged people? Are the magistrates likewise unknowing or purposely blind to their plight?* I thought all the way home about how to approach our minister, the Reverend Mr Treffry, about what I had seen and what our Methodist Chapel and the Circuit is doing to prevent hunger and the criminal acts that result. *Obviously, it is not enough, whatever it is.*

I ran downstairs to the basement and into the new location of the small study and opened three volumes of calculus mathematics. I quickly flipped the pages to my current lesson. I pulled out my paper and quickly wrote down an equation. *Best to look busy and get into the lesson immediately, without questions,* I advised myself. My tutor entered the room. My tutor was Father.

I saw the look on his face. *He knows.* He pulled up a chair across from me and sat down in it, slowly. I realized it would be best to relate the incident now, as it appeared he had already heard about it from Jacka. I explained it to him as if I had no fear about the situation at all and that I had learned a great deal from it. I did not mention the fish knife.

To my surprise, he was quite impressed with my response to the attackers.

"Quite right that Jacka and Ann responded so impressively! I must make an effort to congratulate them. And you. I am proud that my youngest stood up to the ruffians, but in a Christian way. I imagine your kindness will not be forgotten! You have given me confidence that you know how to handle yourself," Father said, admiringly.

"Now, what about the knife?" he asked. "Jacka said there was a knife."

"Oh, so you know about that then. Yes, there was a knife, but it was merely a threat without actual intent," I said as calmly as I could.

"I see," Father mused. "It was a threat that could have cost you your life. Next time, you and your companions must be better prepared."

"We will be, Father. I am very grateful for Jacka and Ann's defense. They were quite brave. You should have seen Ann brandishing the horsewhip."

Suddenly, Father laughed loudly, with his head tipped back, and slapped his leg with his hand, the back of his chair hitting the shelves behind him in the small study.

"Ann would have horsewhipped those scoundrels if given the chance." He laughed so heartily, tears came to his eyes. I had not seen him laugh like that for a long, long time. "A fearsome sight, to be sure." He continued laughing, and I could see him conjuring the image in his mind. After a while, he regained his composure.

"I heard you were also brave, Bess. Now, are we ready for our lesson?" Our lesson went on as planned. Although, given the slight smile that would curl on his lips every so often, it seemed to me that Father was savouring the image of Ann and the horsewhip.

***

My heart sank the next day as I awoke and realized I had forgotten my writing box at Boscawen Un. I went to reply to a letter I received from John Stuart Mill, our friend from the St Michael's Mount walk. *I left it in the grass near the Quartz Stone.* Mr Mill's letter was full of news of his more recent walking tours and queries about my thoughts on women's education, when any education women had was "limited" to that provided from home. I was eager to respond to say that home education had plenty of benefits over a man's public education.

No matter. It will give me an excellent reason to go back to the farmer to give him proper thanks. The terror of the incident nauseated me and made me shudder each time I thought about it. I hoped it wouldn't continue to play out in my dreams.

I rushed to get ready for the day ahead because I had promised Father I would come to the bank with him to learn bookkeeping. *I am anxious to learn it as it sounds rather interesting and I have always liked and done well in mathematics – yes, I think I will like bookkeeping.* We walked the short distance along Chapel Street to our bank. *I admire the red brick and red trim on the windows and door, which make our bank very inviting,* Father opened the red front door, and we went inside. Father went in first and walked over to speak with the manager while I waited in the hall. I heard two of the younger, more junior men in the small office next to the hall whispering to each other.

The first young man asked the second, "What is *she* doing here again?"

"How would I know? Except that her father *owns* the bank," the second replied with a low sneer. "I have a mind to go ask her."

"You would not!" the first said in challenge.

"Watch me," said the second.

I stiffened. His face appeared instantly in the doorway. He was a tall young man with neat brown hair, cravat, waistcoat, and black jacket.

"I hope you are not thinking of taking a position here just because your father owns the place," he whispered. "That would not be fair to all the men that are out of work and looking to work at a place like this," he said vehemently. Then, in a flash, he was gone.

"Better keep quiet if you want to keep your own job, mate," the first said in a hushed tone.

Father came back to the hall and suggested we begin in his office, which was a very pleasant room with inlaid bookshelves stocked with leather volumes. He sat in his large wingback brown leather chair. I sat across from him, where I could see out of the large bay window overlooking the comings and goings on Chapel Street.

My face was hot and red. *How disappointing of those young men to resent my presence here. Of course, I will have to prove my merit, but up against those odds, who would measure up?* I sighed. *No time to worry about this now,* I thought, pushing their comments to the back of my mind.

Father sat an enormous book down in front of me, entitled *A Practical Treatise on Banking,* by James William Gilbart.

He said proudly, "Brand-new third edition, just published."

I quickly flipped to the end to see how many pages it contained. Over five hundred, I saw.

"Do you know Mr Gilbart, Father?" I asked, looking up at him.

"Yes, oh yes, I do, Bess. Perhaps you will also meet him someday." He smiled. "What you have here before you are a set of principles for banking. If you turn to page one hundred and fifty, you will see how the principles of bookkeeping work. It is this that I would like you to read and then we will set upon a practice."

"Yes, Father," I said, eager to find page one hundred and fifty. As I flipped the pages, there was a loud knock at the door.

"What is it?" Father growled. He was thrown into a foul mood at the disruption, breaking our concentration.

"There is a gentleman here to see you, sir," Philip Marrack, the manager, announced. Mr Marrack was a man of feeble body but mighty brain. He managed Father's affairs and ran the bank when our family was away on its travels, which was frequently.

"Show him in," Father said, in an annoyed voice, probably hoping his intruder would hear and think better of his interruption.

"Sir, if I may, you may want to see your visitor in the open office." I suspected that Mr Marrack sensed that the visitor would not be appropriate for me. He waited and then cocked his head to the side, with a slight nod towards our other and vacant office. He seemed tense. Father acquiesced.

"Oh, very well, then," he grumbled as he trudged out through his office door to the next room. Having been in Father's office many times before, I knew that if I went to the adjoining wall, I could just make out what was being said. I sat in my chair and pretended not to notice Mr Richards as he walked by the slightly ajar door of Father's office. He was neatly dressed in a gold-coloured silk waistcoat and dark blue jacket. His short, straight black hair was slicked back from his face with pomade, which I could smell as he passed by. His black boots were shiny and spotless. After he passed, I moved to a small chair next to the adjacent wall.

"Ah, Mr Richards. Here to discuss your loan, perhaps?" Father asked, trying to be cheerful.

"No. Another matter entirely," Mr Richards said, curtly.

"Well then, what can we do for you today?" Father asked, trying to get to the point quickly, which was Father's usual style.

"I have an interest in your daughter." Mr Richards smoothly moved on to the purpose of his visit.

I did not like the sound of this and instinctively braced myself for what might come next.

"I have come to discuss obtaining your permission to ask for your daughter's hand in marriage," Mr Richards stated pompously, as if he was the one that owned the bank.

"Caroline is of age, but ..." Father stammered.

"No, not Caroline, Elizabeth. I know she is a bit young at eighteen, but I would like to ask for a lengthy engagement," he said, firmly. My mouth dropped open. I thought I might scream out, so I clapped my hand over my mouth.

A second or two passed in silence. "Does Elizabeth know about this interest?" Father asked, with his voice low and trembling with anger.

"No. I wanted to ask you for permission first, and then make my intentions known to her," Richards responded casually.

I was in shock. *I cannot believe what I am hearing.* My head was pounding with my own heartbeat. My mouth was dry.

"I know you are an ambitious young man," I heard Father say, quite calmly. "However, despite your interests, which I suspect are nefarious at best, Elizabeth is young, still receiving her education, and not available for consideration of marriage under any terms!" He ended his last sentence with a loud bark, making me jump on the other side of the wall. "She will finish her schooling, which will take quite some time, Mr Richards. I suggest you find another family that will meet your needs. Good day to you, sir!"

Completely unruffled, Mr Richards said, "Perhaps at another time we could discuss her best interests, that is, if my offer is still available. For now, I will leave you to think about my good name, my good standing, and my sizeable account in your bank."

"Your inquiry is quite impertinent, sir. I have no reason to think of anything with regard to you. Now, good day!" Father snapped, clearly on the defensive.

"I see. Let us hope that your bank continues to suit my needs. I trust Elizabeth has not been entrusted to anyone else's hand and if so, I may have the right of first consideration. I will keep an eye out to ensure that she continues to be of good merit in the community and of pure standing. We all know how vital good standing is," he hissed.

"Is that a threat?" Father said through what sounded like gritted teeth.

"Let us just say that it is a note of caution. I will be on my way but will leave you with this thought. I ask you, who in Penzance, or in all of Cornwall for that matter, would suit her better than I? No one. So, in the future, have a care with how you treat me. Many a family would jump at my offer. Good day to you, sir." His unhurried footsteps indicated he was leaving the room at his own arrogant pace. I knew Father would be back in the office within seconds, so I leapt out of the little chair and back to my place across from the window immediately. I was shaking.

"My God!" I thought I heard Father sputter. "The appalling nerve of that snake!"

Horrifying. Never in my life would I have expected that! Thank goodness Father put him off. Father will not want to discuss this. Concentrate. Breathe slowly. Appear as if you heard nothing. Look down at the pages. I must write something. Here he comes. Father re-entered the room.

* * *

That night at dinner, we sat in our dinner finery and made light conversation about our day. The candle flames danced merrily on their wicks, but I barely noticed. I silently begged Father, *Please do not bring up what occurred with Mr Richards at the bank earlier today. I am mortified by his interest. Please, please do not mention it.*

"Someone came to see me today, asking about Elizabeth," Father said, looking down at his folded hands and his napkin in his lap.

Not knowing what to say, I tried to change the subject. I asked Grandfather, "Grandfather, I was at the bank today to learn about bookkeeping from the Gilbart treatise. Have you read it?"

Grandfather looked up, surprised at my interruption.

"It was Mr Richards, from the Copper Company," Father continued.

Grandfather asked, "What did that peacock of a man want?" His tone was again, surprised. Before I could form my next word, Father spurted it out.

"He asked for Elizabeth's hand in marriage," Father said, words bursting from his mouth. "I apologize for raising this at the dinner table, but I have been so aggravated by it. It has weighed heavily on me. The audacity of that man to think he could have Elizabeth's hand in marriage!" he spewed, shaking his head.

"Oh, what an exceptional offer!" Caroline exclaimed sarcastically, from her seat next to Grandfather. Grandfather was not amused.

"Caroline, sarcasm is not ladylike," Grandfather admonished.

"Yes, Grandfather," Caroline replied with a heavy sigh.

I was horrified and I could not keep my composure. Tears pricked my eyes and I tried to blink them back. "You turned him down, I hope. Oh please, Father. No," I cried, my voice shaking. I knew that he had turned Mr Richards down, but I wanted Father to know my exact feelings on the subject in no uncertain terms.

"Do not worry your head one moment, Bess. I did turn him away and for good. I would not allow you to be married to a man like that. You, of superior intellect to that – snake. I would never allow it – never in my lifetime."

"Exactly right, Joseph," Grandfather chimed in.

"Never any man in your lifetime," Caroline mouthed across the table to me.

I was relieved beyond measure. "Thank you, Father, for your faith in me," I said, my hand on his arm.

Father was tired of the conversation, and so was I. Neither of us ate much that night.

* * *

The next day, I had arranged to return to the farm with Ann and Jacka, gifts in hand, determined to pay proper thanks to the farmer and anxious to retrieve my writing box, hopefully undamaged, laying on a cushion of grass rather than in the mud. Not knowing what a farmer might need as a gift, I took a very plain and sturdy tan tablecloth and some jellies as gifts. I wore a light, charcoal-grey frock that was neither too fancy nor too plain, with thick black leather boots, and a bonnet with a woven straw brim, black ribbon and crown. The underside of the brim was decorated with a thin layer of pleats. *Perfect for all my needs today. I do not want to dress in any way that would emphasize a class difference between myself and my new farmer friend.*

"Jacka, are we quite well protected?" I asked as we climbed into the Brougham, our light, four-wheeled, enclosed, one-horse carriage. Ann and I were seated in the back and Jacka hoisted himself up onto the dickey box. Today, I took time to admire the carriage. *Today, I must enjoy the inside of the carriage. I love the shine and the smell of the leather interior! It smells like a delightful adventure!*

Ann, in her middle twenties, besides acting as maidservant, also kept house for us. She was very loyal to the family and assisted on looking after my grandfather. Jacka, slightly younger with a very trim build, besides being our coachman, also worked in the stables along with the stable lads, taking care of the horses and keeping the carriages in good repair. Neither knew how to read or write, much to my dismay. I had offered several years ago, along with Father, to allow them some time to learn, but neither could see the benefit at their age.

"Quite well, miss!" Jacka answered, indicating that he had brought the shotgun we had shown the ruffians earlier. We set off for Ednovean Farm, rattling and swaying, with the intention that we would drop the gifts at the farmhouse, bestow my sincere thanks, and retrieve my writing box. Then, we would make our way back towards Penzance to Market Jew Street to do our shopping in preparation for our new occupants, our cousins, who would shortly be arriving in our home. Finally, it would be back to the study with my German tutor in the afternoon. I resolved to speak German to myself along the way to the farm, naming objects and describing them in German.

While we were all (especially Father) in deep mourning for the loss of Uncle James and Aunt Charlotte, I for one was delighted with the opportunity of absorbing five bright young souls into our lives. *It seems to me they will brighten up our sombre house. And I know it is what Mother would have wanted.*

Ann had reservations about all the additional work. "Can you imagine the trunks of clothes they must 'ave? They will be a handful for me, and no mistake!" she moaned.

We had not seen them for quite some time, and we wondered what to expect. *Will they be orderly? Will they be quiet and studious and fit in with the demeanour of the household?* Sister Caroline insisted that we list all the clothes that the children would need for paying calls, chapel and Sunday School attendance. I had different ideas.

To me, as a young child, I learned most, and I learned best when I was out and about in the fields with the other children of our neighbourhood, creating and playing games of all sorts, along with sports. I intend to buy plain, easy to wear, comfortable play clothes that the children will be wearing as they make mud pies, climb trees, play football, build forts or gather blackberries. I am determined to advance all of these important lessons daily through outdoor play, now that the children have no parents to advocate this for them. It will be a joy to watch. What lessons will the children learn in tight-fitting clothing that has to be kept clean? They would learn to be stiff. That not getting dirty is more important than running; that sitting in place neatly is more important than jumping in piles of leaves; or that lace and leather are more important than freedom, spontaneity, and creativity. So wrong!

As I rode along the muddy, rough roads in the carriage, it occurred to me that these trappings of social convention – formal clothes from fancy materials, studied manners, and the protocol which enforced them – were merely trappings of the wealthy and were made to mean more than just the things themselves, in ways which conveyed arrogance and status difference, setting those who had all above those who had little. If one had these things, one had stature and grace. Without them, one could be labelled inferior. *How petty and insignificant these trappings of wealth really are. Plain, rough-and-ready farmers can be just as intelligent or brave as someone with fine breeches. How conventions and the trappings of a well-dressed society get in the way of achievement! How they create lines that have no true meaning but often have great implications in terms of education and status! Henry Pearce, as another example, could be intelligent enough to attend college, if given the chance, which he will not. Ann is bright enough to learn to read, if it had not been instilled in her that she would have no use for it. Status symbols create artificial lines and gaps between people that are destructive and cruel. I will impart this to the cousins, in conjunction with our Methodist teachings.*

We reached the stones, which I could not resist walking amongst for a short time. The solitude of the stone circle in the midst of the fields was fortifying. I touched each stone I passed. They felt cold, rough and slick at the same time. I tried to transfer their solid strength to myself through my hands. I tried to imagine their immense weight as I looked for my writing box. It was gone. *I hope the farmer picked it up for safe keeping, but I do not remember him doing so.*

I sat down and let my grey frock with small black buttons up to my neck billow around me on the grass. I stroked the grass so that its texture could calm me and I took a deep breath of the clean, warm, summer wind. I stared at the centre stone, angling up to the sky, and tried to will it to tell me its purpose. I wanted to ask the stones for help. My black and woven straw bonnet protected my face from the hot sun. I sat in the thick, dry grass and thought. *I have quite a duty laying before me, which appears to be defining my future already. I am glad to have an honourable, meaningful purpose to hold on to in these times. But it is daunting and intimidating. What is my greater purpose? Will it be to devote my life to my family's legacy and missions? Is it to teach my cousins that class distinctions can only lead to one type of thinking and one type of empty life? I am grateful but will it mean I have little time for a family of my own? What about what Father and Richards said? Certainly, the word will spread that Father would never entertain such a marriage proposal again!* I grimaced at the prospect. In the graceful solitude of the stones, wind lapping my face, I decided I felt sound and strong in my family calling and its meaning. The stones were standing tall as they had done for centuries. *I must stand tall with them. Tall and strong in my own purpose as they are in theirs.*

I stood and walked through the grass, looking for a few flowers I could attach to my gift for the farmer. I found yellow gorse and several lingering red campions, surprisingly still hanging on to their beauty at this late season for them. In a way, I felt like a guardian to the stones and them to me. Many years before, it seems, someone had stolen a stone from the circle. I could not imagine who would do such a heinous thing as to spoil a magical, historical place where we are the keepers of their legacy. I felt compelled to check on the stones, to keep them safe, as if I could do that as an eighteen-year-old young woman. Inwardly, I laughed at myself.

We drove up to the farmhouse through a lane to a gateway in the substantial stone wall piled four feet high that surrounded the property. A small wooden carved sign hanging on a white post at the end of the lane bore the name of the farm:

"Ednovean." Before me stood a two-storey, grey granite farm-house speckled with white quartz stones here and there. The granite house had a sloped, thatched roof and ivy crept up one side of the front of the house to the roof. Grass and hedges stretched out inside the stone boundary wall. The front door with iron cross bars unlatched and opened slightly with a squeak as soon as our carriage stopped. Two little blonde heads, about thigh high, popped out; both had missing teeth.

"Please stay in the carriage. I won't be long," I said to Jacka and Ann.

"Hello!" I called out softly. "Good morning!" I said brightly to the two heads. I carried my packages in front of me.

"You a princess?" asked the first head, a girl of about seven.

"No, not at all," I said, amused. "Is your mother at home, please, or your father?"

"Mum's 'ere. I'll run and fetch 'er," the other head said. "I'm Amos and this 'ere is Ellie," he said. He was long-legged, with trouser legs above his ankles, and an abundant number of freckles. Before I could introduce myself, he ran back into the depths of the house.

"Hello, Ellie. It's nice to meet you," I said.

She stared at me, her mouth open. Her bright blonde hair was pulled back from her pretty face in a braid that went down her back to her waist. She wore work clothes and had a straw hat in her hand.

The mother appeared at the door, with Amos at her side.

"Ello, can I 'elp ye?" she asked, timidly, peeking out of the barely open door and wiping her hands on her apron.

"Hello, Ma'am." I started my rehearsed speech. "I met a man near the stones yesterday who I assume is your hus-band?"

"Oh yes. Seems he did mention it," she said guardedly, keeping the door only slightly open.

"Yes. My name is Elizabeth Carne. I live with my family in Penzance, on Chapel Street. I came here today so that I could properly thank him for his help." I paused. She cocked her head as if to ask a question.

I jumped in to fill the gap. "I would like to give you these gifts as a small token of my sincere gratitude for his help with two ruffians. Is your husband about?"

"I am Jane. We are the Freethy family. We are the tenants here at Ednovean Farm. He ain't 'ere now. He's in t' lower fields with a sick cow." She held her hand to her forehead, squinting. She and Ellie resembled each other, with their blonde hair and pretty faces. Jane's face looked quite weathered from the sun but had a look of joy about it.

"It is very nice to meet you, Jane. In that case, would you please give him my card and tell him I stopped by to thank him? And I would like to leave these gifts with you and your children." I knew she was a busy woman, so I wanted to be brief.

"Thank 'e. Thank 'e kindly." She smiled.

"I am sorry to trouble you, but did anyone here find a brown wooden box with paper in it? It is a writing box that my grandfather gave me, and it is very precious to me. Did anyone find it?" I asked, hopefully.

"Yes, miss. William, that's my husband, found it by 'em stones. Come ye in and I will fetch it for ye."

I entered the front room, which was a narrow hallway with low shelves about knee-high, which held several small pairs of boots and various hats. Around the corner was the kitchen with an old black iron stove in a bricked chimney that had whitewash around the sides. The room was bright and clean with wooden candle holders and handmade furniture. The chairs were the type where the small wooden logs formed an "H" on the back of the seat. The seats themselves were woven from straw. Several children's drawings were strewn about on the floor. The stone floor was nicely swept, I noticed.

Jane handed me the writing box. I heaved a huge sigh of relief; it was intact and unharmed.

"Oh, I am so thankful and relieved," I said. "Thank you ever so much!"

As we drove down their lane, the children ran after the carriage, dancing and waving. I waved back from the back window. *What a pleasant farm!* I thought.

I would like to return and perhaps bring lunch for them and my cousins, at Boscawen Un, and perhaps some drawing paper, I thought, clutching my precious writing box. I ran my finger over the gold embossed letters on its lid, E. C. T. C, my initials.

When we arrived back in Penzance, the shops on Market Jew Street were full of people darting this way and that, busy shopping while the weather held off, as an angry storm was now brewing out over the Channel. Large, well-formed clouds looked dark and heavy in the sky with the promise of what smelled like rain. The wind picked up my skirts and tossed them around my ankles.

"Let's do hurry, Ann, and get to the tailor's directly." Mr Hewitt's tailor shop was at the end of Market Jew Street, closest to the harbour and on the high side of the street, over the elevated walkway. This elevated walkway, five feet higher than the other side of the street, with stairs appearing at regular intervals to give access, was there to accommodate the slope of the hill. Mr Hewitt's shop had a lovely white exterior with black shutters and black trimmed windows. Above the first set of windows was a cornice in the shape of a loose ribbon, which added both a lovely ornament and a fitting element for a tailor.

"Yes, miss," Ann replied over the freshening wind, hand on her bonnet. Jacka stayed with the carriage and the horse.

"We will be as quick as possible, Jacka," I called out.

"Yes, miss," he replied, steering the horse and carriage out of the wind.

Thankfully and oddly, the tailor's shop was empty. We bustled in and shut the door that the gusty wind wanted to blow open. A brass bell over the door announced our arrival.

"Good day to ye, ma'am." Mr Hewitt, the tailor, stood behind the polished counter and seemed unusually stiff in his greeting.

"Good day, sir," I replied, quickly. "We would like to place a large order with you, and we are in a bit of a hurry."

"A large order, you say, Miss Carne? I was just about to close my shop for a few minutes but give me a few moments to take care of a shipment in the back, and I will return quickly," he said, eyes darting left and right.

"Certainly, Mr Hewitt, but do be conscious of the weather and that we would like to depart soon for Chapel Street."

"Of course, miss," he said, and he hurried behind the thick tan velvet curtain that divided the front showroom from the back storeroom.

Ann moved to the back of the showroom, looking at several lace shawls and commenting on their beauty under her breath.

I toyed with several ornamental tassels mounted on a stand at the front counter. On the way into the shop, I noticed that the shop next door was vacant. *I wonder if Mr Hewitt might expand his business.* I saw jostling and what seemed like erratic movement behind the tan velvet curtain, which made me curious. I turned slightly so that I could see a small sliver of the storeroom through a slit between the curtain and the door frame. A man stood across from Mr Hewitt and ran a hand through his loose hair. His hair, I noticed, was dark and very greasy looking. The hand that I saw was gnarled. *What? Who is that?* I saw the man land a large package covered in brown paper on Mr Hewitt's storeroom countertop, which was about level with the one in the showroom. Mr Hewitt pulled its contents partially out of the package, examining them with his immaculately clean and smooth hands. He fingered what looked to be a sizeable amount of pristine white Breton lace – the kind Mr Hewitt displayed for sale in his shop. Both men were whispering, so as not to be heard.

"Yer daughter's frock was an excellent hiding place at the harbour. No customs man would go lookin' there, now, would they?" The man sniggered. Mr Hewitt grimaced. He handed over a leather pouch that clinked and looked heavy – *payment for the lace,* I supposed. I knew a little about the smuggling that used to be carried on by the townspeople and even sometimes the customs men all around Penwith. *I remember reading that as many as ten thousand people across Cornwall in times past have been involved with smuggling, although now it is very much in decline, as the former duties on imported goods have been greatly reduced or removed altogether. It is not right, of course, but it seems a necessary evil, especially to those who are starving or have difficulty making a living – and nearly everyone has shared, however indirectly and unknowingly, in the benefits of what has been commonly regarded as "free trade" all around the coasts of Britain.*

"Be gone now. Out the back. And don't be noticed, Pixley, and next time, leave the lot in the empty building next door like I asked you before," Mr Hewitt hissed.

My mind raced and I felt a panic come over me like I never had before. *Greasy hair and those hands. Pixley!* I slid back ever so slightly and silently from the counter.

The man nodded. "Till next time," he growled. "And say hello to that pretty blonde-haired dau'er of yorn."

I hid my face as well as I could with the side of my bonnet. *Should I leave the shop? Will I come face to face with Pixley, my tormentor from the stones, outside?* My mind raced.

I couldn't turn my eyes away even though I begged myself

to. I saw Mr Hewitt slide the white lace into a glossy wooden cabinet that he had unlocked with a tiny key. I jerked my head back. Ann seemed to notice nothing as she was fawning over the hats, turning them over and fondling the material and the feathers, on the right side of the back of Mr Hewitt's store. *Thank goodness she is not near the big bay windows at the front of the shop,* I thought to myself. *Pixley cannot possibly see her and therefore think she might have heard something if she stays where she is.*

Mr Hewitt returned to the front of the store with a sickly smile pasted on his sweaty white face. I heard the clank of the bell on the back door.

"Now then, Miss Carne, how can I help you?"

***

It was glorious to go to the services at our Methodist Chapel, just a short way along the street from our home, on breezy summer mornings. My father, my sister and I could not agree as we were leaving the chapel, which was more edifying; the singing or the sermon. Our chapel was quite old compared to the many that were now being established everywhere. It had been built in 1814 in the new revival style.

I stood in front, admiring the array of arched windows in the front of the large grey granite building, waiting for my cousins to gather around me as we came out. I was in deep thought about the sermon as we stayed awhile, chatting to people we knew among the crowd, lingering on the chapel's spacious forecourt; but, as happened frequently these days, my concentration was broken by a young cousin drifting off somewhere. Father and Caroline had walked on down Chapel Street towards the harbour and our house as I tarried to keep the children in order.

When I had gathered them all together and we started to

walk along, they followed me like a brood of baby chicks. I was pleased with how well my cousins had become accustomed to their new home in such a short time. By all accounts, all five had settled in nicely and were quite well-behaved during chapel services. Now our large house was full to the brim with lively youngsters who brought a new energy and demeanour to the seriousness of our home. My cousins' names were Edward, aged twelve; Francis, aged eleven; Catherine, eight; Anna, seven; and Charles, all of six. I supposed that now our Carne household had become similar to most families like us, with two or three generations living together. Certainly, the cousins had mollified the hollow feelings of loss we had endured. So much loss in such a short period of time was, however, still difficult to bear, even with the bubbly laughter of the children in the house.

Today's sermon interested me. Mr Treffry discussed the dangers to civilization and to all people under God. He spoke about the current topics of liberty, using the United States' internal conflicts as an example, and variety. Variety, he said, was a good thing for people unless it was too stimulating with too little rest. The wrong sort of variety and liberty is not a good thing, and should be kept in check, so that the two do not undermine themselves and each other. I vow to remember the sermon as it strikes a chord in me. To achieve harmony in life, one must strike a balance between liberty and variety. I was thinking of additional applications of the sermon, such as to differences in status, when my concentration was broken yet again.

"Elizabeth, could I speak with you briefly?" It was Henry Pearce, smiling, who had come out of the chapel some way behind us.

"Of course. Children, this is Mr Henry Pearce. He is a friend and a mine purser and surveyor," I replied, also smiling.

"Yes, that's what I wanted to talk to you about." Henry

said, taking off his tall hat. "You see, I think I have you to thank for that."

"Oh, I sincerely doubt that, Henry," I replied, a bit awkwardly.

"Our captain has said that he had been instructed to resume the surveying and prospecting that we had been doing, and extra help was coming on to the mine. Apparently, this had been at the instigation of the Copper Company. I can only imagine that you had a part in that," he said, seemingly full of gratitude.

"I think you have done that all on your own," I laughed happily. It was becoming warmer in the noonday summer sun, and the children were anxious to change out of their Sunday clothes by the look of it, given how a few were tugging their collars.

"I wanted to thank you and give you this," he said, pulling a small item wrapped in cloth out of his blue jacket pocket. It was wrapped in a cloth that one might see at Christmas time. As I gently unwrapped it, its deep indigo blue crystals sparkled in the sunshine.

"Henry!" I exclaimed softly, knowing exactly what the mineral was and its rarity and value. "I could not possibly accept this rare piece." It was a piece of vivianite, a new discovery in Cornwall and, therefore, unbelievably valuable to us for our collection. I was at a loss for words.

"It reminds me of you. I want you to have it. From me," he said. In that moment, he touched my heart.

"Thank you. What a kind gesture," I said, glowing, putting the stone away securely in my brown leather reticule. *How could this stellar stone remind him of me?* I wondered, quickly trying to think of what to say next.

As I did, a thought and a question came to me. I summoned up my courage to ask about it.

"Henry, I have had an idea, and I wondered if I might

discuss it with you?" I asked, tentatively.

"Of course!" he replied. "I would be interested in any idea of yours."

I continued. "It may be warm now, but the autumn and colder weather will soon be upon us, and life will be harder in the struggling mining communities. The rebuilding of St Mary's is nearly finished, and the congregation will be back. If they are willing to help, I would like to take some gifts from there, and from our chapel and my family to the mine children and their mothers, as soon as possible. I would like a guide to help me find the people who are most in need. I can provide a carriage and support the effort. Would you be my guide, please?"

By having a guide, I would be able to reach people far beyond lower Chapel Street and the harbour. I want to be able to continue my grandparents' and parents' work and investigate the living conditions of the impoverished for myself. With a guide like Henry, I will be less likely to be rejected as an outsider. I could then take this information to the local parishes and inspire the church vestries and our chapel ministers and deacons to feel the concern more keenly. The fact that they do not do more between them to alleviate the pain has bothered me since the incident at the stones.

"I can, and I would be most delighted to help you in this mission. When shall we start?" Henry asked, energetically. My heart was pounding so loudly I could barely hear him.

"There will be lots to do and to arrange. Can we meet, say, at the end of next week, here at the chapel with Mr Treffry, and discuss the preparations we will have to make? Will you be able to identify some places where there are people in need?" I asked.

"Yes, I can. I can invite my sister Mary to join in, as she will be interested. We might be able to bring a cart to help carry everything. Do send word when you have arranged the meeting with Mr Treffry. Good day to you, Elizabeth, and I look forward to your mission." He tipped his tall hat and strode away. My heart leapt out of my body.

Chapter Five

Country

September 1835

William Freethy, my farmer hero, and his wife, Jane, looked nervous. Their four children, however, shouted and waved at me wildly from their wagon. It was a lovely, warm day at the end of summer, full of breezes and sunshine. As usual, the grass at the stones smelled fresh and lush. I was nervous about how my young cousins would react to these farm children from another world.

"Hello!" I cried out, standing among the stones at Boscawen Un. My large dark blue day skirt billowed in the wind. My black bonnet ribbons fluttered. I smiled and I was so happy I felt as if the sun shone right through me. A large, quilted blanket was spread out in the middle of the stone circle with baskets set around the edges. Ann, wearing a large white cotton apron, was busy unpacking the baskets laden with food. Jacka stood by the carriage, holding the horse by the bridle. He gave me a quick nod. Alongside him stood the five Carne cousins, hands by their sides, dressed in informal blue woollen clothes, with corresponding head coverings and polished boots. They seemed to me to be little soldiers, standing ready to meet the unknown.

"Come, come and meet everyone!" I called cheerfully, waving my outstretched arms to beckon my silent, slightly apprehensive cousins.

The Freethy children tumbled out of the worn brown hay-filled wagon onto the grass, each one blonder-headed than the last. They were clean and combed but also ready for running and tussling about the grass, as was their custom.

"When I call your name, please raise your hand so that everyone can know who you are. First, I will start with our guests, the Freethys. Children, this is Mr and Mrs Freethy, who live at Ednovean Farm. Their farm has a big wall of granite stones around it and lots of chickens, if I remember correctly. The Freethy children are William, Margaret, Amos, and Ellie. Well done, Freethys. Thank you for the proper hand wave. Thank you to all the Freethys for accepting our invitation to our Boscawen Un picnic. Now, that leaves the Carne children. May I introduce Edward, Francis, Catherine, Anna and Charles? Nicely done, Carne children. Welcome, all. To begin, might I suggest a game of hide and seek with refreshments for the adults? Mr and Mrs Freethy, would you like some refreshment?" Ann was pouring cider from a large pewter pitcher into matching mugs.

"Don't mind if I do," Mr Freethy said. He nodded his agreement to me, returning my smile.

The children all darted about amongst the stones, some crouching and others standing tall against the side of a stone so as not to be seen. Others hid under a hedge nearby.

"I will be the seeker. You be the hiders," I said loudly, covering my eyes. "I will count to twenty. If you make it back to this spot where I am standing without being found and tagged, then you win!" I shouted. *I will count dramatically, "One, two, three, four ..." so that each number seemed to have a special dramatic tone.*

The adults looked on with interest. "She knows 'ow to please a crowd," I heard Mr Freethy say to Jane and Ann.

Ann smiled. "Our Bess is a blessing to us all," she said, stressing the word "all." *How kind of her to say that*, I thought. *I have never heard her say anything like that before. Surprising.*

Ann continued, not seeming to care if I overheard her. "In the Carne house, you don't age in years. You is as old as needed to do what the Master asks you to do. Bess is comin' up on her nineteenth birthday. But she runs the household down to the last bag of sugar. She is her father's scientific assistant. Without their poor mother, she and her sister Caroline, who is just two years older, between them act as the lady of the house. The Master works 'em like horses, minding those rock collections, the cousins, us servants, the house, the garden ... Quite demanding, he is."

Mr Freethy let the topic drop.

I quickly thought about what I had just heard Ann say. *Not such different worlds after all the way Ann describes us. We do work very hard, but it is a pleasure for me, truly. We all do what is needed to survive, and both our world and the farming world are certainly fraught with hard work.*

The children squealed with delight and changed hiding places at the last count of "twenty!"

"Children are the unifiers, are they not?" I asked Mrs Freethy, who was standing on the edge of the stones while the children were hiding with my back turned.

"Playin' games like one family," she replied, warmly.

I swarmed around the stones, arms outstretched. "Where can I seek the little hiders?" I asked, in a teasing voice. *I want time to stand still, or perhaps stretch out, so we can enjoy this happiness for much longer than it will actually last.*

William Junior, the tallest and oldest Freethy, sprinted into my spot handily, his long legs moving in a blur, barely making a sound in his brown overalls and thick boots.

"I see we have a sprinter in our midst!" I laughed, hands on hips. "Now, I must find some more little hiders. But where?" I asked, looking to the sky and across the fields. "Have you seen any children hiding about? I shouted to a nearby cow, who let out a long moo in response. *I love creating fun for the children and being a bit dramatic. Look how they jump right into the game.*

The adults laughed at my antics.

The two oldest Carne children, Edward and Francis, teased me as I tried to tag them in their hiding places but was too slow. The game continued, gleefully.

"A mighty beautiful carriage, this one," I heard Mr Freethy say to Jacka, who stood by the carriage near the stone entrance, admiring the gleaming polish and the fine leather interior.

Jacka agreed. "Yes, it's a dandy. I take care of all the Carnes' carriages, and the horses. Mighty glad you came along when we was here last."

"Oh, that. We farmers try to keep an ear out for each other. Thieves and poachers, ya know," Mr Freethy said. "Miss Carne was right brave. And kinder than most to them ruffians and smugglers."

"That she was. Kinder than most of her sort. Her parents and grandparents raised her up right. The Carnes do good by people," I thought I heard Jacka say. *So kind of him! He has been such a loyal friend to us, and we are fortunate to have him caring for us.*

"Well done, well done. You have roundly beaten me at hide and seek," I said, breathlessly. "Now everyone, please be seated on the blanket, and we will have our luncheon."

"Luncheon? Wha's 'at?" little Ellie, the smallest Freethy, asked Catherine Carne, who was about the same age.

"Oh, we're going to eat! Come with me!" Catherine replied, taking Ellie's hand. Ellie looked up at her with a questioning look but took the hand anyway, anxious to get a place on the blanket.

As everyone sat around the blanket, the adults helped serve the smaller children honey-glazed ham sandwiches on fresh baked bread, Cornish potatoes, and berries with a cup of fresh milk. The older children politely waited until the younger ones had their plates in their laps. The adults leisurely added more cider to their mugs and were seated with their own heaped plates.

"I have asked Francis to lead us in the blessing. Children, it is important to give thanks to God for all the blessings we have this day. Please hold your hands together as we pray. Francis, if you please," I said, sternly, bowing my head and pressing my hands together in prayer.

"Bless us, oh Lord, for these thy gifts which we are about to receive from thy bounty through Christ our Lord. Amen," Francis said, a bit reluctantly, as he was with new people, I assumed.

"Amen," everyone firmly said.

"Now, everyone. While we eat our lunches, I would like to go over a bit of a history lesson with you," I announced firmly, trying to command their attention.

William, Francis, and Edward let out simultaneous stifled groans.

"Oh, this history is a story of ancient lore, including pirates," I said, coyly.

Sighs of relief and exclamations of excitement came from all around the blanket. I laughed into my hand, despite myself, because the children were lovely and so sweet.

I continued. "About eighty years ago ..."

"Will there be a shipweckth? Oi likes shipweckths," Amos said, through his missing teeth.

"You will have to listen very carefully to see if the story has a shipwreck, Amos," I responded, as calmly and patiently as I could. *Being interrupted always seems to try my patience.*

"As I was saying, about eighty years ago, and that is a very long time ago, a man was buried in Gulval churchyard, in the same parish where he was born. And on his tombstone was carved this emblem." I quickly produced a pad of paper and a piece of charcoal I had hidden behind my back. The children watched, mouths open, fascinated by the drawing. I quickly drew a picture of the tombstone, with a skull and crossbones at the top; and I put two eyebrows on the top of the skull.

I held the drawing out for all to see, like a schoolteacher.

"This is the story of the pirate John 'Eyebrows' Thomas." I could not wait for my next trick to see their reaction. I turned my back to the audience for just a second and when I turned back around, I had stuck two small and long pine twigs with green needle fringes underneath the top inner pleats of my bonnet, to suggest that I was now John "Eyebrows" Thomas. My head was cocked at an angle as I displayed my "eyebrows." The crowd roared with laughter.

"It was written in his will that he had quite a lot of money to leave to his friends and family and that he had three houses." I quickly drew three modest houses with my charcoal.

"Ooh," the younger children cried. The older boys folded their arms across their chests, skeptically.

"Now, I ask you, how did he achieve this wealth?" I asked the children, most still seated before me but a few jumped up when I showed them the houses.

"He was a pirate," William replied, a bit sarcastically. His mother gave him a disapproving look. He shrugged his shoulders and had a look on his face that asked, "What did I do?"

"If that is so, how is it that he, a treacherous criminal pirate, was allowed to be buried in his own home parish churchyard?" I asked.

"Huh?" asked Amos.

"If a person is a criminal, he or she is not allowed to be buried in their home parish churchyard," I added.

"If he was not a pirate, why would he have a skull and crossbones on his headstone?" asked Francis.

"A fair point," I quickly answered. "No trade was listed on his will, and with the skull and crossbones, does that mean he was a pirate?" I asked. "Perhaps he liked pirates, or someone thought he was a pirate and made the tombstone that way?" I continued.

"Or he was a farmer!" cried Ellie. Everyone chuckled.

"Also engraved around the edges of his tombstone was a strange message. The message was thus:

'Study to imitate, you won't excel.

If you would live beloved and die so well.'

"Now, I ask you, what could this mysterious poem mean? Someone put forth great effort to engrave it there." I asked, furrowing my brows. One of the pine twigs fell out of my bonnet, which I quickly replaced as if nothing had happened. The children covered their mouths and giggled.

"No one knows what this means?" I paused. "Clearly, this is a historical challenge. He has no trade listed. He has a skull and crossbones on his tomb, suggesting that he might have been a pirate. His tombstone has also left us a mysterious message. And there is a path in the churchyard leading directly to it. What does this all mean? We may think that we have an answer, but we need to know more facts, do we not?" I questioned the children.

I heard Mr Freethy whisper to Jane. "I see where she be goin' with this. It's a bit 'o mystery for the older ones."

"Ahh," she replied, seeming to be glad for the tip.

"John 'Eyebrows' Thomas was known to have boarded many ships right off the Penzance coast. These ships were

French and sometimes from other foreign lands and were captured by John Thomas and his crew, each one, and their cargoes taken."

"That's how come 'es rich!" said Amos.

"Most probably. Does that mean he is a pirate? Or could he be doing a job, say for the King?" I asked, with a royal air and wave of my hand.

"The King?" Several children spontaneously sighed.

"Yes, as it turns out, John 'Eyebrows' Thomas was on a mission for the King. A sort of Royal Navy of one. He was given what is called a 'Letter of Marque' from the Crown. Anyone with this letter was allowed to ward off, plunder, capture or sink – if they had to – any enemy vessels. But only enemies, not British ships of any kind. So, was he a pirate?"

"No," came the answer.

"No, not really a pirate, because he had what?"

"A Letter of Marque from the King!" they all said.

"And now, back to the poem. He suggests that if you merely study to copy someone else, your effort is what?" I asked the group.

"Lost," said Francis.

"Yes, very good, Francis. And, if you do what instead, will you be more successful?" I asked again.

"If you try to be beloved," said William, with a calm confidence I admired. *I think he will be quite successful someday. It is his calm demeanour that appeals to me. He is confident but not arrogant, which is critical. But what about his education on the farm? It worries me that he will most likely grow up with little education. He has such a wonderful way with others.*

"Quite right. Very good, William. He was trying to tell us in his will that he thought it important to be a beloved person. Can you be beloved if you are a treacherous, law-breaking criminal?" I asked, looking puzzled.

"Nooo!" the crowd howled back.

"Very good. And so, children, perhaps he wanted to be a true pirate. Perhaps he wanted others to think he was a pirate and have a legend to his name. Perhaps the pathway leads us directly to him in the churchyard so that we will see his message. We will never know exactly why his grave has a pirate skull and crossbones on it. But he did emphasize being a good person, and he did the King's work. The letter of marque had made him a privateer instead of a pirate. And, we can guess he must have had special eyebrows!" I gave a bow to end my performance. Everyone cheered.

"Now, time to run and play!" I shooed them off the blanket and out among the grass and stones while I joined the adults.

"Now that was a proper tale!" Mr Freethy said.

"Thank you. I enjoy a bit of history disguised as a tale." I laughed.

"I can tell! And more to come, I hope," he replied.

"If I am not being impertinent, how do you manage your children's schooling?" I asked Mr and Mrs Freethy.

"William, being the oldest, completed his third year. But he is needed at the farm most days," Mr Freethy replied.

"Yes, I can understand he would be most helpful at the farm. I wonder, if a school was closer by, would that enable you to send him to school and still work at the farm? The other children as well, of course," I asked.

"Might do," said Jane. "But there ain't no school close by."

"Yes, I understand that difficulty. It's just that I have had an idea and wondered if I should pursue it." I pursed my lips together in thought.

"What idea would that be, if I can ask?" Mr Freethy asked.

"Well, the idea is that Penzance could use more schools closer to the villages, hamlets and farms where the schools now are too far away. My idea is that if Penzance had more education, our children and then their children would prosper and be able to avoid the up and down fortunes of the mines, and good and bad harvests. Perhaps, with more education, more choices in life would be open to them to work with engineers or doctors or engage in science and many other things. As the world moves on, our children would be educated to keep up with it and prosper from it," I said.

Mr Freethy looked at me as if he had not heard any woman speak in such a way before. His mouth hung open a bit. Jane was surprised as well. She said nothing.

"If the new things be here to stay, and someone prospers from them, then best if it were we," he said, strongly, gesturing with his hand.

"What about things for your farm. Are there any implements that would help you prosper?" I asked. "Perhaps with them, you could spare William a bit more? *I ask with good intent. I do care for the Freethys, and I hope they will allow us to become friends and maybe allow me to provide some support.*

"Implements and tools cost money. Money on a farm is hard to come by, ye see," he said.

"Yes, I see. Let us think about that a bit more. Could I come by the farm at some future date, and we could discuss this? Perhaps we could think about some new implements and whether or not it could be profitable for you?" I asked.

"You mean, you could work out things like that?" he asked, as if he wanted to be sure of my meaning.

"Yes, exactly," I said.

"Mum, is it cake time yet?" Ellie asked, tugging on her mother's sleeve.

"It is, love. Wipe yer hands and come along." Jane winked as she led the way to the cake.

"We brung heeva cake. Come and git it!" she yelled. I could smell Jane's buttery cakes being cut and the sweetness of the raisins made my mouth start to water. The children cheered.

"Miss Carne, I am glad, mighty glad, we came today," Mr Freethy said as we walked over towards the slices of cake.

"I am so glad to hear that," I answered, feeling as one with him. "You saved my life and I wanted to thank you."

"Consider us even, then," he said, earnestly. *He wants to shake my hand, I believe, but he does not quite know how to do it appropriately, given that I am a woman.*

"I would like to consider us as more than even. I would like to consider us friends, Mr Freethy."

"All right by me, but why would a young girl in your station, if you don't mind me sayin', want to be friends with farmers like us?" His eyes were squinting from a combination of the sun and concentration on the question.

"I admire you, one and all," I said. And with that, I linked arms with him and we strode off towards the cake.

On the way home, I sat silently in the carriage, thinking of the possibilities the future might hold for the Freethy children. The carriage bumped along, falling into holes, rocking us back and forth, and jolting us over the muddy, uneven lanes.

Someone on horseback pulled up beside my window, going in the opposite direction. The lane was small and barely big enough for our carriage. I could smell the horses' acrid sweat and hoped they would squeeze by without incident. *It is a bit rude to ride up so close on this narrow lane. Who would be riding out here in the middle of farmland?*

"Why hello, Miss Carne. What brings you all the way out here amongst the farms?" he said, tipping his tall green felt hat with a wide satin trim. It was Mr Richards, on his gleaming horse with his gleaming tack and black riding attire trimmed in the same colour green as on his hat. He was accompanied by two men, both young, one on a beautiful white horse, the other on a dappled grey.

I would like to ask him the same thing, but I do not dare seem impertinent. "Out having lunch and some games with the local children," I responded, happily.

"Cavorting with the locals?" he asked, his eyebrows raised. "Why on earth would you want to do that? They are another breed, you know." He sneered. The other two men snickered.

"No, I did not know," I replied sharply, clearly disgusted, and hoping none of my cousins had heard his foul comment. "Good day, sir. Jacka, drive on please."

We drove onward, their deep, haughty laughter ringing in my ears.

Mr Richards called after the carriage, "I will see you again, Miss Carne. You can count on that."

Chapter Six

Poverty

October 1835

For most of September, I had been working with Mr Treffry, the vicar at the chapel, and other helpers for a few hours each week to pack up all the clothes that were coming in as donations, mostly from the chapel membership after appeals had been made at the various Sunday services and mid-week meetings. Mr Treffry was ordinarily a man of few words. He was a tall, thin, solemn man with grey hair and a wrinkled face, especially on his forehead.

"Miss Carne, a word, please." He motioned me over with a bony-fingered hand.

"Yes, Mr Treffry?" It was almost time for me to leave and return home. I supposed he wanted to show me another pile of coats to be gathered for the mission.

He looked down at me and said, "It is a good thing that you and your family do to aid the less fortunate. You have the spirit of God flowing through you. It is as if a light of goodness shines through you. Through your donations, it is as if you are helping us see there is light among us."

"Thank you, sir, but I am only an ordinary person trying

to make conditions bearable for a handful of needy people." *I am certainly no saint. No, I am as worldly as the next woman.* "But thank you, sir, for your help and encouragement in these times. Everyone needs to help others so that we can all get through our difficulties with mining. And we all rely on your good words," I replied. "I feel like it is what I am meant to do. Does that sound strange?" I asked, looking up into his sage face.

"Not at all," replied Mr Treffry, clasping his hands together. "I think you can do a great many things, Miss Carne, if you allow yourself to follow your heart. You bring people together with your spirit and light. God willing, do more of that. This world needs someone like you, Miss Carne." He looked down on me with kindly eyes and my doubts faded away from the strength of his smile. He bade me good day but I felt ill at ease. *I will continue my missions. But how can I follow my heart when it is my father that I must follow?*

* * *

In the days to come, I thought more about what Mr Treffrey said, and I felt a bit guilty. *I have more on my mind than only this philanthropic mission, if I am honest, Mr Treffrey.* Henry was often on my mind. *I have no need to feel guilty. I am working with Henry so that he can introduce me to the mining communities we are going to visit. That is all. There is no sin in that,* I argued with myself, making ready to meet him at the appointed time and place. *Yes, he is extremely handsome. And he is kind and a true Methodist. He is everything every man should be. But I am only asking for his help, which he seems inclined to give, because it is a mission.*

But as the days passed, I became uneasy. I joined Miss Ann in the kitchen for a late lunch mid-week.

"How about some lovely rabbit stew to give you strength?"

she offered. Her rabbit stew was truly delicious, as it contained fresh thyme, as well as carrots and potatoes from our garden in the back of the house. She always put a small piece of toasted crusty bread on top that I used to dip into the stew. "Stew will fix what is ailing you, and I can see something is amiss," she said, looking into my solemn face.

Miss Ann was middle-aged and average height. She was plump in the waist but I could tell she must have been a beauty in her younger years. She mostly listened to what I had to say and never commented on or judged my thoughts. She was very kind to everyone but had an inner strength that commanded respect. No one ever tried to take advantage of Miss Ann. She commanded the pantry and kitchen with velvet gloves, Father would say.

"Yes. Something is amiss. You see, I am uneasy about something Mr Treffrey said to me when I was at the chapel bundling clothes to donate." I said, stirring my stew around with my fork.

"Oh? Uneasy in what way?" she asked, in her usual cordial tone.

"He said I was doing right by helping the less fortunate and that I have a light shining within me. But, Miss Ann, I have thoughts that may be considered sinful, just like anyone else."

She paused for a moment. "I see. And those thoughts are bothering you?"

"Yes, they are," I replied, sullenly.

"I wonder if it depends on whether the thoughts are truly sinful." She responded, kindly.

"Yes. Having kind thoughts, loving thoughts even, about someone deserving is not a sin, is it?" I asked, seriously.

"Most of us sin at some point, as you know. But loving thoughts that are well intended for a deserving person would not be on a list of sins that I am aware of." She smiled. Then I smiled. Her words had grounded me once again.

***

On the arranged day, we met at the Methodist chapel, I with my carriage and our servants and he with his oldest sister, Mary. They had a well-worn, two-wheeled cart which, old as it was, had a nice coat of red paint and was quite sturdy – a welcome sight.

"My family would like to contribute these sacks of peas, and my mother and sisters have made several fruit pies," Henry said, proudly.

"How wonderful!" I exclaimed. Mary was going to drive the cart, while he rode with us in the carriage in order to explain the places where we would call and provide Jacka with directions.

"Please do thank your family from all of us!" I said to Mary. She smiled and nodded. Henry and I smiled at each other. Ann looked away, I noticed. Mary gave Henry a stern sisterly look, and I felt rather awkward. I could only assume that my affection for Henry was clear to everyone even though I tried my best to hide it. My face was red, I was sure of it, but I was happy all the same.

The cart and carriage were now packed with blankets, coats, bread, cheese, ham, apples, socks, mittens, and hats, mostly collected from the chapel and several family friends. Ann and I sat on one side inside the carriage, Henry on the other, and Jacka expertly drove the four horses from the dickey box.

Along the ride, I decided to ask Henry about the greasy-haired man. I wondered where he was from and if he was known in town. I would definitely stay away from him and any place he might frequent.

"Henry, do you know a man that might be involved with smuggling, a man with black, greasy hair and rough, gnarled hands?"

"That describes many a man in Cornwall, Elizabeth. How would you know about smuggling?"

"I have read about smuggling in Cornwall and know it still carries a heavy penalty. I believe the man's name is Pixley."

"Right. I imagine you mean the younger rather than the great grandfather, Pixley? The older Pixley was a famous smuggler of over one hundred years ago," he replied, with a questioning look.

"Yes, I am familiar with the notorious John Pixley from our local history. But who is this younger Pixley?" I asked, trying to seem nonchalant about my repeated inquiries so that Henry would not guess that I had had an encounter with Pixley myself.

"He is the great-grandson, recently returned from a mining venture in Peru," Henry informed me. "He apparently did not find fame and fortune there and has returned. He is a known scoundrel. Not someone anyone would want to tamper with." Henry turned to look out the window.

"No, indeed," I replied.

Ann smirked knowingly.

"Why do you mention him?" he inquired, one brow arched suspiciously. Henry leaned forward in his seat as if I now had his full attention.

"I saw him in the tailor's shop dropping a package full of Breton lace and receiving what appeared to be payment, and I wondered if I could turn him into the authorities. That is, I think it was him. I saw only a glance through the curtain and heard the tailor refer to him as Pixley," I said, levelling my eyes with his.

"It could have been him. Or it could have been any number of other ragged men. To turn him in, I believe you would need stronger proof," Henry replied, softly.

"Yes, quite so," I answered, evenly. The thought of him stealing and escaping freely did not sit easily with either one of us. And what of the tailor? He would also be guilty. However, it seemed he was supporting his daughter, Talwyn, a sweet girl, and her three sisters, and I dreaded to think that she was complicit in the deed as well.

"Perhaps, this was an example of 'too much freedom' of which Mr Treffry spoke at his sermon back in the summer," I said, thinking out loud.

"I believe you are right. Too much freedom with the law combined with greed and need. A poor combination. We are nearing our first call. Allow me to introduce you and your mission," Henry suggested.

He had directed Jacka to the first mining settlement on our itinerary, near the Botallack mine, which was on the point of stopping altogether and throwing the miners out of work. Its future was uncertain. The mine itself was perched on a high rocky ledge with crystal clear waters below. *It is incredible how the miners dug down in that ledge. It appears as if the mine might be swept off the ledge by the sea at any moment, it is so close to the water's edge.* Father visited this mine and confirmed that yes, he could hear the waves pounding overhead as the miners worked under the surf carving out and harvesting rocks and ore. *What would that feel like, to be down under the sea and under the sand where one could safely walk about and hear the waves crashing overhead? Would I be brave enough to go down in that mine? To think of all the miners working there that do that every day. What must go through their minds? Being crushed by rock and water?* I shuddered involuntarily at the thought.

Thankfully, our arrival at the cluster of cottages near the mine shifted my attention away from the depths of the mine to the mission at hand. Luckily, and despite his youth, Henry had already spent several years working around the mines of the area and knew many of the miners and their families here well, with their many children. The miners had been freely allowed to use the mundic stone from the mines to build these thatched cottages, and there were six of them in this small settlement. Children and dogs ran about the unpaved lane in between the cottages. Women and children sat huddled by outdoor fires in small metal grates, trying to keep warm in their inadequate clothing on a cold day – it was already the first frost of winter. I saw people coughing, clutching their throats. *My eyes are stinging from the cold and the smoke from the fires, and I have only just arrived. What do I say to them?*

Henry introduced me to several of the women whose husbands he knew. They were seated, cleaning potatoes to make ready for the next meal or weaving baskets to earn a little income from the Penzance quayside dealers. They had grown the potatoes themselves over the summer on the small plots that most miners had by their cottages. The potatoes would be boiled in their skins along with dried codfish, when they could get it. They seemed indifferent when they first saw the carriage. I stooped down and opened my arms to the children, who came running towards me.

Jacka and Ann helped Henry, Mary and I divide the food among the families, who became friendlier once they saw we meant only good. Children's hands, obviously trying to feed their hungry bellies, groped at the packages in haste. *I hesitate to call out good wishes, for what kind of future is in store for these indigent and desperate people?*

I smiled, nodded, and sat down on a stool and took out my writing box to sketch for the children. I produced a sketch of one of the smallest boys, who squealed in delight at his likeness. The other children clamoured for more sketches. I then drew another sketch of a little girl standing next to a stone wall with a gorse bush hanging over it.

"How are you getting by? Henry tells me your husband has gone in search of work in America," I asked Mrs John, who appeared happy to meet me.

"Yes, miss. He's been gone now two months. We moved in with my sister to share watchin' over the children and takin' in others' washing. I sent my oldest girl, ten years old, to work as a servant in a house in Falmouth," she answered, sadly.

I nodded and said, "I see. What hardships you face. You are doing good and right things for the betterment of your family." I had a difficult time understanding sending a small girl away to work with another family. But what did I know of starvation or of living without much heat in cold weather?

I bought several cleverly formed baskets from the women with some coins I had brought along. We bid them good day and promised to return soon. Many of the children ran behind the carriage, waving goodbye.

"Jacka, might we carry on a bit further and see the cliffs at Cape Cornwall? I would like to view the striations."

"Yes, miss," Jacka called back.

Once we were at the Cape in its magnificent glory, I described the rock formations we saw. I pointed out how the striated or striped rocks about the cliffs have the same makeup as those lower down on the shoreline. The view was one of the most spectacular in all of Cornwall.

"Why do you think they are the same, Henry?"

"I could not say, Bess," he replied, smiling, the wind ruffling his hair.

"Because they too used to be underwater," I said, with certainty. While the others enjoyed the scenery for a few minutes, I sat on a nearby flat boulder and sketched the outline of the cliffs and indicated where the striations would be. I would finish the sketch later at home in my study.

After walking along the wide expanse of green grass of the Cape, we carried on towards the Levant mine, where Henry had previously worked.

"More of the same here, I am afraid, Elizabeth," he said as we arrived.

"Let us do what we can for now," I said, hopefully. On the cliff paths, we had encountered several miners on their way to or from their work. They would be here in all weathers, hot and cold, rain and shine, light and dark, year in, year out. Hot and wet working hard in the depths of their mines, at the end of their shift, they would have a long climb up the ladder roads to the surface; and then, still wet and very tired, they might have to walk several miles home. Some acknowledged us with a slight nod. Most were simply too exhausted.

On the ride home from Levant, I was deep in thought. Ann was engrossed in a pasty we had saved for her. *I am continuing with donations as my parents and grandparents had done for years. But how can we continue this in any truly meaningful way? I am happy to give, as are most of the wealthy landowners in their parishes all over Cornwall and across England. Yet, there is a limit to what people are willing to give. Giving odds and ends is not reaching all those in need and is only a small temporary way to placate the consciences of the wealthy.*

"Henry," I asked. "What would it take to fully rescue these poor people from this condition, and their poor health? All we have done is provide them with aid for the present. How can they be free from this poverty?" The answer came to me before he could respond. My mind was working fiercely and clearly.

"Education. Schools. Teachers. Books," I said excitedly. A larger mission was taking root in my mind, and I was glad of it.

Chapter Seven

Empathy

November 1835

"Wonderful Sunday school teaching today, Father," I said cheerfully, wanting to set a bright mood for supper after the Sunday services. We were all seated at our dining room table, Father, Grandfather, Caroline, and I. A cozy fire blazed away in the limestone fireplace. Six different candelabras, holding five white candles each, lit the room as well, flames dancing on top of the candles. *Of all the rooms in the house, I would say the dining room is the most cheerful by candlelight, with its polished wood floor, oval table and chairs, beautiful dado rail moulding of scrolls and Greek vases overflowing with grapes and vines, and clean white linens. The enormous round-fronted cupboard holds our crockery for special occasions, which is painted spongeware in a pretty white flower design. It all reminds me of Mother: clean, fresh smelling and festive.*

As a family, we always had our meals in this room, and the servants ate in the large kitchen below, although I would often eat breakfast and luncheon down in the kitchen with Miss Ann, who had become like a mother to me. She always welcomed me and seemed to know what I was thinking, even though she had no children of her own as a reference. I could smell her delicious roast pork coming up from the kitchen, and I knew eating roast pork, his favourite meal, would put Father in a good mood.

"I am glad you enjoyed it, Bess," Father said. He often taught Sunday school, as did Grandfather before him.

I could see Father had no interest in discussing the Sunday school class, which in fact had been rather boring and sombre. Father tended to provide a lecture, his mouth often turned down into a scowl, which made him appear even more solemn. The pupils left the room quickly afterward, I noticed, without asking further questions.

"I have received a letter from my dear friend, Caroline Fox," I said, trying again to engage Father in conversation and brighten his mood.

"Ah, how are our good friends the Foxes in Falmouth doing? Well, I hope," Grandfather chimed in. I could always count on Grandfather to help me carry on a conversation.

"Yes, how is that fine brother of hers, Barclay, with his long side whiskers?" Caroline asked sweetly. She had changed into a lovely burgundy gown with a square neckline and her shiny brown hair looked lovely in a chignon with a large curl swinging down.

"Caroline Fox and her sister Anna Maria seem to be doing well. For the others, I cannot say," I replied, looking at my sister with a penetrating glance. "Being Quakers, they do not marry outside of their religion, as you know, Caroline."

"More is the pity," Caroline sulked.

"Did you know that Robert Fox paid his children to write in their diaries daily?" Father asked Grandfather.

Grandfather let out a snort of laughter. "If it started them off with a good habit, so much the better," he replied, shaking his head.

Father nodded as he took a sip of his white wine.

I then told Father, Grandfather and Caroline about my mission experiences. I described the often squalid conditions for the numerous children and how food was scarce. I told them about the mother who had to send her child away to service.

"How can food be scarce if the mines are doing well?" Caroline asked, as she placed a small piece of roasted pork on her fork.

"Many of the mine wages cannot keep up with the financial demands of a household," I replied, coolly. "And some of the mines, like the ones we visited, are now in some difficulty."

"The needs are many and exceed a miner's wage in bad times, my dear," Father replied. He continued. "Often wages are squandered on drink and gambling as means to balm the harsh conditions and stress of daily injury in the mine. Or sometimes the wives do not manage the household very well."

At that, the conversation lapsed. *I am hoping Father is not pointing a finger at Caroline and me regarding our own household management. I do not think it fair of him to blame women for the miner's state, but it is disagreeable to argue at dinner. I will bring this up with him another time and ask about his logic in this instance. For, if the women are not properly educated, as we know they are not, then how can we expect them to properly balance their household income against their expenses? And, furthermore, plenty of educated women are known to have difficulty managing the expenses of a household in Penzance, so I think he is pointing to a class difference that I disagreed with. I hoped someone would change the subject.*

"I have just been reading a serial by a new author, Charles Dickens, in a pile of magazines I have been lent. They say that he is a journalist at the *Morning Chronicle* in London, and his reputation is growing," Caroline offered.

"Does that interest you?" Father asked Caroline, monotonously.

"Yes, Father, it does," Caroline replied, vexed. "This serial has a strange title, *Sketches by Boz*. Does that not sound absurd?" she said, laughing down at her plate.

"Hmm," Father grumbled, suspicious of literary innovations. Caroline frowned.

There was another long pause in the conversation. *Poor Caroline,* I thought. *What must it be like for her, living with a family of geologists whose favourite topics of discussion are erosion and rock formations?*

"I would like to read that as well, if you still have the loan of those magazines?" I asked, showing sisterly support. "Mr Dickens sounds like he will become quite popular, from what you have just indicated." Caroline nodded and looked pleased.

"Caroline Fox and I have been discussing a new society that is beginning in Falmouth. It was first thought of by Anna Maria." I was about to put forward the idea of contributing to the Fox sisters' plan for a technical society and was testing the waters with Father. I hated to see him so glum, and I thought this idea would surely spark his interest.

"Oh? And what kind of society is that?" he asked, chewing heartily on his pork and peas.

"The idea is to form an educational society whose purpose will be to generate discussions and exhibitions of innovative art, science, workmanship and industry provided by anyone, including local townspeople. Prizes will be given for the best exhibits. They refer to it as a polytechnic society."

"A polytechnic society for the encouragement of local townspeople? A brilliant idea that corresponds to your educational notions, Bess," Father answered.

"I was hoping you would find it interesting, Father, because the Foxes and even Mr Mill are supporting the idea and contributing to the funding. It has been under serious consideration for well over a year now. Mr and Mrs Fox intend to attend the first meeting which is now being planned." Caroline was busy finishing her meal and did not seem to engage with the idea.

Grandfather leaned forward and said, "A polytechnic? Never heard of such a thing. A wonderful idea, however. Joseph, you must match the Fox funding. You will want your name on this, to be sure. Bess, will you enter your sketches and watercolours?"

"I prefer to see what others will offer and maybe, if invited, to take part in reviewing the exhibitions and prize giving, Grandfather," I said. He shrugged. "The society is not only for education, but also for showing the work of our own skilled local people. The exhibitions will generate pride and encourage craftsmanship and innovation," I added. I wanted also to say that the society would bring in new ideas that occurred outside our own class, for the betterment of all. I thought that I might mention this as the possible crowning outcome of the society once the basic concept was well understood. I waited to listen to Father's reactions.

"Capital is needed, of course. I will look to it straight away," Father said.

"We, the Foxes and I, see that the polytechnic society would bring together the topmost talents in the arts and sciences and share knowledge between different sorts of people," I emphasized.

"Quite right – Joseph, will you mention this to your business colleagues, who can give support and maybe provide speakers?" said Grandfather.

Father nodded. "Our mineral collection would yield some fine topics for discussion. Yes, let us think about the best way to further this great cause," Father suggested.

Delightful, I can not wait to write to Caroline and Anna Maria to share the good news. Further establishment of the Cornwall Polytechnic Society! A new way to educate more people across classes!

Henry and I had discussed the advantages of the Polytechnic Society several times during our continuing charitable
work and excursions, which also included occasional visits to
geological sites of importance. Sadly, we were all too aware
that the educational needs of the mining communities were
far more elementary than what the new Society would be
offering. Many could not read or write, as Henry noted.
Nevertheless, we hoped the society would encourage and elevate thinking across all the varied stations in life. Henry was
an enthusiastic advocate and his energy was exactly what we
needed to bring the Society into being.

***

Days full of sunshine are scarce in November, so when one
came along on a Saturday early in the month, I dropped my
studies and my books and went with Ann, Jacka and Henry
(who happened to be at home with the family that weekend)
on a short visit to another mining community, on the way to
Pendour Cove near Zennor. This time we went on horseback,
and it was a good hour's ride. Ann, never confident in her
riding ability, had to be persuaded a little; but the fine weather
and an opportunity to leave the house for a while encouraged
her to go. I was always trying to give her more practice with
managing a horse. Now that we were more fully aware of their
likely immediate needs, we took as much salted fish and as
many blankets as we could carry in our saddlebags, and on
another horse which Jacka led. We also intended to spend the
rest of the day looking at the geology of the area. The mine
had a large, three-storey engine house of the usual form for
pumping the water out of the lower levels and employed
hundreds of workers. Although the beam and pump rod were
moving majestically up and down as usual, keeping the mine
from flooding, Henry said that work was suspended at present,

and the miners were not being paid. We gave our food and blankets to a group of appreciative wives who lived across the road from the entrance. They said that, because of our gifts, they would now have more than enough to eat that week. I asked about the children's education in this, a fairly remote location. They had almost none. I left a small amount of plain paper and some pencils so that a few children could draw. With a heavy heart, I bid them good day, and then we rode off on the road towards Zennor.

The road was narrow, windy and undulating with the tall hedges on either side curving over almost to form a tunnel, as many of the hedges did on the Penwith roads. Several times we had to move to the side of the road so that a carriage could pass. We decided from then on to ride overland through the fields where Henry knew there was a right of way, and we quickly reached the fork in the road by the old Zennor church, the White House built only the previous year, and the Tinners Arms, an old tavern, where the landlady was more than happy to meet us in the courtyard outside.

"I will gladly care for yer horses, miss," she said, putting down her broom. "I have some nice bread and cheese just inside for your walk. I will fetch it for ye."

"Oh, we do not want to be a bother ..." I trailed off as she had already ducked inside the inn.

"Here ye be," she said, a bit out of breath, handing me a wrapped parcel. "Will you be stayin' for lunch, then? I have just made a pot of carrot and coriander soup and we have some very nice ham," she offered, looking up at me on my horse, her hand shading her eyes from the sun.

"In that case, lunch sounds lovely," I replied.

I had always admired the charming nature of the Tinners' Arms. Some of the walls, it was said, dated from the thirteenth century. It was also said that the masons who built the parish church and tower across the street and had to have a place to rest and take their meals and drink, so they built the single-storey Tinners' Arms, all in stone. The floor was a solid piece of stone, it appeared. The building had windows along every wall and a beautiful garden in the back. Inside, two fireplaces burned, one on the north side of the room and the other fireplace on the south wall, closest to the kitchen. The kitchen, which was in the back, was said to be original as well. Despite the time of the year, colourful flowers lined all sides of the entry to the tavern, giving it a very cottage-like feel. On the side of the White House, a two-storey building with a kitchen and several bedrooms to let next to the Tinners' Arms, was the path leading around the farms to the headland and coves

I adored the rugged Zennor headland jutting out to the open sea. I had been working diligently at my studies for weeks, reviewing my Latin and the mathematical theorems buried in huge leather-backed volumes. My German tutor had complimented me on the most recent essay I had written on a German literary classic. All of that seemed distant now and lacking in importance as we made our way along the headland path.

The path was narrow and rose up and down sharply like a wave, flanked by tall gorse bushes loaded with yellow flowers, dried bracken, ferns, and thick and spiky bramble thickets, making it somewhat difficult to reach the flat rocky areas where we had the best view. Gnarled roots of brush formed the most interesting-looking wooden sculptures, and the little bunches of lush green pennywort on the ground reminded me of tiny cups that I thought fairies drank from when I was younger. In front of us, the blue sea appeared calm at first sight; but on our left, waves smashed dramatically against black and grey granite cliffs and boulders far below us at Pendour Cove, which was the shape of a funnel with an open front, small end pointing inland. From above, the pools of water around the small beach were the colour of a blue-green tourmaline or emerald stone. Light orange seashore lichen covered the jagged and pointed white granite that jutted out along the cliffs in beautiful vibrant puzzle piece patches burnished in gold. Henry and I moved on and off the tops of the rocks, and continued along the path to Zennor Head itself, the vantage point for the best view of the sea and the cliffs of the coastline.

"It feels like we are on the bow of a ship, does it not? Out in the open sea?" Henry asked, laughing, his arms outstretched.

"Yes, it does. Where does our ship sail for today?" I asked him, laughing, holding the straw brim of my bonnet against the wind. The sea breeze and the roar and froth of the waves below were calming and comforting to me. I felt most at home here among the cliffs and granite formations. I again marveled that several varieties of flowers were still in bloom this late in the season. Gorse, chamomile, hemlock, and meadow saffron clung on to their stalks blowing in the wind about the rocks. Nothing in this world made me happier than these cliffs that looked as if a giant had taken an enormous spade or axe and hewn them along the coast like cutting a piece of cake. I wanted to burn this fresh happy day in my memory to recall during times of sadness in the future. I was hesitant to truly feel happiness when it did come along because it seemed profound sadness was always just around the corner. I tried to keep a happy, positive outlook and insisted to myself that a day like today was one of life's jewels.

"Our ship, called the *Elizabeth*, sails the world in search of fortunes of the future," Henry said, poetically, his arms and hands mimicking the action of a spy glass.

I laughed. *How good natured he is*, I thought, *and how rare that is.*

"Fortunes of the future – those could come in many different varieties, don't you think?" I asked as I sat down on a patch of soft green grass on the headland outcrop. Henry walked over to the grassy patch to join me.

"Yes, anything can be a fortune for the right person. Elizabeth, I have wanted to tell you that what you have been doing with the charitable work is a wonderful effort. You seem to understand their dilemma better than most," Henry said, one foot on a large piece of granite, his eyes overlooking the sea.

I ran my hand over the cool grass, drinking in the sunshine and clean, moist sea air. At that moment, I felt like I could stay here at Zennor Head for days and weeks, never wanting to leave. Maybe I would like a position on one of the farms whose fields bordered the sea path. The colours were so lively in contrast with each other: the orange, white, grey, green, blue, and black. Not only was the sea view spectacular, but looking behind us at the rolling farm pastures with their green hedges and fences lined with the thick carpet of heather asleep for the winter, was also stunning. The vivid scene in all directions was like something described in a fairy tale.

"You mean, I understand them better than most in my situation in life, do you not?" I questioned.

Ann and Jacka were at some distance back on the path, eating the bread and cheese the matron had provided. He seemed to be in no hurry to rush back home to finish off his weekend tasks in the stables, and she would be laying out the cousins' Sunday clothes for the morrow, as well as her other household duties, which still had to be done. They, too, were enjoying the sunshine and the opportunity to get away from it all for a while.

"Elizabeth, I do not wish to sound impertinent, but what of your future? What do you intend to do in your life?" Henry's question pulled my mind out of my fairy tale and, at first, I thought he might be joking, but his expression was serious.

I thought for a moment.

"I think my mission is with my family here in Penzance. Somehow, I think Father has a large future he is planning for me. I do not know what that plan is, but he insists I continue with my education, just the way a son would."

"And is that agreeable to you?" Henry asked tenderly.

"Yes. Yes, it is. Somehow, I relish it. It is a bit daunting, to be sure. Perhaps I will also have a family of my own if I am lucky enough. But, yes, I think my future lies with building up this community. That is, making it better for us all and for those to come," I said, arranging yellow gorse flowers in my hand.

"No one better for the job, I would say! I can see you leading in efforts to reduce poverty. I truly can, Bess."

"Now, let us hear about you. What do you desire in the future?" I asked.

"For me, I would like to become a mine captain. Have my own family. Take care of my mother and sisters, of course, and I would like to write the way you and Miss Fox do."

"Write! What a wonderful idea! Would your writing be about pirates of old? Sea battles of ships and men fighting for God and country? Shipwrecks?"

"No, nothing that brilliant," he said, looking off into the hazy blue distance. "I have been thinking of writing about mining, actually. I could write about the people and what it is like to strike a paying lode of copper. It is quite glorious, you know," he said, with a wry smile.

"Perfect," I replied. "Write about your observations of mine captains, the challenges they face. What about Richard Rowe? He seems quite the competent fellow."

"Now that we have our futures determined, and those futures are prosperous and bright, I have something to ask." Henry sat down across from me. He started in. "I would like to ask if you would attend the opening festival at St Mary's Chapel with my family and me, which we are planning to attend. So, would you like to? That is, sit with us."

"Oh, I see. Of course, I am flattered," I said, stunned and

taken aback. "Truly. But the decision is not mine, and Father is unlikely to agree to it, Henry. I can think of no one that Father would approve of. I am sorry. But I would hope to see you there." He looked stoic, with no reaction on his face.

After a moment, he asserted, in rather a low voice, "You pretend not to like me on a personal level, I think."

"On the contrary. I do not know how to pretend, Henry. It is not in my nature." I felt awkward, my hands and face moist with perspiration. "I am not what you would call a loveable person and I cannot help it, even though I have the most cordial regard and esteem for you. I do know there are many kinds of admiration one can have. I do know that I care for you and admire you," I said, honestly. "You represent to me all the good that youth and Cornwall have to offer, wrapped in one person. I do respect your hard work and diligent efforts, your inquisitive mind, and your friendship. Beyond that, I am not ready to ... that is, what I mean to say is ..."

Henry held up his hand to stop me. "In that case, I will have to ask someone else. Someone like Talwyn Hewitt," Henry said, matter of factly, again, staring off into the vastness of the sea.

"She is lovely, like a wildflower, delicate and sweet," I said, looking down at the flowers in my hand.

"Yes, she is quite like a flower. Colourful and bright. Flowers, however, fade and are not long-lasting. They wilt easily. They are delicate and are easily damaged. She's not solid. Solid and pure like you," he said, trying to be light-hearted, and I assumed he was referring to my disposition and my brain. "No, not solid like you. Not solid and true like a snowcapped mountain or immutable like the vast blue sea. Not solid like a sparkling slab of granite or quartz. Not solid like a brilliant natural gem that one wants to hold and never let go."

"It would be quite difficult to take a mountain or a slab of granite to the chapel festival," I said, sadly.

He boldly took my hand and kissed it. His hand was the warmest and strongest I had ever felt. I looked into his eyes to convey how much I admired him. He pulled me forward to him, very lightly and his other arm encircled me, giving me an embrace that was so quick, it was over before I knew what had happened. For a brief moment, our heads touched, and I had never experienced such a powerful moment of impending union. Upon release, he kissed the top of my forehead. His eyes were pensive. He seemed to hesitate, just for a few seconds. Then, he stood up, backed away slowly and returned to the path and started the walk back to the Tinners Arms and our horses. I felt suddenly very downcast. *Have I made a mistake?* He waited for me on the path as it was about a half-mile walk back to the tavern. The path was narrow, so we made our way back single file. I was confused as I watched him from the back navigate the rugged path, not knowing what to say or when to say it.

He stopped, turned to me, and said with a large smile, "If you change your mind, you will mention it, won't you?" I reached up and touched his face lightly. We both laughed.

As planned, we stopped for a late lunch in the Tinners Arms. A husband and wife sat by the fire on one end with their two large black dogs. The dogs gazed at us approvingly as they thought we might drop some crumbs they could lap up. I patted one of the dog's heads and he laid back down, since at that moment I had nothing to give him. Another woman and man came in after we sat down. She had grey hair that stuck out in all directions, resembling a gorse bush. I could not be sure if she intended it to look like that or it was severely windblown. They sat down quietly in a corner. The landlady ladled out carrot and coriander soup from a large tureen and we each had a slice of soft wheat bread with a delightful crust that was about three inches thick in total. She piled on slices of ham.

"Now there's a good Cornish meal for ye," she said, aware of our hungry looks and appetites. We ate happily. Then Jacka said, "Henry, you are always good for an amusing tale. Tell us a tale, one of this place. Ye know the place well enough." Henry and Jacka had a close bond and they got along like brothers.

"A tale? Of this place?" Henry said in an exaggerated tone, swallowing a mouthful of food.

"Yes, if you please!" Jacka urged, ruffling Henry's hair with his hand.

"Yes, please!" I chimed in.

"If you must," Ann laughed.

"Well then. You know the tale about the mermaid of Pendour and the lighthouse."

"Yes, yes," we all said.

"But do you know that tale of the mermaid of St Senaranthe, the old church of Zennor, the church right outside this door?" he asked, leaning in, as if to tell us a secret or a bit of gossip.

"No," we replied.

"Let's hear it, then," Jacka said, leaning back in his chair and crossing his arms over his chest in anticipation of a nice long story.

Henry cleared his throat and began. "Huddled between the moors and the cliffs, here sits the old church of St Senara. In the church, carved on the end of a bench, is a strange figure of a woman with long flowing hair, holding up a mirror and a comb. Legend has it that many years ago, probably right after the church was built, a beautiful lady would attend church. No one knew who she was. Many people asked about her, because not only was she a beauty, but she also had a lovely singing voice. One of the local men, Matthew Trewella, decided to pursue her, and he too had an amazing singing voice."

"And they decided to join a choir, did they?" Ann asked, with a note of sarcasm in her voice.

Henry continued, ignoring her quip. "Matthew, according to legend, decided to follow her one day after services, down to the cliffs. He never returned to Zennor."

"They never do," Jacka sighed, shaking his head. We all laughed.

"Years passed and Matthew's unexplained disappearance was forgotten. His body was never found. Then, one day a ship's captain was sailing past Pendour Cove when he heard someone singing in a voice so beautiful, he tried to follow it. He saw her. The beautiful woman said she must return to her husband Matthew and her children, and could not stay to sing any longer. The captain found his way to Zennor and told the people that Matthew had married a mermaid and they now had a family near Pendour Cove. The people became afraid of this fate, so they carved an image of the mermaid on the end of a pew as a warning. To this day, the town has not lost another man yet. And that is the mermaid tale of Zennor." Henry made a slight bow at the table and we clapped and laughed for his dramatic tale.

"Well then. Let us see it," Ann exclaimed.

"I agree. Let us go to have a look at this mermaid carving," I echoed.

We rushed over to the church but entered respectfully. No one was in the building, so we crept through it looking for the famous mermaid.

"I see it there!" I exclaimed. I had found the historic carving.

Just as he had explained, there it was – a quite large and detailed depiction of the mermaid, mirror and comb.

"It is quite lovely and detailed!" I said, admiringly.

"Imagine that ..." Ann trailed off, as if she was imagining life underwater in the cove.

We came out of the church into bright sunlight. Jacka and Henry brought the horses round and discussed their readiness for the ride back. Jacka, Ann and I were quiet as we mounted our horses a bit earlier than we planned for the ride back to Madron and the Carne country home where I was currently living. So was Henry. Ann gave me a questioning look, but I looked the other way. Eventually, we reached a fork in the road that would lead to Henry's family home.

"My time is running short, and I must get back. There are things I have to do on the farm," Henry said, looking over his shoulder. "Thank you for a most memorable day." His eyes lowered, his bright disposition vanished. I reined my horse closer to his and tucked a sketch of him from earlier that day in his jacket pocket. Despite our enjoyable lunch, from the wounded look in his eyes, I suspected that it might be our last such excursion together.

***

As promised and on time, the work to replace the ancient chapel opposite our house on Chapel Street was finished; and the newly built St Mary's Chapel opened on November 15, 1835. Penzance, although a fairly large town, was actually part of Madron parish, whose church was two miles away in the village and near our country home. St Mary's was a "chapel of ease," built and consecrated for the convenience of the people in the town. The Church of England and its creed was still the established religion of the realm, and in earlier times long past, church attendance had been compulsory. Even though we were committed Methodists, we were full of enthusiasm for the renewal of St Mary's, and had made a contribution. Father, Caroline, and I went to the opening and had a goose dinner with all the other families. Grandfather was not well and stayed home in bed to rest.

Despite the weather turning wet and cold, we did not mind standing outside the front of the chapel admiring it while awaiting our turn to go inside. Although we lived directly opposite, we did not really have a very good view of the entire building. Our view enabled us to see that the masonry was built from beautiful West Penwith granite and had a slate roof, so we were quite interested to proceed with the internal tour.

"Father, do you think the style is made even more Gothic by the granite?" I asked.

"Yes, Bess, and it gives it a very elegant appearance, more elegant than other churches," he declared and I agreed. A lovely slim tower dominated the skyline over the other roofs in Penzance and was our new landmark from out at sea. St Mary's overlooks the holy headland which gives Penzance its name. It is "Pen Sans" in the Cornish language where "Pen" means headland and "Sans" means a sacred church site. The ancient chapel which stood on these same grounds prior to St Mary's being built was named after St Anthony. St Anthony's had a carved stone figure set in its east wall. It had become badly damaged over the years, and it was difficult to ascertain what the figure represented. It seemed as if it was a mother holding a child – Mary and Jesus, presumably. I was glad to see that it had been moved to an honourable site at St Mary's, next to several cemetery plots. I recollected all this to myself with pride, in admiration of the chapel and our long history.

We inspected the interior and saw that the architect, Charles Hutchens, had created a five-bay nave, with full-length aisles and an additional bay for gallery stairs. The terraced head of the inner doorway carried the Lamb and Flag against a cross, taken from the seal of Penzance. He created a meeting room in the absence of a church hall. The nave was well lit and spacious and had a separate roof from the aisles, each of the four centred arched sections with slim wooden strips forming square panels. The nave ceiling had a large "M" in a rose at the centre, which I pointed out to Father. The entire ceiling was comprised of squared trim overlaying a deep red colour, creating a striking and majestic atmosphere.

"Father, look at the alms box which came from St Anthony's." I pointed to an ancient box with very ornate trim. "And I hear the architect has kept a stoup dated 1612," I exclaimed. We admired the alms box which looked like multiple boxes forming a statue of sorts, about three feet high.

"Yes, Bess. I would that they had been able to keep more of the ancient pieces," Father responded, sullenly.

The pulpit was wooden and painted white with gilded mouldings and a carved panel for the lectern.

"Bess, did you know that the original chapel here was spared in the Spanish raid of 1595 because they knew that Mass had been celebrated in it previously?" Father asked.

"No, Father, I did not know that. At least they had the decency to show some respect before they burned down the remainder of the town. I hope we will be able to hear the bells ring a full peal today," I said. "That would be a most glorious sound!"

"We shall see, but I expect we will hear them at the end of the proceedings," he replied, giving my arm a little squeeze.

At the back of the church was a wide pathway that led to a large, grassy area suitable for outdoor events. From this area, one could see the harbor and the open sea stretching out far beyond it. For the celebration, a marquee had been erected, and volunteers had arranged many tables and chairs for dining. Caroline had gone to join our family friends, the Bolitho's, at a long plank table. I saw my friend Emily Bolitho sitting there with her family. They beckoned to us to join them. Father and I circled the table, happy to join long-time family friends and sometimes business associates, as they had their own set of bank branches.

As I rounded the tables, I saw the Pearce family sitting at a table near the side facing the large stone wall perimeter. I smiled genuinely at them as they were all devout, caring people. Henry sat at the end of the table, Talwyn Hewitt by his side. I paused. *So, he did invite her.* Henry and I did not know how to greet each other – he seemed embarrassed from the look on his face. I gave a quick nod and turned away. I sat frozen at the table with the Bolithos, but no one seemed to notice. *I want Henry to be happy,* I told myself repeatedly. Yet, I was not happy seeing him with Talwyn. *You have no right to be unhappy. Perhaps I could have at least asked Father if I could attend with the Pearce's.* I thought, sadly, having missed my chance.

I tried my best to be conversant and pleasant. I thought Caroline would be interested in the alms box, given her love of antiquities.

"Caroline, did you see the ancient alms box from St Anthony's?" I asked her, trying to be pleasant.

"Why, yes, I did. I admired it very much." Was her limited response as she then returned to her conversation with one of the Bolitho's on her left.

As we left the church to walk home across the street, the bell ringers must have given mighty pulls, because the bells rang out loudly and clearly for the first time across the whole town of Penzance. It was a glorious finish to what had been a glorious day for all. I hoped that we would be fortunate enough to hear those bells toll long into the future, whatever that future would bring. *But will it be prosperous and bright, as Henry said that day on Zennor Head?*

Chapter Eight

Journey

July 1836

"It is the largest turnout for anything Cornwall has ever seen," I exclaimed under my breath to my sister, Caroline.

"Chapel Street is lined with people on the way into the house, and there are twenty-four carriages outside, some standing in Quay Street as well," Miss Ann said. "It's astounding."

"That many? That is more than I was expecting," I gasped, looking out of the parlour windows towards the street.

"He has been a towering strength for us all, for the whole of the community, Bess. He will be missed. God rest his soul," Father replied quietly.

"All the establishments in town are closed for the funeral," Mr Fox said quietly to Father as we were gathered in the parlour around Grandfather's coffin. "However, I daresay more business dealings will be conducted today than in the last two months."

We turned to greet our dear family friends, Mr and Mrs Bolitho, whose family were also bankers in our area and in East Cornwall, and whom we had seen at the St Mary's opening festival. They had also come inside the parlour to pay their respects.

I asked Caroline, "Can you see Caroline Fox? I must find her." The house on Chapel Street was crowded with people paying their respects. All I could see were the shoulders and backs of people.

"People have come from all over Cornwall, Wales, and London for the funeral of William John Carne of Gwinear near Hayle, Cornwall, who died at the age of eighty-one," my sister Caroline said, as if she was a newspaper journalist and trying to add a light humour to our sorrowful day.

"He was my bedrock," I told her, sadly. Caroline simply nodded. Finally, I saw Caroline Fox and her parents make their way through the crowded parlour over to me. *Thank goodness. I need her comfort now.*

"Oh, Bess! I am so sorry to hear this sad news. I know you are heartbroken!" Caroline Fox said, clasping my hand. "Next to your father, you were the closest family member to him. What a sad day for us all but a happy one in heaven," she said as we stood in the parlour next to Grandfather in his coffin. Black crepe draped the windows and mirrors, and the family portraits had been turned around in accordance with the local superstition that doing so prevented evil spirits from haunting those in the frames. Ann had insisted despite my weak protests.

"Yes, but it is good to see you. So many people are here I was afraid I would miss you. Will I see you at the church in Gulval and at the breakfast here afterwards?" I asked her, anxiously. "We are sending him away with ham, his favourite."

Caroline stifled a laugh. "I will be at both places and by your side if you like. You look tired."

"I stayed up with Grandfather all last night, so yes, I am tired but being the youngest, it was put to me to stay with him," I answered.

"Poor you!" she replied.

"Nothing to do but move on. That is what Grandfather wanted us all to do, in His name," I stated, which came out in a rather monotone voice. *I am so very tired and deprived of sleep.*

When it was time to take Grandfather to the funeral service at Gulval church, we stepped outside to climb into our carriages. *It looks as if people of all descriptions are waiting to walk behind Grandfather on his journey: miners, mine captains, townspeople, fishermen, bankers, civic dignitaries. Grandfather was like that. Someone that people of all descriptions followed when he was alive. Fitting.*

"I see even a few men from Harveys are here," Father informed me. "See them jostling for their places in the procession? I also see members of the wider Boase and Bolitho families," he added.

Some Branwell relations are here, but not their Brontë cousins, Charlotte, Anne, and Emily, as Yorkshire is such a distance away.

The carriage ride to Gulval, our family burial place, seemed to take hours, even though it was only two miles from Penzance and even though we were riding in our finest carriage. The slow procession of people dressed in their finest, some walking, some riding, and the twenty-four carriages plodded along slowly behind Grandfather, in honour of his life. *Long ago, he had been a miner,* I remembered *being told. Then he had become an adventurer who invested in mines, a shipowner, and then a banker – and above all else, he was known as the father of Wesleyan Methodism in Cornwall. He had been a strong-willed man and a force of nature. How did he manage so well in so many different occupations?* We all sat quietly in the carriage, containing myself, sitting with Father, Caroline, and my oldest sister, Mary, who had come for the occasion from London. *I imagine we were all wondering the* same thing. *That being, what would a future without Grand-father mean for each of us.*

After the internment, mourners milled around in the churchyard. Mr John Stuart Mill walked slowly up to Caroline Fox and me. My sister Caroline was standing next to us.

"My deepest condolences to you and your family, Miss Carne."

I simply nodded. *I would like to converse with him but I feel drained of energy at this point.*

"And what will you write about this grand event in your diary, Miss Fox?" he asked.

"I will say it was the most solemn and most well-attended gathering in all of Cornwall," Caroline replied.

"Quite true, Miss Fox. I say, Elizabeth, I did find your reply on the schooling of women and men at home to be very logical with enlightened reasoning. Thank you for your many consequential and deep responses. I hope to receive your point of view on the subjugation of women and the implications for society. Shall I write to you with my position on that?" It seemed to me that Mr Mill wanted to take advantage of seeing me face to face for his additional requests, as many of the authors, bankers, politicians, and scientists in the crowd were also doing with Father and amongst themselves.

"Yes, of course, I would look forward to such a distraction, Mr Mill," I replied. Mr Mill tipped his hat to all three of us. *He has only aged slightly and still a charming, thoughtful man.*

Following close behind him was John Sterling, a very handsome man with a fine, chiselled face. The Sterlings were longstanding friends of both the Carne and the Fox families. I considered him to be almost an older brother. *He is a highly educated author whom I admire, both for his intellect and, also, his courage to endure his struggle with tuberculosis.*

"I enjoyed your lectures at the Royal Cornwall Polytechnic Society, Mr Sterling," Caroline Fox said. "I hope we will benefit more from your oratory skills in Falmouth."

"Indeed, that would be my greatest wish as well. My sincere condolences, Miss Carne, for your enormous loss," he added.

"Thank you for your kindness in attending today, Mr Sterling," I replied. "I quite enjoyed your last draft of poems and would like to see more, if you have them."

"It would be my pleasure, Miss Carne," he smiled, happy to receive my request.

We stood facing the church on the lower grassy terrace, underneath many enormous trees that provided much needed shade. Flower beds adorned the sides of the church and provided beautiful contrast to the many ancient headstones which reminded us why we were here.

My uncle, John Carne, himself a widely published author, walked past our group. He had been such a prolific writer that Grandfather had allowed him to follow his literary inclinations to write and publish and to become ordained in the Church of England rather than having to pursue mining or banking as a career. He walked to the top of the steps, with green grass slopes on either side, which led to the church. He turned, facing the crowd below. He held his arms up over his head in a wide "v" shape.

"My friends, my friends," he said in a loud voice, attracting everyone's attention.

"Oh, I do hope he is about to tell a story!" Caroline Fox said to me. "It is said that your Uncle John is such a renowned storyteller that he has cleared many a room in a party to gather around him and hear his tales."

His hands clasped before him, he said, "We have come today to honour the life of our father, William John Carne. I say our father because he was a father figure not just to his family, or the town of Penzance, but to all of Cornwall. When he was much younger, he met John Wesley not far from here on Newlyn Green, where Wesley was preaching about a new way of faith, which came to be called Methodism. Now, we all know what a tough lot hard-working and hard-drinking Cornwallers can be. But apparently Wesley did not. Wesley came away a bit shaken from his experience saying, 'Those wretches must be true Cornwallers.' He said the adoption of Methodist principles could go no lower and that he was 'beating the air.'" The crowd laughed. "In fact, the crowd was so rough that Wesley commented on their brazen language and said they were pushing each other off nearby cliffs." John laughed and the crowd laughed with him. "My father embraced these teachings of God alongside his good health."

"William Carne rose up and accepted a mission – a mission to be an early leader in this new nonconforming faith. He gave it respectability, not to mention a little capital," John said, behind his hand. The crowd laughed again. "He provided Methodist teaching and books for education, even in his own home." Several in the crowd nodded. "He gave us a better way to live. He improved our hearts and minds with his teaching. He has been called, the 'Father of Cornish Methodism' here in Penzance for his work. I was proud to call him Father. I think many of us were. Thank you for being here today. May God be with us all." And with that, he sauntered down the steps to murmurs of "Aye" and "God be with you."

"True words, Bess. Your grandfather was a legend and will be as long as we remember him," Caroline Fox said.

"He was all of that," I replied, nodding. "He will be missed by so many," I added.

Out of the corner of my eye, I spotted Henry Pearce approaching. I had not seen or heard from him in months. He stepped up at an angle and I did not see the gloved hand in the crook of his arm until it was too late.

"Hello, Bess. We are sorry for your loss. Your grandfather will always be a legend to anyone who knew him," Henry said, only his side facing me, due to the crowd.

"Henry!" I exclaimed. In a moment of weakness, I grabbed his hand and then the crowd parted, and I saw the gloved hand on his arm. He was with Talwyn Hewitt, the tailor's daughter. I dropped his hand like a hot ember. I felt my cheeks burning. I forced myself to hold my eyes up and put a smile on my face.

"May I introduce you to my fiancée, Talwyn Hewitt," he said, plainly.

My face froze. I was stunned. "Hello, Talwyn, nice of you to come," I stammered.

"Henry, Talwyn," Caroline Fox said, with a slight curtsey. Caroline my sister did the same.

Henry and Talwyn departed as quickly as they came.

He brought her here, to my grandfather's funeral? To make his announcement? I am alarmed and saddened that he has chosen this day to....

"The surprising things you discover at funerals," Caroline my sister, said, sarcastically.

"She appears the right sort for him and will likely make him a perfect wife," Caroline Fox said, as if to say aloud what they must have been thinking. *Right. There can never be a future for me with Henry. I am an heiress. He is a humble mine purser.*

"Caroline, would you like to take a closer look at these exquisite roses? That fuchsia one is a most striking colour," I said, taking her elbow and steering her away from the crowd. We walked past people sitting on black wrought-iron benches, talking in low voices, and stood, intent on the roses while I tried to compose myself.

I reached out to lightly touch the lone fuchsia, so unique in colour, which was just past bud and pushing towards full bloom in the July heat. The sun beat down directly on the rose's face and its petals seemed to glow in the light. I said to myself and to the rose, *I know what it feels like to be different, to be unique, and to be alone. You seem quite happy as one of a kind in your garden. Will I be happy in mine?*

"Too bad we are not at Madron Church, where we could visit the holy well for advice." Caroline tried to make light of the situation.

"An appropriate time to look in a well for advice, I would say," I said. *His fiancée! I am stunned. What a dreadful situation to find out about their engagement here.*

"What is that verse one should say, staring down into the well?" Caroline asked, smiling. She did not believe in the powers of the well any more than I did, but it was said that if a girl gazed into the water and chanted the verse, the future of her beloved would reveal itself. If the water was clear, all was well with the beloved. If the water was cloudy, trouble was near.

"I do not recall it, but it is a lovely well all the same. Despite what must be cloudy water today," I replied, solemnly. "Given that," I continued, weakly. "I would like to return home now." We turned away from the rose garden to make our way down the stairs and back to the carriages.

"Elizabeth, please come and meet Mr Gilbert from the Geological Society." Father saw us and waved me over.

"Yes, Father." I had to straighten up and push forward, following Father, with what little energy I had left. *Must be polite. Must be gracious.*

"Hundreds of people are due back on Chapel Street for the funeral breakfast. I must go and attend to Miss Ann and the servants," sister Caroline said as she walked towards the carriages.

After a series of introductions to her father's circle, Caroline Fox returned to her parents' sides and I stepped into my carriage. I had no words. I peered briefly through the carriage window then looked straight ahead as it drove away.

There will likely never be a man that understands me the way Henry does, I thought, dejectedly, alone in the carriage. *If there is one, I cannot imagine how I will ever find him.*"

Chapter Nine

Promissory

September 1837

Life at home was difficult without Grandfather's good humour. Father and I moved on with our studies and work, and Caroline with the management of our household, with Charity, Miss Ann, Ann and Jacka.

Months passed from warm summer to windy autumn. My studies included spending weeks reviewing the geological data from our family friend Mr Charles Fox, who was Caroline's uncle. I felt ready to discuss my conclusions with Father. We sat in the second-floor study overlooking Chapel Street, situated between my bedroom and Caroline's. Father's bedroom was across the hall from Caroline's. The second-floor study was lined floor to ceiling with books, which had now become a mixture of mine and Father's, after the moves we had made to include our cousins into the household. Father made it my job to catalogue all of our books and note their location in this small study, in the basement study, and in the Methodist reading library in the basement next to the kitchen. This was no easy task as family members often pulled books out and did not return them to their proper location. We pulled our chairs against the room's one large window to obtain the best light. Outside, Chapel Street was awhirl with shoppers and tradesmen.

"Father, today I would like to discuss Mr Fox's data with you and his draft paper on the geothermal gradient. It is a most fascinating discovery." I patted a seat near a pile of papers and drawings, indicating where he could sit. It occurred to me that while most young people of my station enjoyed looking out of the window at the street fascinations, I read, studied, and analyzed. Hours would pass and I would barely notice; I was so engrossed in my work.

"I asked Mr Fox if you and I could look over his data and findings as part of a review and summary of his article," I continued. Father nodded.

"He and I have discussed this research. It goes back to 1821, I believe," he said, folding his arms across his chest.

"Yes, he has been collecting data in mine shafts for quite a while and studying the geothermal gradient."

"Definition, Elizabeth?"

"Yes, Father. The geothermal gradient is the rate of temperature change as depth increases in the Earth's top layer of ground, called the crust."

"Correct. Continue," he said.

"Mr Fox has found that temperature does increase as depth increases. But what causes that temperature increase?" I asked.

"You tell me. You are the geologist," Father said.

"According to Mr Fox, the heat comes from deep inside the Earth."

"Yes. Is that all?" he queried.

"No. The Earth's outer layer serves as a blanket to keep the heat in, but when the blanket is torn, heat escapes – where the crust is thinnest, or where fault lines cause weaknesses."

"Ah ha. And are there any other possible causes of this

underground heat?" he asked, quizzing me.

"What part does pressure play, Father? Does pressure from the weight of the crust cause heating as the pressure increases with depth? And if the Earth's crust was hotter in early days, is that why komalites are no longer formed?" I asked, as pointed questions came tumbling out.

"So many questions at once!" Father laughed, which he rarely did. "One at a time. One at a time!"

Just as he was beginning to answer, Charity came in.

"Sir, will you be having tea here, or would you prefer the parlour downstairs? she asked, her head tilted at a deferential angle. Charity admired my father greatly for being well-spoken and a scholar particularly; she herself did not know how to read, to our mutual regret. *When she interacts with him, it is as if she thinks she is speaking to Socrates himself.* I stifled a little laugh.

"Here, as we are in the middle of working on an assignment," Father replied.

"Yes, and I have received a letter from Caroline asking us to participate in Mr Fox's discussion of this paper at the next Polytechnic meeting, Father, so we need to prepare questions for Mr Fox as well," I replied.

"Sir, Miss Ann has made several sorts of cake for your tea today," Charity interrupted.

"I have been thinking about what John said about those buns. We can have Miss Ann's cakes later, for dessert perhaps. Charity, do go up the hill to Market Jew Street and fetch us some of those saffron buns that my brother goes on about. You know the place?" Father asked.

"Yes, sir," she replied quickly, nodding, and turning to go back down the stairs.

"Father, do let me go to Betsy Allen's shop on Market Jew Terrace! I know exactly where it is. I would love a bit of time outdoors, and I would be very quick about it," I pleaded.

"Very well. Put it on our account. When you return, we shall get back to your questions and prepare for Mr Fox's presentation," Father replied, emphasizing our continued work.

"Of course, Father. I look forward to that. I will only be a few moments." I exited the front door with a quick and happy step. I had put on my navy wool cape, the one that had frog fasteners at the throat with a large hood hanging down the back. It had recently been raining, and I was delighted to be outdoors in the fresh, brisk air, which smelled so much like the sea I could almost taste the saltiness. I walked up the Chapel Street hill on the narrow pavement and watched the gulls swoop down to the ground and back up again in the wind. I walked carefully up the hill, avoiding the dung piles and mud. The granite paving in wet or frosty weather could be slippery and cause a fall or a twisted ankle, so I took care to watch my step as I dodged the crowd of shoppers in my haste. I turned right in Market Square, and I made my way along Market Jew Terrace to Betsy Allen's shop at the far end.

Her shop was not much to look at from the outside. It was a one-storey, very rudimentary block building. But the smells coming from it! I floated on the scent from the pavement outside to the door and I ducked my head to enter through the low doorway, savouring the delicious scent of crisp buttery muffins. My eyes devoured the macaroons, gingerbread nut, heeva cakes, currant cakes and her famous saffron buns arranged in rows along her shelves on the left side of the shop on brown paper.

"Good afternoon, Mrs Allen," I said, trying to decide which of the macaroons we should have and taking stock of her supply of saffron buns. Looking around the shop, it surprised me that no one else was in there because she was one of the most popular bakers in Penzance.

"G'day to ye. What'll ye 'ave then, Miss Carne?" she said,

wiping her hands on her apron. She was an older woman with a softly wrinkled face and brown wavy hair with streaks of silver in it. A few of her stained teeth were missing. Mrs Allen was famous in Penzance for her smart sense of humour and the quality of her baking. She stood before me in her smudged white apron over a blue cotton dress, also smudged with flour. Behind her was an old black cast iron stove with two ovens below the hob. A pair of bellows sat in a basket next to the stove. From the look of the bowls, spoons, sacks and pots strewn about, she had had a busy morning.

"Father would love some of the saffron buns. The ones that Uncle John likes so much, please."

"Yes, yes. Mr John Carne came into my shop just the other day and he said, 'Betsy, give me one of your saffron buns. I have been through the Holy Land in Palestine, and over many other parts of the world, and nowhere have I been able to taste such cakes as yours,' he said. 'One of the first things I do on coming back to Penzance after a long journey is to visit your shop to enjoy your capital cakes.'" She beamed.

"Yes, my father agrees wholeheartedly with that!" I laughed. "Could we have some of those pretty macaroons as well?" I pointed to some light pink macaroons. *I will give one each to Miss Ann, Charity, and Ann as a treat for all their hard work.*

"Ah, those is me raspberry macaroons. Will 'ey suit ye?" she asked courteously.

"Yes, quite," I replied. "I would like to put these on our account, if that is quite convenient," I said.

"Certainly, ye can. If ye is a Carne, ye can," she laughed, her eyes crinkling at the corners.

As she filled my order, she said, "I 'ave another customer says that while he does not know what heaven is like, my macaroons help him better understand what it might be like!"

Mrs Allen was also a delightful storyteller. She was always

cheerful, but I could tell she worked very hard, baking and standing on her feet all day long, with sweat on her brow and wisps of grey hair escaping from her kerchief. *What must it be like to be her?*

"Mrs Allen, how did you become such a fine baker, if I may ask?" I was curious.

"It's in me bones, from generations, on me mother's side. That an' hard work and plen'y o' it." She sighed from the strain of bending as she was leaning down, using a spatula to extract my order and place the items in a bag.

"I see," I replied. "The perfect combination then. Perhaps that will work for me as well," I said with a smile.

She looked at me a bit askew, just for a second, as if wondering what kind of hard work I might be involved with, given my family's name. Then she quickly said, "Work, like life, is 'ow ye treat people. 'At's the most impor'ant thing." She nodded, placing the packages in my hands.

"'Ave a good day and come back soon! And give me regards to ye uncle John," she said as I gave her a quick nod.

"I will, and thank you, Mrs Allen." I smiled goodbye as I ducked my head under the doorway again as I left.

How you treat people, she said. Of course, she was exactly right. This baker knows what is important in business and in life, perhaps better than those more educated than she. People of different classes have equal worth and importance, in that she works as hard as any banker or solicitor, I daresay. Class distinctions bother me greatly –_especially where Henry is concerned. Class distinctions lock those "without" into place and do more harm than good to society, I thought, vehemently.

I walked on, thinking more about Mrs Allen and her shop. *Father will be well pleased with these for his tea.* I crossed over Market Jew Street back to Chapel Street.

The bells at St Mary's were beginning to ring. I could hear them from the top of Chapel Street. *That's odd. It is not time for services. Someone must be having a wedding or a christening.* I frowned as I considered why the bells were ringing. I kept walking quickly, concentrating on getting back to my studies.

I was just passing the Admiral Benbow tavern, when I saw a black carriage slowly pull out of the gate of our chapel and onto Chapel Street. Apparently, the bells were ringing for them. My grip on my packages loosened and I almost dropped them. I saw a man's face in the carriage window as the carriage rolled by heading up the hill. It was Henry Pearce, wearing a black suit with top hat and seated next to him was a blur of white. He was smiling. Then his expression went completely blank when he saw me. I stared back, equally blankly, my heart dropped, and immediately started to ache. Then he was gone. Henry was just married, presumably to Talwyn Hewitt.

He did not tell me and I was not invited. I have made a terrible mistake. I have made a terrible, permanent mistake. A binding one that is unbreakable. I stood there, frozen. I do not know for how long. My hand started aching from clutching the packages. *What did you think would happen?* I chastised myself. I walked numbly up the steps to our front door. I handed the packages to Charity in our large hallway, without so much as a word, and climbed the front stairs to rejoin Father in the study as if my feet were made of lead.

He said, "Right, now let us continue with your questions."

What would have been the most enjoyable part of my day had turned into something quite bland and uninteresting. I responded to his questions in an offhand, indifferent manner, showing none of my earlier energy or enthusiasm.

"My dear, you seem to be sinking in this topic rather than being buoyed by it," he asked, with one eyebrow raised in a questioning look.

"Yes. I have just seen Henry Pearce and his new wife drive

by in their wedding carriage," I responded, dryly. *Now she will be sharing his life and his love,* I thought forlornly.

"Oh, I see," Father said, slowly, clearly seeing the hurt in my eyes. "And did you wish to be in that carriage, destined for a life of marital bliss?"

"You and Mother were happy, had many children, and built a wonderful life together," I stressed, not willing to be overruled in my sadness.

"Yes, and I would say that we were blessed and fortunate in that regard," he said, looking down at his folded hands.

I turned to face him and forcefully said, "Father, you seem to have a plan for me, for my future, but I am not sure what that plan is."

"I'll not deny it. Elizabeth, you have tremendous potential. Even John Mill said so, and he is now becoming revered by thousands. John Sterling commented to me at your grandfather's funeral that your keen intellect is a gift. Your intellect is a power for good. Would you want your power of good limited by a man who is likely going to want to keep your abilities at bay?"

"No, no I would not. But a man might exist who would welcome such a wife!" I hurled at him, defensively.

"It is possible, but is there really any man who would be willing to commit himself to your mission, to our mission, of raising up the community?" he asked, patiently.

"What if there was such a man, but he came from a different class and understood the importance of my mission, even shared in my mission?" I asked, as theoretically as I could. I did not want to anger Father but I refused to succumb on this topic.

"My dear, gaps between the classes are a social problem that concerns us, yes. Our family is in banking where credibility and the right business and personal relationships are essential. However, what I am trying to say is that with a man inevitably come children. That is the burden to weigh, not the class in this situation. Do you take my meaning?" he asked, reaching for my arm, gently. He was referring to Henry Pearce, of course, and the consequences of a woman having a family.

"Yes, I see," I replied, downcast. "But, Father, you will support Henry, will you not? Can you look after his interests and see to it that he has opportunities? He has a strong mind."

"Yes, I can make inquiries and do what I can," Father said, gently. He added, "You may not believe me when I say this, but I would rather you marry someone like Henry than that rake Richards. I know you are fond of Henry and that he has greatly helped you with your missions. That is all fine and good. But, Bess, you are so very young and Henry Pearce wants to move forward with his life. Are you truly ready for marriage and children? Probably many children? This is the real issue, Bess, not money or class. And what then? What time would you have for science, mathematics, and writing? Think about your poor mother. She had eight children in about as many years. She had no time for anything other than childbearing, weaning and rearing. What time would that leave you for your mission? Not to mention the dangers of childbirth! If you assembled ten thousand men of Cornwall or any other region together, you, Bess, would have more intellect than any of them. You have a grand and wondrous future ahead to do the Lord's work freely. Can you see that?"

"Yes, Father. And I am happy for it. Truly. But surely brother William would have the right to step in before me. He has a college education, and I do not! I have read everything from Lyell to Byron, but will never have a university degree like a man. In addition, it would be unusual, and probably socially unacceptable, for me to work in commerce or industry, even though I have the legal right to do so – and society would also frown on me owning property while unmarried, for that matter. My only real options would be to become a governess or perhaps a teacher."

Father raised a large hand gently to silence me. "Your brother may not follow this path, given his current dealings in France. He may be part of the executorship of my will, certainly. You, Bess, are the one I see moving our legacy forward. That is what I have in mind for you, however surprised you seem."

"Yes, I am thoroughly surprised. Thank you, Father, for your confidence in me," I said, taken aback. "I am surprised because I do not see myself, as a female, achieving what you have done, to be honest. How will I accomplish this without a university education behind me? I am not you."

"Nor would you want to be me, Bess. Be yourself and you can do anything. People warm to you more than they do me," he said, laying his hand on mine. "I can and will prepare you with the right relationships and backing," he said, smiling.

"Father, I have to live my own life and I adore children, you know that," I said, slowly to emphasize my point.

"Of course. Of course," he said, now patting my hand. "I want you to live your own life. However, I know that you can and will succeed where other women have not. We will prepare you with stepping stones. One step at a time. Tomorrow, we will begin by looking at our holdings. I will teach you about looking out to the horizon with our assets: the bank, our ships, our lands, our other properties. We will discuss and learn about investments, risks, and returns," he said, and sat deep in thought for a few moments.

"How? How do you know that I will be successful where other women would not?" I urged him to answer.

"Because of who you are inside. You have every element you need – intelligence, grit, determination, resolve, kindness, and faith. We have had a most fruitful conversation, my dear!" he exclaimed, confidently.

"If that is the case, Father, I have a few ideas I would like to discuss with you," I said.

Father laughed, as if I had just proven his point. "Such as?" he asked, one eyebrow raised.

"Such as, you remember the farmer, William Freethy, the one who assisted us at the stones that day we encountered the ruffians?"

"Yes," he said, dubiously.

"I would like to visit his farm again and determine whether he could apply new methods and tooling to improve his yields and the working of the farm. If so, I would like to draw up a loan that he, perhaps with additional farmers, could apply for, to share an investment in new implements. That way, he might be able to send his children to school instead of having them work on the farm. And thus, improve the standard of living for them as well as other farmers near Penzance."

"An excellent learning example. Do you think Freethy is a good risk? Are farmers a good risk as a whole?" he asked.

I know where he is going with this. There is too much risk, with so many things beyond a farmer's control – such as the weather and sickness in livestock. The list is endless.

"Could we not spread the risk in some way, Father?" I asked, beseechingly.

"Let us develop an approach. I will ask Marrack, our manager, to join us in the discussion at the bank. But do not mention this to the farmer. We do not want to get his hopes up," Father warned.

"Very well, Father. As you wish," I said, trying to smile. *He is very influential, my father, and the thought of being a practitioner of science, an author, and a banker does appeal greatly to me, strangely. I fervently hope we can help the Freethys. I will discuss my ideas about the schools another time with Father. One step at a time, as he said.*

"Now, I would like to sink my teeth into one of those

saffron buns!" Father said, as he helped himself to the plate that Ann had left in front of us. He seemed relieved and happy as he devoured his bun and drank his tea with a bit of a slurp. *Teatime is a time for him to relax. I enjoy seeing him have a bit of happiness. But that makes us one.*

I will miss Henry deeply. I sighed to myself, staring down at the table remembering our fond moments at Pendour Cove. *I will always care for him and hope for the best for him. I cannot simply change how I feel about him, so it is no use expending energy to try.* I pushed back the pain as far as I could in my mind, picked up the nib pen and pulled a pile of papers towards me. *I must move forward, again.*

***

After a few months, and several days of Polytechnic meetings in Falmouth, my sister Caroline, Father, and I set sail on Father's schooner, the *Joseph Carne* bound for south-east Italy. I had enjoyed our Polytechnic meetings tremendously and was proud to have given the award for the best work in the exhibition to a miner who had made a miniature model that set out to be an exact replica of the mine where he worked. He said he had paid seventeen shillings over a couple of years for the materials to make it, which was quite a sum. Everyone applauded his work, and he was so proud. It was truly gratifying to watch because those moments made the dream of the initiative come true. A miner had created an incredible piece of skillful art for all to admire. *A wonderful example to all that class distinctions matter little.*

Time exploring the horizontal layers of the Cenozoic sedimentary rocks in the cliffs at Torre Sant'Andrea in Lecce province would be an interesting diversion. Father needed well-deserved time away from the bank and away from the shadow of the family vault at Gulval. He had become more sombre over the last several months. This trip would give him new geological sites to write about and I would sketch the formations and discuss them with him. We had also discussed visiting the Italian Alps, part of the highest and most extensive mountain range in Europe, if the weather remained warm enough. Caroline was happy to go with us and take a rest from the management of our large household for a while. We engaged several nannies, who, along with the tutors and Ann, would look after the children while we were gone. Ann was in a somewhat quarrelsome mood as we were leaving, as we were giving her more work to do in our absence – and more responsibility.

After the long walk down the old pier almost to the lighthouse, to the deeper part of the harbour, we boarded the schooner in our best travelling clothes. Caroline wore her red pleated skirt and bodice trimmed with black, and a black hat with a lace veil over her face. I wore a similar costume of pale grey trimmed with black and my usual black bonnet with white ruffled lace under the brim – my usual conservative apparel. Ann saw to it that our luggage was properly stowed below deck and then grumpily went on her way to return home. She had said goodbye without much of a smile by saying, "I will see you when I see you, and if it is sooner rather than later, I won't mind a bit. Take care of each other."

I turned to Caroline, the wind hitting my face. "I am excited for this voyage. I think this is exactly what we all need," I said through the wind.

She replied, "I hope you and Father are not intending to visit quarries again, like we did on our last journey."

"Of course we are! I have identified two of them already where we can look for geodes," I said, excitedly.

She groaned. "Dreadful."

"I hope you have brought Mr Dickens with you so that you will be in a cheery mood on this trip," I replied. Caroline was now a great Dickens enthusiast, and avidly read his works as they appeared.

We both looked towards the people milling about the docks.

"Is that someone waving to us?" she asked, squinting her eyes against the sun's glare.

I recognized the person immediately.

"Is that not a nice send off for the family?" she said, with a wry smile. "These days, you never know if you will ever see someone again, with all the shipwrecks and cholera which I earnestly hope and pray we shall avoid. Better wave back, silly."

The person Caroline was referring to in the crowd, with his arm up and waving, was Henry Pearce. He gave me a solemn wave and faint smile. I gave a faint smile back. He grew smaller in the distance as the schooner set sail and slowly pulled away from the harbour. I thought about bringing the blue vivante stone, the one that Henry had given me long ago, on the voyage. Then I remembered Mother used to say, "Never take anything with you on a journey that you cannot live without. It could be lost and gone forever. Best to leave valuables at home, where they are safe and sound."

Caroline said, rather smugly, "You seem far away, dear."

"Yes," I answered. "Very far."

Chapter Ten

Integrity

March 1838

"I have seen something that ain't right, Miss Bess, so I thought I should come tell ye about it," Ann said, nervously, as she came suddenly into my bedroom where I was separating my heavy winter clothes from those I wore in the summer, putting them away into black metal trunks for storage under my four-poster bed.

"What have you seen, Ann? You look like you have taken quite a fright," I said to her, trying to calm her agitation.

"Two odd things, miss. With the Pearce's," she said as she shifted her weight back and forth on her feet.

"Yes, go on, but I am not sure this is any of my business, Ann. Or is it in some way?" I asked cautiously, sitting down on my white chenille bedcover.

"First, I saw Mrs Pearce, Henry's young wife, come out of the narrow alley Tower Hill that goes from next to the Turk's Head pub down to the harbour. That's a smuggling passage, that is," Ann said, wringing her hands together.

"I see," I said slowly. "Isn't that alley used as a faster way down to the harbour if one is prepared to go down the steep slippery slope of the path?" I asked, incredulously. *A minute ago, I was folding clothes. Now people I know are using a smugglers' passage? My brain is not moving fast enough for this.*

"Sometimes women use that alley to bring smuggled goods in and out of town, miss, to and from the harbour to be sold and what not," she said, seeing my face trying to catch up with her. "There is a long tunnel from the basement of the Turk's that is arched and lined with large, flat stones, but it is only high enough to crawl through. That is a real smuggling tunnel but difficult to use as a woman because you have to crawl through it. It comes out right at the harbour and is covered with an arched door concealed behind a bush. The door has cross beams on it."

"Ann, it sounds like you have been inside smuggling tunnels and you seem quite aware of their uses," I said, my hands on my hips and a questioning look on my face.

"Oh yes, miss. We've all been in the tunnel. In our youth, that is," she said, looking down at her shoes.

"Go on. You are sure it was Talwyn Pearce?" I asked.

"Oh yes, miss. I am certain. Because when she got to the shallow harbour, he was standing there watching her come down the hill. Her dress was heavy and swinging, just like she was hiding a load of smuggled goods under her skirt," Ann said, cautiously.

"Who do you mean was 'he'?" I asked, full well knowing who it was.

"Why, Mr Henry, miss. He was very put out at the sight of her. I was down at the bottom of the hill looking at the Matthews store for a bit of fishing tackle. I moved in closer so I could hear them. He was angry that she had been at a pickup, he said. He said he did not want her doing any more runs for her father and that it was wrong to deal in smuggled goods, and did she not know this? He said she was in danger and she could ruin his family's reputation. He did. He said those exact words, miss," Ann finished.

"I see. Thank you for telling me, Ann. I am sure Mr Pearce will keep Talwyn as safe as possible. No need to worry, Ann," I soothed.

"Yes, miss. Shall I pull out and hang your spring clothes?" she asked, bustling around the room.

"Yes, please. I shall see to my shoes and the rest later," I said, as I left the room.

Oh dear. What a troubling situation! I grabbed onto the banister on the stairs going down to the first floor for support. *What on earth, if anything, should I do?* I thought on the way down the stairs and into the parlour. *Henry already knows about this, and it is his to deal with. Still, this does not sit easily with me.*

"Miss, excuse me, miss. I did remember one bit more." Ann had followed me downstairs and into the parlour.

"Oh? What is that?" I asked, turning to face her.

"At the end, I remember hearing Mr Henry say something like, 'I will accompany you tonight, and this is the end with Pinky, for good'. He said something like that."

"Thank you, Ann, for telling me. You have done a very important thing telling me this. That will be all," I said, now shaking a little at the name "Pinky" which must have been Pixley, the ruffian from my encounter at the stones.

I know that smuggling is still quite common in Cornwall. Many of those involved now are just steps away from poverty. One can hardly blame common folk who resort to smuggling to try to make ends meet. I can try to justify the actions, but my own words sound shallow and weak. It appears that the tailor, Mr Hewitt, and his daughter, Talwyn, Henry's wife, are deeply involved, and with Pixley of all people. What a stressful family situation. Of course, I side with Henry. Mr Hewitt has a nice and flourishing tailor's shop, but he also has four girls to take care of. Still, greed and smuggling are not the answer, I said firmly to myself. *But what to do? Henry will be in grave danger if he tries to intervene.* I was worried, with conflicting emotions. *Should I go to Henry and tell him Pixley will be armed and dangerous? Is it any of my business? I do trust Ann completely, so I take her story to be true. My only conclusion is that Henry is dear to me and I will make it my business to keep him safe. But how? Go to his home and warn him? What if he is not there? How would I explain my visit to Talwyn if she was there?*

After lunch and her trip to market to find fish for the evening dinner, Ann rushed up to me as I was helping Miss Ann in the kitchen.

"I have just seen Henry going hot-footed in the direction of the tailor's shop at the end of Market Jew Street, near Miss Betsy's shop, Miss," she panted. Miss Ann gave me a questioning look. The three of us exchanged uneasy glances.

Now is my chance. He will be nearly there now. I must hurry. I ran up the stairs leaving the two Ann's speechless behind me.

***

Although it was not very far to go, I went in one of our carriages for safety, with Jacka to accompany me. Caroline had recently been out and had returned the carriage; therefore, it could go out immediately. I arrived at Mr Hewitt's shop just in time to see Henry stride vigorously along the path to the shop, arms swinging at his sides, in what looked like a high temper. As he approached the steps to the door, he heard my carriage coming to a stop on the pavement and turned towards me. I quickly opened the carriage door and stepped out, not knowing exactly what I would say next.

"Why, Henry, hello," I said. I was happy to see him safe

and in one piece. Jacka gave Henry a wave from the dickey box. Henry only replied to Jacka with a quick nod.

"Hello, Bess. What brings you out so late in the day?" he asked, a bit oddly, as it was clear he was fuming.

"My cousins are growing like stalks of wheat! Francis is almost as tall as me and the girls, well, they are of the age where clothes matter to them, perhaps more than they should ..." I paused mid-sentence. "Henry, you seem disturbed. What is the matter? Is something wrong?" I asked in a low voice so that no one could hear.

"Yes, my life is very wrong, come to think of it," he said in frustration.

"How is that?" I asked. *If I can engage him in a conversation, I might be able to persuade him not to go to meet Pixley.*

"My marriage is full of lies and deceit about smuggling, Bess, to be honest. We are caught in a web of lies and thievery, and try as I may to curtail it, it continues," he said, his voice trembling with emotion. *I have never seen him so emotional. It is as if his world is caving in around him.*

"Henry, I must tell you something very important," I started but was interrupted before I could continue.

"If you will excuse me, Miss Carne. Henry, a word, please. Now!" It was Mr Hewitt who was standing in the open doorway of his two-storey shop. I could see past him to the counter and the tan velvet curtain.

"I must go and finish this," Henry said. "Excuse me, Bess." He moved past me to go up the stairs and into the shop. *What do I do? Do I stand here? It is not my place to get involved.* Thoughts raced through my mind. *Think. What can I do?*

"No more. Finished tonight. Do you understand me? No more smuggling or involving my wife!" I heard Henry say through the door, still open, and he had grabbed Mr Hewitt's jacket in his fist. *Mr Hewitt looks very small, almost like a child, compared to Henry. This is all happening so fast. Think.*

"I know. I know. However, we must finish our agreement with Mr Pixley. If we do not, I cannot say what will befall us," Mr Hewitt stammered.

"I know what will befall you if you do not end this tonight," Henry said in a threatening voice. "I will turn you over to the authorities on smuggling charges."

"You would not dare to do so, and you have no proof," Mr Hewitt spluttered.

"I will. I am going along tonight to end this treachery. I have asked you too many times only for it to fall on deaf ears. Tonight, I suggest you have a care." With that, Henry strode through the open door and slammed it shut.

I was waiting at the bottom of the steps.

"Did you hear and see that?" he asked.

"Yes, I did," I replied.

"It is a nasty business." Henry was angry. "Being angry with family is the worst kind of anger," he said, looking back up the steps to the shop door. Mr Hewitt was nowhere in sight.

"You are referring to the smuggling," I stated rather than asked.

"The smuggling and the marriage. Both based on greed. I am sorry to complain and tell you my woes, Bess. The intensity of the greed is something you know nothing about."

"I would not say that I know nothing about it. I work in a bank, as you recall," I retorted. "I see high levels of greed in all kinds of transactions, but it is called by another name: industry. Henry, you cannot, must not go there tonight to stop Pixley," I said as quickly as I could because I could see he was anxious to leave. *I have to stop him,* was my only thought.

"I warmly recall our friendship and your integrity, so that I know it is still possible to have goodness in the world," he said, sadly. "But I must go!"

"No, Henry. I myself was held at knifepoint by Pixley. At the stones. A few years ago. He will be armed. He is extremely dangerous. Do not go," I said, in as commanding a voice as I could muster.

"Good evening to you, Miss Carne." A cold voice filled with contempt interrupted me. "What a cozy conversation you two are having, I daresay. Are you in need of a proper escort?" It was Mr Richards' sneering voice as he walked up to us in his dandy's dress coat and cravat. My immediate reaction was one of loathing of him and I am sure it appeared on my face. I quickly controlled myself and my ability to respond civilly, even though it was clear he was trying to provoke us both.

"Good evening to you, Mr Richards. I am not in need of an escort as I am going home. Thank you," I said. He tipped his hat, smiling.

"I see. Until next time then, Miss Carne. It is too bad you must rush off," he said, as he waited to see me leave for my carriage. "I am sure you would not want any backward glances coming your way, given the company you are keeping? Especially for someone who has a credible banking position such as yourself."

I turned my back to go to the carriage and whispered to Henry, "I must be pleasant, Henry, as I have business dealings with him. Ignore him. He is trying to provoke us."

"He is heading in the right direction if that is where he wants to go. If you say so. I must say, he seems a rather slippery sort to me. Why did you not tell me about the encounter with Pixley? Is that why you were asking me so many questions about him in the carriage that day of our mission?" he asked quickly, so it would seem like he was bidding me farewell by the carriage.

"Promise me, Henry Pearce. Promise me that you will not go tonight or any night," I begged.

"I cannot promise you, Bess. I am going to save my wife, despite the fact that our marriage is a shambles. Why did I marry her?" he lamented, looking up at the sky and shaking his head. "Did you know that I have taken charge of finances for a Penzance shipping concern?" he asked, again very forlornly. "I was trying to get a more stable position, one that would convince her to stop the smuggling."

"Thank you, I will. I must be getting home. I have the household budgeting to do for this month tonight as well as tutoring for Edward and Francis," I said loudly, over Henry's shoulder, so that Mr Richards, who was peering into a shop window and trying to look occupied but was clearly trying to eavesdrop, would think our conversation was coming to a seemly end. *How can I convince Henry?* I asked myself. *What can I say with Mr Richards standing so near?* I asked myself, fervently.

"Yes, I did! Congratulations. My father told me. That sounds like a brilliant position, Henry," I said, genuinely and more loudly, then back down to a whisper. "But right now, you must send for the constables, and not risk losing your own life and Talwyn's."

The horses were fidgeting. The harness jingled slightly as the horses stomped, impatient to get home to be fed.

"Get going, miss?" Jacka called down from the dickey box. He gave Henry a questioning look, not understanding the delay. It was as if Jacka sensed a problem, if he had not per-haps heard part of the conversation directly.

"Yes, Jacka," I called up.

"Promise!" I whispered as we slowly rolled away.

The image of Henry standing there, his hand up in a slow wave, with such a grave face, was burned into my mind. *I may never see him again.*

***

At home, afternoon became evening, and then it was bedtime. I could barely sleep thinking of all the different things that could be happening at the smuggling rendezvous, all of them ending poorly for Henry. I lay in bed, filled with dread and nausea. Everyone in our household was in bed. I counted the succession of footsteps as all the servants went up to their rooms on the third floor. Jacka would be down in his room next to the stables in the garden. I could hear Father snoring in his room across the hall from mine. I held my book close to my candle and tried to reread the sentence I had just read but could not recall what it said.

Suddenly, I heard a loud crack. Gunshot! It was unmistakably a gunshot. Then another. Two gunshots, no mistake! They seemed to be coming from the direction of the inner harbour, which I could not see from my windows. All I could see in the bright moonlight was the side of St Mary's church and the bottom of Chapel Street. I was suddenly in a panic and scrambled out of my chair, threw on a robe and stuffed my feet into some shoes. I stopped to listen to see if anyone else was awake and alarmed by the shots. No one was about. I crept as silently as I could to the study window which had a limited view of the harbour, but I saw nothing amiss. Father's room had the best view of the harbour.

Dare I go in there to get a better view? I went to his door and turned the knob. *Locked!*

I skimmed down the stairs as lightly as I could, barely touching any of them. *Now what?* I asked myself, now really alarmed.

Someone was at the back garden door. I drew in my breath sharply in fear but saw that it was only Jacka at the door. I unlocked the door and let him into the parlour.

He whispered, "I heard gunshots down by the inner harbour, miss. Henry may be down there. I'm going." Before I could utter a word, he slipped back out the door and went out through the gate in the garden wall. He disappeared into the blackness.

Should I go out? Should I wait on Chapel Street? To do what, exactly? I listened by the stairs to determine if anyone else was awake. No one was. *They could be anywhere by now,* I thought, frustrated. I sat down at the dining room table and looked out into the garden, trying to think of a way to help. It was late and I heard no one about on Chapel Street. All was quiet.

I quietly went back up to my room and blew out the candle. *There is nothing I can do at this point.* I went through my room to my windows. I slipped open my shutters and looked up and down Chapel Street but saw nothing. *All I can do now perhaps is to gather some bandages in case Jacka finds someone wounded.* I turned to go back downstairs when I saw a shadow on the street out of my left window. I backed away from the window and looked out from the lower corner. *Now I am imagining things in the dimness.*

I looked again and clearly saw the outline of someone in the dark on the street, hiding under the shadow of the large stone wall that trimmed St Mary's. Long dark hair, wearing a fisherman's raincoat. He waited, his back against the wall, not moving. I then saw another man slowly walking up the hill from our side of the street across from St Mary's. I recognized the man's gait. *It is Henry!* Before I knew what I was doing, I lunged from the window and to my bedroom door, where I used a black iron crab pot weight as a door stopper. I grabbed the weight and spun around back to the window.

In one motion, I slid the locking mechanism open, pushed the window open, and heaved the weight out the window and into the night, to the right, away from the hiding man. It bounced on the cobblestones with a few heavy and loud clanks. I went to the far-right side of the right window. *Did the noise alert Henry and distract the hiding man?* The man crouched down and started creeping away from the noise when he ran directly into Henry. Henry grabbed him from behind and started squeezing and pinning the man's arms to the man's own waist. It looked like Pixley.

"Help! Call the constables! Help!" Henry bellowed.

Men came running from all directions, it seemed. I saw Jacka reach Henry first and then deliver a stabbing punch to the stomach of the man with a sickening thud sound. After that, he was quickly subdued. I ran out of my room and ran directly into Father.

"There has been a crime. A man is in custody outside in the street." I said, in a flurry. I ran down the stairs and through the entry hall to the door.

"Do not open that door, Bess," Father called sternly from the stairs. He had followed me faster than I thought he was able.

***

I dressed for the day, my hands shaking as I tried to fasten each button, but the stress of not knowing what had happened or how Henry was caused my fingers to fumble.

As soon as I came downstairs, Ann handed me a sealed note. *Thank God, a note from Henry. That must mean he is safe.* I read the note, stuffed it into a hallway table, and ran out the door. "Ann, please tell Father I am going to the chapel," I said over my shoulder.

I nodded a greeting as I passed several women whom I knew, who were in the large entryway of our Methodist Chapel, organizing food donations and putting them into crates. As I entered, I saw Henry sitting in a middle pew. *The chapel feels like a second home to many of us as a safe and quiet refuge.* It smelled of hymnals and new wood flooring. Several members of our Connection were milling about, resetting for the next service.

"I received your note and came at once," I said softly as I

slid into the pew and sat beside him. We both faced the pulpit.

"Thank you for coming. And I wanted to thank you again for coming to my parents' funeral last month. It was a terrible time for us, given how unexpected it was," Henry said, twisting his body to face me.

"Cholera strikes like that. It spreads quickly. I am sorry for your tragic loss. You know I was fond of your parents," I said, glancing at him with all sincerity. *I am afraid to ask why Henry is here in the chapel. His face is so stricken with pain.* In all propriety, I continued to face forward.

"Was it you who threw the stone out of your window last night?" he asked in a hushed voice.

"Yes, it was a door stopper – a weight from a crab pot. I hoped it would be a distraction or alert you that trouble was quite near," I said quickly.

"It did! You were so brave and smart to think of that. You saved my life, Bess. I would have walked right into his blade had you not alerted me." He sighed.

"Something terrible has happened." At this, we both turned to face each other.

I drew in a breath and tried to prepare myself for whatever was coming next.

"Talwyn and Mr Hewitt were murdered last night on the old pier," he said, in a strained, scratchy voice.

I shook my head in disbelief and my hands flew to my mouth on their own. My eyes welled up with tears. I tried to blink them away, my eyes never leaving his. He too had tears in his eyes.

"Oh, how terrible!" I whimpered.

"They were conducting a smuggling transaction with Mr Pixley, who you remember. Turns out he was every bit as dangerous as you and others have said. You warned me. Talwyn warned me. But I was too caught up in my own integrity, trying to stop the grip of greed that smuggling had on them to listen to her. It's my fault they are dead now, Bess. It's my fault," he said, darkly. *I feel like I have a huge, heavy and empty black cauldron in my stomach, weighing me down.*

"How could it be your fault?" I asked in disbelief.

"It was dark. I ran down the pier to stop the drop and tell Pixley the agreement and use of my wife had come to an end. As soon as he saw me, he ran a blade through Mr Hewitt's neck and then he shot Talwyn. It was hell to witness. My poor Talwyn. We were not well suited in our marriage, but I never wanted something like this to happen to her and never, never wanted her dead."

We sat, both still from shock and horror of the tragedy. *Shocking. How brutal and cruel. What should I say? I cannot even think straight at the moment.*

"All I wanted was steadier work, instead of the ups and downs of mining. But even my new position appeared not to be enough to reduce the need for smuggling," he said, coldly.

"Henry, I am so sorry to hear this. It is too awful to be real. How can I help you? Please, let me help," I said, tears in my eyes. I felt so helpless to do anything.

"I would like to tell you what happened. You can tell me if what I did was truly wrong," he said.

"Tell me then. What happened?" I asked, trying to be calm but my heart ached for everyone involved: Talwyn, her sisters, her father, and my poor Henry.

His voice was cracking, and he bent forward at the waist, gripping his hair as if to pull it out. He was in agony recounting the scene. It burned through him painfully. It was plain to see.

He sat up but in a slumped position. "I went down to the Turk's Head tavern, the old one, across the street. I thought I would have an ale before I had to go to the old pier and confront my family in their sordid business with Pixley. I dreaded it. Going to the old pier at night to pull my wife away from a smuggling operation! Hideous. Looking around, I saw the usual sort. Many fishermen supping after a long day on their boats. As I was drinking, I noticed a man a few tables over with his eyes on me. Initially, I paid no heed. Until he got up and came to my table."

Henry continued. "He said, 'Might I have a word? It would be to your benefit.' He was a round man, middle-aged, with very bad teeth and poorly dressed in filthy trousers and shirt.

"'Who is asking?' I asked him. I did not know who he was, you see."

"Go on," I said.

"He whispered to me, scowling and looking side to side, that he knew my affairs. I told him to state his business and be quick about it," Henry said. "He said that he could offer me some goods that I might be interested in, as if he was making me an offer I could not refuse," Henry said, sickened.

"I told him I did not know what he was talking about. Then came the dreadful information that he had seen my wife at the Turk's Head and then in the Tower Hill alley. So, Talwyn was deep inside smuggling by the sound of it, to my deep despair," Henry said.

"I told him I was not interested in any goods, nor was anyone of my family," Henry continued. "But then he said he would be meeting my father-in-law and Talwyn at the Turk's Head during the week. 'We will see what he has to say,' the man said," said Henry. "I doubt I will ever live this down."

"So that is how you knew where Talwyn had been. My maid, Ann, confirms that. She told me prior to me seeing you and Mr Hewitt at his shop that she had seen you and Talwyn by the harbour, and that Talwyn had come from that alley," I said.

"Yes. So, she saw us, did she? I was angry earlier in the day at the harbour, but by evening I was livid. I headed down towards the old pier where the meeting would take place as darkness fell. I wanted to make sure I got there early enough not to miss catching Talwyn and Patrick, my father-in-law, in the act. I decided to wait behind several large barrels on the old pier, which was an ideal place for their meeting because it was seldom used after dark, and isolated. The old pier was already deserted. No one came near. I had a pistol ready but prayed I would not be forced to use it. I waited," Henry said, taking a handkerchief out of his pocket and wiping his eyes and nose.

"I thought maybe Talwyn and my father-in-law would come to their senses and there would be no need for me to wait for them. Unfortunately, and as expected, Talwyn and her father appeared in the moonlight as if their meeting was an everyday, lawful occurrence. Bess, it was as if they thought they were entitled to smuggle."

I do not know what to say to this. I just nodded slowly, trying to comprehend what happened.

"Boldly, they marched up to the end of the old pier where a small fishing boat appeared seemingly out of nowhere. The sails were furled, and it was moored quickly with Patrick's help. Talwyn and Patrick carried nothing. Talwyn quickly boarded the boat while Patrick waited on the edge of the pier. I did not know if I should run out and trap them at the end of the pier so that I could deliver the message that this was to be the final run and stop the transaction. I was in a panic, Bess. I asked myself, 'What if the boat leaves with Talwyn?' I strained to hear what they were saying, but only heard muffled voices. The voices seemed urgent. Time seemed to stretch out end-lessly as if hours were passing as she remained on the boat even though it was mere minutes. Then the incoming fog swept over the boat and the surrounding water, making it difficult to see and hear."

"Very frightening," was all I could say. He was right. *How bold of Talwyn to go out in the moonlight to face a suspected thief and possible murderer. How unsafe.*

"I began to think something was wrong because it was all taking too long. I started to run down the pier. I had gone no more than two steps when Talwyn alighted from the boat and another head appeared. I saw a man with greasy black hair and shabby fisherman's clothing illuminated in the pale light." At that point, Henry began to stutter. He had to pause to regain his composure.

When he was able to continue, he said, "Talwyn stopped as she saw me and put a hand up to halt me, but I continued down the pier. Patrick yelled out something I could not understand. He rushed towards the boat. I saw the glint of a blade at neck level and then Patrick dropped like a stone. A shot was fired. In an instant, the mooring line dropped, a foot pushed the boat off the pier, and it swung around, sails unfurling. A man jumped on the pier and raised a gun. Another shot fired, grazing my left arm."

"Are you badly hurt?" I asked. *Inflammation. Henry could die from this injury yet.*

"No, not badly," he said, showing me the bandage on his upper left arm. "The worst image I have is what happened next. My poor Talwyn staggered towards me, looking like a broken doll trying to walk as I ran towards her. She was lunging and her dress swung around wildly. She fell on the pier face forward; her blonde hair spilled out of its cap with the impact of her body on the pier. I ran to her, as if in a dream where I ran but made no forward motion. As I reached her, I gently rolled her over. The front of her bodice was red, flowing outward in all directions, like a flower. Her body was completely limp, her arms drooping behind her. I felt her neck for a pulse. There was none. You always said she was like a flower," Henry sobbed, thinking of the bloody image, I imagined.

"Now she's dead. Oh, my God! My poor girl, she's dead. She was like a limp flower, with her eyes open and lifeless, like a drooping, wilted flower. Her bodice was soaked in blood within moments. I felt along the length of the dress and felt hard lumps, bulky under the black material. Then under the dress I found six wrapped packages tied to the shift beneath her skirt."

"Henry, it is not your fault," I said. "You were trying to save her, save them both." I tried to console him, but it was no use.

"My wife is dead because of my damned integrity. She managed to live through childhood, and a small portion of adulthood, only to be ruined, not by disease or failure, but by ruthless greed. I am to blame." Henry sniffed and paused.

"The man with the weapon ran past me as I knelt next to Talwyn's body. A few men came running out of lower Penzance as apparently they heard the shots. But the men were too far away to grab the gunman as they ran towards the pier. I pointed down at Talwyn to the approaching men as I stood up and ran after the gunman, who we now know was Pixley. I wished it had been me and not her, Bess. Oh, God," Henry said, his head in his hands.

"You did a valiant thing, trying to save her from that trap of greed. I know smuggling is still a commonly accepted thing, but you and I know that does not make it any less dangerous. You tried to protect her, which is the right thing to do. Protection for safety is closer to justice than integrity, in this case," I said slowly. "You did the right thing, Henry. For better or for worse, remember? You promised God in your vows that you would protect her. You were doing God's work to save her from harm, not your own work to protect your integrity. Do you see that?" I asked, in calm, caring tones.

He went on, his face contorted in anger. "I wanted to kill Pixley myself. I ran after him with a speed I did not know I possessed. I ran up Quay Street, looking for him. Once I got up to Dock Lane, it was so dark in the shadows, and there were so many hiding places I did not know which way to turn. I could not think straight, either."

"That's when I threw the weight down, I am guessing," I said.

"Yes, thank heaven for you. You know what happened next but you did not see the final end," he said, bitterly.

"What final end?" I asked.

"After Jacka punched him in the gut, the jolt of the punch loosened my grip, he staggered away, reached down into his boot, pulled out a fishing knife, and slit his own throat."

"What?" I said, aghast and in disgust.

"Probably knew he would face the noose for sure. Ended it quick, the coward. There will of course be an inquest, and I have already made a statement to the head of our new police force here. Yet I doubt if any of your people will understand when it all appears in the papers and is embroidered and exaggerated as it circulates in the town gossip," he said, cynically.

"Yes. People do love to gossip. I have often thought that the distances and differences between classes separate us from justice," I agreed, regretfully. "But people will see that what you tried to do was right."

"As I sit here today in the house of God, I will never marry again. The struggle and pain are too much, unimaginable, Bess," he whispered.

"Do not say that. There will be another worthy of you some day." I tried to soothe him. I laid my hand on his for a brief moment.

"No. I do thank you for trying to understand, but there will not be another. I have no more energy or taste for such a union. As inappropriate as this sounds, Bess, I love you and always have. I know we can never marry. But even if we could, I would not be able to marry you now or ever. Never again." He gritted his teeth and spat out the words. "I have lost hope in humanity," he said, clutching my hand.

I gave a sad sigh. "I too will most likely never marry. My father has told me I am likely to be his successor, meaning I will have little time for children if I am to protect his legacy. I will be married to my legacy, I suppose. But, when you love someone, the burden is no less if you are not married. You do not have to be married to care for someone your whole life." My eyes searched his, searching for his understanding, and I pulled my hand away slowly.

"I have nothing and no one left to care for but you, Bess. But I know I will care for you the rest of my life. Could you care for me, Bess? For the rest of yours?"

Without hesitation, I nodded and said, "I know that I will."

Mr Topham, our new minister now that Mr Treffry had sadly passed away, entered the chapel at the front by the pulpit. He stood looking at Henry, waiting, and it was apparent that he needed to speak with Henry about arrangements. *What a horrid set of plans Henry must make now, when he is at his lowest.*

"Henry, I am truly sorry for your losses. I wish we both could have prevented this disaster. I want you to know this. I am glad you are alive and fairly unharmed. Our worlds are more similar than you think. My father works us like horses at home. The men at the bank seem to resent my presence. Father's colleagues resent my involvement in their interests. I work hard for and still worry about the future of my five cousins and my sisters. Life here is a struggle for us all. I deeply sympathize with your conflicts and pain, I do. But you are on the right path, Henry. Keep moving forward with the things God asks of us. Stay on His path," I said with all the emphasis I could give. I got up from the pew and walked to the chapel door.

He nodded slowly and sadly, as if he knew that moving forward would not be enough to enter my world.

"You are the best any path could offer," he said. The misery and hopelessness in his eyes were unmistakable and penetrating.

"*Let us keep our youth as long as we can – its simple means of enjoyment, its simple power to enjoy; for by so doing we shall escape many temptations, and lay the foundation of a stronger and happier manhood.*"

- Elizabeth Carne, *Country Town*, 1868

Part Two

Being

(1858-1873)

"Time for drawing up, pausing, looking backwards, and forwards, and then stepping on with fresh vigour along the path appointed for you – not anybody else's path, however it may exceed your own in goodness and brightness and usefulness; you would blunder and fall there, even with the best intentions."

- Caroline Fox, January 1858 to Elizabeth Carne in response to Elizabeth's letter to her wishing her a happy new year.

Chapter Eleven

The Youngest Successor

1858–1860

It was near midnight. The candles were burning low on the mantle. *Caroline should have left hours ago. She has worked all day looking after Father and the household, and I can see the toll it has taken on her mentally and physically. Father's illness has dragged on for months and months. Mentally, she seems to have lost much of the cheeky spirit she once had. Physically, she is drained, tired, and thin. Her hands are so red and chafed from having them in water and soap too much.* She motioned to me to come outside the bedroom with her.

"Bess, I will say goodnight. I am bone tired. Too tired to sleep most likely," Caroline lamented.

"Yes, you have had too long of a day," I whispered back so as not to wake Father.

"When we are free of this, what will we do with our time?" she asked, showing some of her old cheekiness.

"We will have freedom. From more than just this bedside," I offered

"Yes. A freedom that we have never had. Think about it. No father and no brothers to abide by. What will that be like,

I wonder?" Caroline looked as if she was in a dream.

"Go to bed and dream of your new freedom," I said, smoothing her hair and sending her off in the direction of her room.

I sat down on the edge of his bed, staring with heavy eyes at my father's empty big brown leather chair with the brass studs, in his bedroom in our Chapel Street home, my shoulders slumped and my body aching. He loved to plan his next day from this chair. The fire was dying down, but I was too tired to do anything about it now. My father's long-running battle with his lungs, a type of bronchitis the doctors said, had worsened, and we were all three exhausted: my sister Caroline and myself from the care and nursing that she and I provided him around the clock, as he would not accept care from anyone else, and him from simply trying to stay alive. *It appears from the look of him that he will not be planning his next day, or any other days.*

He barely had the strength to cough, this man who had been a tyrant, a revered industrialist, complex problem solver, a challenger to world order through geology and a Sunday school teacher. At seventy-six, he had lived an outstanding life, serving his family and community, but had become so weak he could barely take in even small amounts of air through his laboured wheezing. Once so strong of mind and body, he could barely move his lips to speak. When he did, it required effort from his entire frame to form and produce the words. His room smelled of sickness along with the mixture of hemlock and turpentine the doctors gave him, to no avail. Since I had been there through all of this last night and every other night for months, I must have smelled like the mixture as well.

"I ... musssttt ... telllll ... you ..." he whispered, barely audibly.

"Father, you have told me all you need to, many times. Your work now is to rest and smile, for we have much to talk about tomorrow," I said, bearing him up.

"Keeepppp the legacyyyyy ... intact," he said, pushing the words out with all his might.

"Yes, of course, Father. It is what we have worked towards for the last twenty-six years. You have thought of everything in your planning and have prepared me so well. Do you think I understand the application of good banking practices, with all your tutelage? I could have no finer," I said, proudly, stroking his hand. Since my older brother William died six years ago from overexposure to the sun on his way home from France, my fate as the inheritor of the legacy and its responsibilities had been sealed, and my full-time banking work had started in earnest

"Yes ...You ... prepare ... nexxxt ..." He was getting frustrated and emotional at his lack of ability to convey his meaning.

"I prepare for my next work?" I asked? I was bone tired and needed rest myself.

He was becoming impatient, and he grimaced. "No ..."

"I prepare the next person who would take my place in the bank?" I asked, now taking his meaning clearly.

"Ye ... ss," he croaked.

"Yes, Father. We have discussed this. If you recall, we discussed that the current managers, Mr Downing and Mr Bodilly, run the bank with tremendous judgement and that I will be involved with the important decision making. In time, we will bring on others in the family, Archie first and then Charles, into the business to keep the bank in the family." I quoted from our last discussion on the topic. Archibald and Charles Ross were my sister Mary's sons. "But as you know, Charles is only ten years old." *I have my doubts, however, if Charles will be up to the task, given his flippant and impulsive nature. He wrote home from school in Brighton recently saying that he wanted to be an actor, something his mother frowns* upon, but for which I think he might be well suited. Something about his demeanour makes me think that as a banker, it will not be an asset.

"The min ... er ... als ... to uni ... ver ... sity," he urged.

"Of course, Father. I will take them to Cambridge and they will have a fine viewing case with lighting, and crowds of people will be proud of Cornwall's finest treasures," I said, soothingly.

"Ye ... ss.," he replied, his eyes rolling back in his head, causing me alarm.

"Father?" I asked. "Father?" I shook his arm.

He gasped, his lips pale white. "You ... have ... been ... my true ... partner. And ... I ... have loved ... you ... so well."

He stopped short of saying anything more or taking another breath, I noticed. His eyes open, he was motionless. He was dead. My Father, who had been my academic tutor, geology professor and mentor my whole life, and the person who I spent the most time with for thirty years, was gone. *He will never make plans in his leather chair again. He will never hold court in the Geological Society again. We will never evaluate an investment together again. I am now a forty-one-year-old heiress of a sizeable fortune, properties, assets, and as of this moment, a partner in the Penzance Bank my grandfather started and my father grew. I am suddenly one of very few women in the whole of Cornwall to manage a bank. Now Joseph Carne is gone, and I am left to continue his legacy. I am desperately alone. I will never be able to replace him as my like-minded collaborator.* Even though I knew his death was near, tears poured down my face as never before.

I could not stay all night with him as is customary. Every fibre of my being was fatigued. After I had awakened Caroline and the household, and then set the servants upon their immediate tasks, I walked the short distance home to 6 Coulson's Terrace, having already sent word. Jacka accompanied me with a lantern. I had decided to live permanently here in this small white house so that I could have some respite from the months of sickness that permeated my childhood home at 29 Chapel Street. Father's illness added a black shroud of misery and death over the entire household. I had to escape from it.

An icy rain beat down on us. I was damp, tired, and completely miserable when I reached my house. I was surprised to see him standing by the black metal gate. Henry Pearce, my long-time friend, who had been deemed an inappropriate match for me in all propriety, was there to meet me in this dark hour. We had always cared for each other greatly and I was always glad to see him. Jacka bade me good night and returned to Chapel Street. I barely noticed. I had told Henry on the street earlier that day that I did not expect my father to make it through the night. However, I did not expect to see Henry here.

Impulsively, I ran towards him, and his large arms encircled me instantly. He half-carried me into the house where Mary, my maid, came quickly to take our wet things and help us indoors. The fire was roaring and crackling loudly, and Mary brought blankets and hot tea. She knew Henry to be a family friend and had already given him the news of my father's death. She passed no judgemental glances or questioning looks our way.

I looked up at Henry from my seat on the couch. The large, dancing fire in the white marble trimmed fireplace gave me the sense that if it could go on, I could as well. Several small candles made from beeswax softly lit the room.

"He will be missed by many, will he not?" I sniffed and gave out a heavy sigh.

"By you most of all, Bess. It will create a vacuum, a gap in your life and for your intellectual pursuits. You must allow yourself time to grieve and accommodate the change, as I know you have in the past. I am sorry for your loss." His tone was strong and sincere, which was one of the things I admired about him.

"Yes, I need time away to meditate about this most recent chapter and the one coming next. My family is well provided for, but I am the one responsible for the ongoing legacy. It is my mission now."

His handsome face leaned into mine, his green eyes, the colour of green grass in the summer, shone in the firelight. "The continuation of the same larger mission you have had since you were nineteen, when we sat by the sea on Zennor Head and I spoke of wanting to be a mine captain," he reminded me.

"Yes, I believe that was the time you said I was thick, like a stone or solid like a mountain. Something like that, I recall." I gave a small laugh and ran my hands across my thick brown hair to put it all back in place, stretching my neck back and forth to relieve the aching.

"Yes, but I meant solid and pure, like nature is solid and beautiful. Certainly not thick. And I still think that at this very moment." Unexpectedly, he pulled me at the waist close to his chest and kissed me on the mouth in the most passionate way imaginable. His hair brushed by my face and the scent of it soft and brown, awakened my senses. His strong arms enveloped me and my exhausted body absorbed every part of him, finding energy and strength where I had none, and filling me with love that had long been deprived. He suffused me body and soul with a man's powerful touch that I needed, electrifying me to the core. I gladly accepted all the warmth, care and bonds of love that he offered, letting it permeate the fissures of loneliness and the cavern of sadness I felt within.

***

After days planning my father's funeral with Caroline, our energy was completely spent. When the last funeral guest had left, I said to her, "It is my opinion that you and I need a mental break from our stress and grief, Caroline. Our business affairs are doing well, and Mr Bodilly and Mr Downing can keep them steady and have agreed with me that you and I need a break. I propose that you and I take a trip. My idea is that we spend the winter and spring in Pau, which is in France, by the foothills and mountains of the Pyrenees. What do you think?"

"I would be more than delighted, but why Pau? What will we do there? Lounge on warm sunlit patios? Dine on luxurious food and drink?" she asked, hopefully.

"Yes, all of that and I would like to ride up to see the splendid views of Gabas and le Plateau des Bijoux Artiques. I see from Murray's travel guide about Pau that I have been reading, that several geological sites of significance are there in addition to the spectacular views. Several quarries." She frowned. "Pau is known for being a resort where the sun is warm, and relaxation is paramount. That is why I have chosen Pau." I was becoming increasingly excited about this trip as we discussed possible plans.

"Oh, if we must. But do acquire magnificent lodgings for us. And some tall, strong local guides if you can find them." We laughed. "Will it be just the two of us?"

"I would like to invite Caroline Fox, but she is busy as she is about to become the guardian of some young cousins of hers and is unable to join us. I have been thinking about inviting Henry to be with us for a couple of weeks while we are in Gabas. Would you mind?"

"Henry who, dear?" she asked, knowingly.

"Henry Pearce, of course," I said, tossing the travel guide at her. "He would be housed in separate lodgings, and we will pass him off as our cousin, so no fear of any backward glances. We may need a strong pair of hands for attaching climbing ropes to rocky outcroppings and hauling gear in the Pyrenees," I told her.

"Strong hands, indeed," she chided. Then she looked thoughtful. "Is this part of the newfound freedom we now have?"

It is a strange feeling. Being able to make decisions according to what I think is best, without having to take into consideration what Father thinks, says, or does. Even though I still live within the bounds of my faith and my duty as a citizen, I now feel more alive than ever before – more alive and more powerful within my own self. I feel as if I am breathing on my own for the first time. I have always had some kind of understanding of "freedom" but have never been free personally at all. It is altogether a different feeling than I have ever had before.

"You have captured a feeling that I could not quite put words to, Caroline. And yes, I do think that a trip of our own making, with our own interests at heart, is a step forward in a freedom we have never had before. I find it a strange and powerful feeling, as if inside me sails are unfurling, one at a time, and I am gaining power and forward momentum," I said, speaking my mind as I rarely did.

"I am not quite as free as you, since you are the principal legatee, but I am free. For the first time, I have my own means that are mine, that I can do with as I please," she replied, with her hands on her hips, smiling. "I am now a "Railway Investor" as opposed to a "Spinster." She beamed.

"Yes, quite right, as long as you do not stray into debt." I tossed a cushion at her, teasingly. "We are quite likely two of the freest individuals in the world. No parents, spouses or male siblings."

"That is one way to look at it," she said, looking a lot like Father when he was about to debate a topic. "Another way to look at it is that we are now as free as many twenty-one-year-old young men are and stay for the remainder of their lives." She smirked.

"A fair point and commentary on the current social norms for women. What will we do with this freedom, and where and how?" I asked her.

"That is the beauty of it," she responded. "It is ours to decide."

Freedom that is ours to decide, I thought. *It is now possible for me to act on needs that I can see and which I think should be fulfilled, as long as I stay within the bounds of the principles that Father has so deeply instilled in me. New projects within my mission, for the church and for children, and papers to write and publish that I think are important works. Ideas that for years I have considered worthy of development are swirling around in my head as if they have all been waiting for this hour to be born. It is as if the world has changed completely for me and now that I am at the helm, I am actually steering the course. Instead of being the captain's mate, I am now the captain.*

***

Our small group arrived in Pau and took up our lodgings in a four-apartment house, where four kitchens steamed, each with its own smells. Madame Française on the first floor imbued us with garlic, to the extent that my clothes started to smell of it. This proximity of kitchens may be why the British prefer separate houses and cottages instead of the apartments used on the Continent. Too many scents mixed together, seeping through the walls and ceilings, night and day, become inescapable.

We had walked for miles in the foothills of the grand Pyrenees, and even though Murray describes them in his travel guide as "round backed" I think them beautiful. The trees were devoid of leaves, and I reminded myself that it was January after all and that the trees were all still asleep. One lone floral plant, one belonging to the Umbelliferon family, was in bloom, a brave signal that spring would not be far away.

"I believe I will write my own travel guide, as Murray's is missing some of the key points about the regions we have passed through," I told everyone and no one as I was speaking aloud to myself. "I will add detail about several of the incredible geological sites we have passed, as well as the conditions of the apartments, like the one we have secured. Murray writes three pages about the cathedral in Amiens, which is most needed as it is a glorious sight, but he then neglects to write properly about the hills, the beautiful coteaux, such as Gelos, which is truly the most beautiful sight we have seen so far. How it shines so brightly in the winter sun!" I exclaimed. Caroline was not as impressed.

"I believe I shall write under a pseudonym to increase the readership of my guide. For what man would buy a guide written by a woman? What name could I use, Caroline?" I asked, puffing white clouds from my breath.

"How about Wititterly, from Dickens' *Nicholas Nickleby*?" she replied, facetiously.

"Brilliant. Yes, Wititterly it is!" I exclaimed.

"You cannot use that name. It is too ridiculous. Can we not return to our apartment now? My feet are not accustomed to these walking boots and my hands have turned to ice." Caroline was grumpily trudging on next to me.

"Yes, yes, we can return to the apartment. Perhaps the loud Anglais above us will have awoken after their late-night revelries, singing and stamping about in their heavy boots, and drinking beer," I responded.

On the way back to Pau, we passed vineyards, where a small amount of veronica was in blossom, with hoar frost on the underside of its dead leaves, a fact that some natural philosopher, whose name escapes me, said proved that dew does not fall from the sky as a soft mist, as we once supposed, but comes from the earth, as condensed vapour in the colder atmosphere. We had, over the weeks, many such walks with our French tour guide in and around Pau. We saw quaint lanes and the nearby castle that included a tortoiseshell crib for an ancient king. In our horse-drawn carriages, we toured wooded glens and viewed the long lines of the Pyrenees beyond the hills with their white and blue slopes, with misty skies that were intensely beautiful and filled us with deep enjoyment. We came down from the hills to see the plains beneath us, which were probably once an estuary of the sea. I noted that the low bank running from the Haute Plante of Pau, past Belhieres, Lons, and Leasear, was most likely once the line of the sea-cliff. In ancient times, water must have covered the Place Grammont, and all the flat areas between Pau and Bisanos because nothing but a covering of water could have made the plain so uniformly level. *I must add this to my guide as a feature of geological interest,* I noted to myself.

Caroline, our guides, and I galloped on horseback past farms and up the slopes of the Pyrenees. We rode over summits on wild country rides that afforded a great variety of scenery. We went on rides where we rode higher and higher, leaving the Neiss behind us, winding round sunny slopes with acres of vines stretching up the hills. We plunged down into little ravines, into brooks, and stopped to look for flowers. Woodcutters stopped and stared at us as if no stranger had been there before.

I insisted that we visit the nearby quarries, where we found splendid geodes. The whole quarry was a mass of them, sparkling with white crystals. *It is times like this when I miss Father so painfully. He would have loved a discussion about how the geodes formed. Were they also on the other side of the coteaux? Had they formed since the conglomerate of the coteaux was heaped upon them, and were they brought by water or ice?*

My personal purpose in all this was a change of scenery and time to reflect, not to run away from Father's death or my new responsibilities. I wanted time to recuperate, not to escape. For me, thoughts of Father and home and responsibilities were the best parts of a good life. The real work of life creates strength within and strength for the soul. I saw much pretension in Pau that could become its own way of life, if allowed, for those of soft minds who enjoyed relaxation and social events too much.

I will include a poem making this point about strength versus soft minds, in my travel guide, as a warning that a holiday is a time to recuperate and should not be a way of life, for that would be soft minded, like a mind made of clay. To me, poems were a way for me to express powerful emotions and contentions that were difficult to put into words or sentences alone. I enjoyed the challenge of writing an effective poem and thought writing poetry would be a productive use of time and a tonic for my own spirit. *After all, wasting time is akin to vanity*, I thought. Thinking about my poem and its purpose, I started considering how I would begin the poem. *Something about long hours of sadness, long hours of a journey, in search of springtime gladness, restoring health ... I wish I had brought my writing box as now I will have to memorise those scraps and fragments of lines.*

We rode and looked for evidence of spring's readiness in the grassy slopes and steep hedges, miles from Pau and our odorous apartment. The saying goes that the climate of Pau has healing properties for rheumatism and breathing ailments. We spent weeks on these little journeys, riding, hiking, climbing, and searching for flowers, most of which I could name. We felt that we had become acclimatised; and that the old saying about Pau, "Have a little patience with the climate and you will feel the benefit in good time," had come true.

However, back in the streets of Pau, the odour was horrendous, as everyone admits. One of our acquaintances said that during the fever which raged in 1857, the English were quite frightened by the foul smell and the authorities, who valued the English purses, had to do something. Since then, they said, sanitary improvements had been made; however, the smell and unsanitary conditions remained. Many of the visitors side-stepped the smell and went to expositions, balls, missionary meetings, and parties. In fact, we found Pau to be a place where pleasure was the main objective. It was my feeling, however, after attending a few of the missionary tea meetings, that they were more about a social gathering than the mission at hand, sadly, and I preferred the fresh air and sunshine to the smell of the streets on the way to the mission meetings or parties.

During one of our rides, we met a family of peasants who lived up in the hills in a small cottage with a garden. Through my broken and badly spoken French, I ascertained that the mother was obliged to send her children to school five days a week because it was the law of the land. As a result, everyone in her family could read and write. I supposed that this law would greatly enlighten this and future generations in Pau and wondered when similar legislation would find its way to Cornwall. I praised the mother of the family as best as I could for her work encouraging learning. Truly, the French here were more advanced than their Cornish counterparts. Despite being extremely poor, they had a treasure that the Cornish in the same low condition did not.

I had invited Henry to meet us at a small hotel near le Plateau des Bijoux Artiques in mid-February so that we could hike to see the famous view. En route for the Eaux Chaudes and Gabas, we rattled down through a gorge and admired the greys of the rocks and the deep blue sky. It was a joyful day for me as I was anxious to see my dear Henry. It had been two months since we had seen each other. I knew he would love to see for himself the cascades whose likenesses were in all the print shops in Pau. We went past the rocky beds and black pools, over ledges and sheets of white snow and past a bridge that must have been a herculean feat of engineering to build. We pulled up to the old wooden inn in Gabas which looked like half inn and half stable, where I hoped Henry would be awaiting our arrival. He would have had a long journey to Gabas, a hamlet in the valley of the Gave d'Ossau in the French Pyrenees and is located at the confluence of two mountain streams. The sides of the mountains are nearly vertical, rising straight upwards from the little road by the hotel. I hoped Henry had made the journey safely. Truly, after a long journey, the hotel appeared to be a mountain refuge.

Henry was indeed there, waiting for us in the canteen, drinking beer with several locals and singing, having a grand time. My heart was overwhelmed with joy to see him, and he and his merry band of friends gladly welcomed us to warm by the fire after our long trek up to Gabas.

"I did not know that you knew how to speak French," I said to him as we embraced, rocking back and forth with happiness.

"I don't," he laughed, his eyes twinkling.

"Then how have you managed here?" I asked.

"Charades!" he joked.

"Have you ever seen anything more beautiful than this scenery?" I asked, sitting down at the table.

"Yes, I have," he said, staring admiringly at me. I stared back at him.

Lavender scented candles glimmered on our table while we feasted on roast duck, pine nuts, and delicious beans grown in the inn's garden. We enjoyed the local wine, and Caroline seemed to be enjoying the local friends as much as Henry did. Our merry table continued talking and singing into the night. Henry took my hand under the table.

"Bess, I have been meaning to tell you something for a long

time, and I want to ask your opinion because I have held on to it with a heavy heart, since Talwyn's death."

"It sounds a bit serious for an evening of revelry," I whispered back, a bit nervously.

"I will simply state it before I change my mind," he said rather quickly. "On the night of her death, I went to my father-in-law's house and found a wooden cabinet."

"I think I remember such a cabinet in his tailor's shop," I mused.

"Could be. However, this one was in his pantry. It was full of pendants in the shape of crosses, laden with gemstones. Very valuable pieces, as it turned out," he explained.

"Go on. How did he obtain these gems?" I asked. Then I quickly remembered the smuggling. "Oh," I said. "The smuggling."

"Exactly." Henry tossed his mug from his left hand and then to his right on the table, clearly agitated. The others in our group were laughing and talking, paying no attention to us.

"I knew they were valuable. I took them to London and had an expert at the British Museum take a look at them. He said they were ancient Maltese crosses from the middle to late eighteenth century, and worth a large sum. At the time, I had Talwyn's three sisters to care for as well as my own two sisters. I had nine pendants and I turned all nine over to the curator for safekeeping. I felt I had to sell them for my sisters' and her sisters' benefit. The museum did in due course decide to buy them, and I put the money in Bolitho's bank so that you would not find out and think ill of me for profiting from the smuggled gems." He looked so weary after explaining this load he had carried for so long.

"I was able to pay for their weddings and dowries. I only used the money for them. I explained the funds had come from their father and said no more. They did not ask for further explanation and I gave none. Do you think ill of me for this, Bess?"

I sat and pondered his outpouring. "How did you explain having these jewels to the British Museum," I asked, curiously.

"I told them that they had been found at the bottom of a trunk of bed linen, among the things my father had left me, which was an outright lie, Bess."

"A very believable one. I cannot judge anyone, Henry. It is not my place. I do see that you wanted the best for your sisters and sisters-in-law. It is right that the gems are in a museum. I would never think ill of you, Henry, for trying to provide for your family. However, I do think your safety was in jeopardy while the crosses were in your possession," I added.

"Yes, quite so. I went to London as quickly as I could and soon thereafter, moved my sisters-in-law to a different home as I feared more loot was hidden in their father's house somewhere. What a nightmare that all was. It still haunts me today. Telling you all this is a way to be clean of it, for good." He slumped down in his chair.

"I am glad you told me. All is well. Let those grey clouds be gone and let us have blue skies going forward. Now, let us plan for our adventure to le petit plateau, starting tomorrow," I said eagerly.

"Our guide told me that if my wish was to go up to le plateau, '*Il faut monter.*' Meaning that we must climb to get to le plateau, and we could be up to our knees in snow, with a biting wind," I said, with a questioning look for Henry.

He nodded, appreciatively. "I am ready for anything. When I am by your side, I feel like more of life is possible."

Chapter Twelve

Modernist

1858-1860

The change coming back to Cornwall could not have been more pronounced. Everything felt damp again! Towels, clothes, hair, all to my delight. Even the sky was different in Cornwall. The windy sky with bright blue openings and whisking clouds, some white, some grey, the rivers, the ponds, all with their very own sense of Cornishness, and I was glad of it. Abroad, I might be taken to be just another of *les Anglais*, but I have always been proud of my Cornish home, as I told Mr Mill all those years ago on that walk to the Mount.

I knew I faced a mountain of resistance in my new position at the bank. I tried to prepare myself for it while in Pau and to gain strength from the mountains I had climbed rather than feel that my own mountains were insurmountable. Now that I was back in Cornwall, I had re-entered the world of men – a world in which it was *their* decisions that were made to be final. It weighed heavily on me. I had written part of a poem in Pau to help me sift through these troubling thoughts and doubts.

Barren is the onward path, and dreary
Darkly hid beneath a cloud of care;
I am footsore, I am worn and weary
Of a world that others find so fair.

My first week back proved to be exactly what I had predicted – a mountain of mortgages to be decided upon, accounts to be balanced, a shortage of coin, pressures from every angle. I went to the office every day so that I could establish myself and oversee the stacks of letters and registers that had to be closed.

Mid-week, Mr Alexander came to the bank early in the afternoon. All were still at their midday meal. I alone was in the bank. The bell on the front door jingled loudly, alerting me that someone had stepped inside. A man cleared his throat.

I came out of my office to see Mr Alexander the colleague of Mr Richards from my earliest meetings with Father, standing there, shaking off the light rain that had begun outside.

"Good day to you, Mr Alexander" I said with a smile. "How may we be of service today?"

"Oh, good day to you, Miss Carne. I am here to see the man who is to be your father's replacement. About some business I have," he said, shaking the rain off his tall black hat.

"I see. I am Father's replacement. What would you like to discuss?" I asked, as firmly and steadfastly as I could. I was bracing myself for this and had prepared a line of thought in response to these "replacement" concerns and issues I knew I would receive.

"Begging your pardon, miss. I need more than a banker to keep my money at present. Is there a partner that I can see?" he asked, getting visibly irritated, heaving his body weight from one side to another.

"I am that partner. Will you please step into my office, and we can sit and discuss your business?"

"Miss Carne, I want to work with a male partner. Are there none to be had in this bank?" he asked, quite grouchily.

"Yes, they are all at luncheon at the present time. I am more than capable ..." He interrupted me.

"Miss Carne, I am sure you are very capable, but you are not the businessman your father was." His expression seemed to say: there, I said it, and I am not in the least sorry for any rudeness.

"No. No one could be the businessman my father was," I said, assuredly. "He was consulted by most of the prominent men in business, in London as well as Cornwall, at one time or another."

"Exactly my point," Mr Alexander replied, irritably waving his hand as if to dismiss me.

"Yes, and I was present at many of those discussions. I alone was privy to those meetings. My father left me many rules and formulas of business that no one else has," I said, as if holding on to a magical business power.

"I see," he said, more interested now.

"I might be able to apply some of this wisdom to your position. Shall we discuss it in my office?"

At that point, the manager and other staff returned from lunch. Mr Bodilly, my partner, had also entered the bank from luncheon. We all stood in the centre of the bank, the men looking at me quizzically.

"See here, Mr Bodilly, Miss Carne is likely a fine banker, but I would like to work with someone who has the experience of a true businessman on my venture, someone like yourself."

"I see," Mr Bodilly began. "You are a most valued customer, and we would be happy to help you."

The tension seemed to drain out of Mr Alexander and the energy returned to his plump, red face in a large smile.

I felt my own face start to redden, and I attempted to push it back down with steady breathing. I felt incredibly awkward.

He must think I sit in my office and write poetry or read the gossip papers, I said to myself.

"I knew you would see the logic," he replied, puffing his broad chest out a bit more.

I began to get very uneasy, but a customer's needs come before my own needs, I reminded myself.

"Your best person for that job is none other than Elizabeth Carne, trained by the best businessman in Cornwall for years, brightest financial student of any I can recall, who actually runs this business. May I suggest, sir, that you step into her office and begin." The air in the office was still and tense.

"Sir, I have my reasons," Mr Alexander puffed, clearly getting worked up and out of breath. "If you could kindly show me the way to your office, then yes, I would like to begin immediately."

"I am afraid I am not the person for the job," Mr Bodilly said quietly. "I will not see Miss Carne positioned as any less experienced than she is, sir. If you cannot work with Miss Carne, you work with no one. Understood?"

The staff made themselves busy at their desks, pretending not to hear.

"You are not the only bank in Penzance, Bodilly." Mr Alexander turned and roughly grabbed the door handle and flung it open, pulling on his coat and hat as he walked out into the rain.

"Let that be a lesson to us all here," Mr Bodilly said, loudly and sternly. "Miss Carne now runs this bank. She is more astute than any man in Cornwall. I will stand by that. I suggest you all do the same." And with that, he strode into his office and closed the door.

I had been standing motionless and silent. I gave a nod to the staff and returned to my office.

In the weeks that followed, there were more interactions

similar to Mr Alexander's. Most customers seemed to gradually become open to working with a woman. Many others did not.

I became very accustomed to the signs, small gestures, facial expressions and kind words that were kind on the surface but had another intention underneath. Both men and women alike expressed their distaste for women in banking, or for that matter, women working in any public capacity. In one instance, an elderly woman gave me a chastising for leaving my children home alone. When I mentioned that I had no children, she said, "What? No children? Are you barren then? A pity!" I had to smile a bit at her rudeness; it was so blatant. Another man refused to have me included in a meeting with Mr Bodilly over a shipping venture. Others would make excuses about not being available for this meeting or that if they knew I would be present. Still others asked that I not be included in their meetings.

After several months of this frustration, Mr John Childs, a shipowner in Penzance, came into the office to meet with Mr Bodilly, who had deep experience with managing shipping matters. I, of course, deferred to Mr Bodilly to handle the meeting. Instead, he insisted that I conduct the meeting without him, as I knew Mr Childs very well through my father.

Mr Childs came into the meeting room and did not seem distressed to see me there. I took charge of the meeting saying, "Mr Childs, so good of you to come to our offices to discuss your salt merchanting business. I understand that the salt market from the Turks and Caicos Islands continues to do well."

"Yes, it does, and I am here today to consider acquiring a mortgage to purchase the ship, *Constance*," he replied.

I proceeded. "The Penzance Bank would be happy to consider a mortgage for that. What are your aims for this vessel, sir?"

"I want to capture more of the salt trade, to be sure," he responded with confidence.

"And are there additional markets opening up for salt that you could also consider?" I asked. Father had always said to watch the horizon before making a large investment to determine how long that investment will provide returns. "My concern would be that additional sources of salt might under-cut your market or that the supply from the Turks and Caicos might diminish. Do you have any information on those issues, Mr Childs?"

"Your father was the best businessman I knew, and I am sorry for your loss. He would have sat here and asked me those exact questions, Miss Carne, to be sure that we would both end with a profit. I appreciate you not rushing to advance a mortgage before we give this our best consideration. Could you assist me with the necessary calculations so that I can be sure I will be able to take on a new mortgage?" he asked.

"Of course, sir. I will work with my staff to gather what information would be needed to make a sound decision and a sound mortgage. In a few weeks' time, shall we meet again to discuss your proposed needs?" I asked him, confidently.

"Yes, taking the time to devise a sound scheme is well worth the wait." He smiled and left the office with something more than he came in to get, I decided. *A success this time, but can I achieve more like this?*

Chapter Thirteen

Geologist and Preservationist

1862–1865

"I am afraid I have some very alarming news, Bess." Thomas Bodilly, now well over sixty years old, a fellow Methodist and my trusted partner from my father's time, came into my office at the bank, looking down at the floor. Mr Bodilly was as sturdy an advisor as anyone I had ever known, other than my father. I braced myself for his news. I motioned for him to sit down.

"Go on. Has someone died?" I asked, my mind trying to stay calm, but all my alarm bells were sounding. So many of my family and friends had died, it was a logical question to ask.

"No, it is nothing of that sort. The thing is, I have just come from a transaction with Mr Richards, with whom I know that you are familiar from past dealings," he said, wiping his brow and looking for my reaction to Mr Richards' name out of the corner of his eye.

"Yes, I know him. Go on," I urged, holding steady and dreading the possibility of another marriage proposal.

"He has just withdrawn a substantial sum, under my authority at the bank, as he has every right to do." He shook his head.

"To what end?" I asked, trying to hurry him along to the alarming part.

"He aims to lease the Boscawen Un land from the current tenant. He has stated that it is derelict but sits on prime farmland, and his plan is to use the land to grow potatoes." He winced.

I was stunned. Tears pricked my eyes. "What?" I asked, incredulously. "We own that land, so it would be illegal for him to attempt to lease it," I argued.

"Yes, correct; however, these ancient land agreements from before your grandfather's day can be complicated and can be misconstrued. Misunderstandings can obviously cause disputes about ownership even now," Mr Bodilly argued back. "He has not actually leased the land yet, but has the capital in hand, enough to pay for several months' rent, I would imagine," Mr Bodilly added.

"Well, he must not!" I blurted out. "We own those grounds. Does he not understand the property arrangements? That land is sacred to my family. He must not be allowed to lease that land." *What appalling news! How could he think he would be able to lease the land that belongs to us? What a strange course of events.*

"Let us think calmly and clearly," Mr Bodilly urged me.

I stood up, abruptly. "Yes. Yes, let us think. How do we ensure that he knows that we own the land, and the conditions of the tenancy agreement? Where is the tenancy agreement?" I asked, trying to get as many facts as I could.

"I will have enquiries made to find out what he knows. Clearly, he is mistaken," he replied, cautiously.

"We must do so at once and notify the tenant that he is not able to lease the land. Is it too late? Has ground been broken?" I was earnestly and desperately hoping that it was not too late to save the stones, which would certainly be removed to make room for the ploughing.

"Historical notes from William Camden in the late six-teenth century describe the stones in detail, which as you know, date from the Megalithic period. Standing stones are sacred historical sites in Britain." I was pacing in the office at this point. *That they could be desecrated in our lifetime after centuries and millennia of standing silent witness to lost an-cient beliefs is unthinkable. Unfathomable. Evil, even. To think how long they have endured in this world, only to become a potato farm! Incredible!* I could not fathom the atrocity of harming the stones.

"Knowing him, and he is a slippery type, I daresay he will not act on a whim. Somehow, he gives me reason to believe that we would have time to stop his plans and we will certainly draw up a letter today informing him that we own the land." Mr Bodilly raked his hand over his face, a sure sign of tension and frustration.

"How did he arrive at considering that piece of land for his potatoes out of all the others he could have chosen?" I won-dered out loud.

"I daresay he has his ear to the ground for all sorts of business opportunities," he said, with a shrug. "You have my full agreement on the importance of the stones. Copper pro-duction is falling, but tin is increasing now, and our business is doing quite well. And now, with your nephew Archie and my son Thomas training with us and learning about our banking methods, we have valuable additional help. So, now is a good time to focus our energies on nineteen ancient stand-ing stones if we need to," he said with a brief smile." Thomas Bodilly was vastly experienced, and we were very like-minded in our conservative business dealings. I could not have asked for a better replacement for Father. "Now, let us ask Mr Downing to find out the facts with haste."

"Thank you, Mr Bodilly," I said. "However, is Mr Downing not in London at present, visiting our agent there? *Mr Downing, now our manager, has worked for the bank a long time, as had Mr Marrack before him. I wish he had been here as I know I could rely on his assistance.* "I simply cannot lose Boscawen Un to potatoes. We cannot. I know my father would agree if he were here."

"That is correct. Nicholas is in London at the moment. I will ask my son Thomas to help and direct him on who to ask. Yes, of course. Your father would have wanted to keep the stones intact. Now, let us take action. I am sure it is not too late." He strode out of my office. *I wish I had his confidence.*

I went home that evening very troubled. After working in my bank office, I often ate my evening meal alone in my study, where I could read, write, and relax. *Times have changed*, I told myself as I remembered how we would dress for dinner and eat as a family when we were growing up. I did miss those times. Because I was now living alone, I did not see the need to spend time changing my dress just to eat alone in the dining room. Besides, I rather enjoyed my writing activities, and I wanted to continue my geological studies after all the training Father had given me.

I was so vexed and worried about the Boscawen Un standing stones that I needed something substantial to take my mind away from imagining what it would be like to physically drag each of the stones away, and the spectres of farmhands digging potatoes from the once sacred land. *The thought of it!* I decided that working on a new geological paper for the *Transactions of the Royal Geological Society of Cornwall* would be the best distraction. I had splendid success with an article that had been published two years previously, concerning the evidence for different shorelines having existed in previous remote ages at Land's End. In all my writings, that was one of my favourite topics and one that Henry and I discussed through the years, both at Land's End and in Pau, during our visit there.

In my new paper, I wanted to discuss and prove the past existence of forces that Father and I believed had been in place to form the Land's End granite itself. An explanation of how and why it was formed where it was would be a significant contribution to the study of geology as a whole and would add distinction to Cornish geological studies. Having already outlined the article, I set out to use my research materials and steadfastly write several hundred words, using my reference texts and sketches. Then, the next time I wrote, I reviewed what I had written and then added several hundred more words. My references and sketches were strewn about, covering my desk completely. As I sat perched on the edge of my desk chair, reading what I had written, I thought critically to myself.

I believe I need to emphasise in greater detail how I know that the grey granite at Land's End was formed several million years ago when a mass of boiling granite forced its way through the underground rocks and came to the surface.

"How do you know this, Bess?" I could hear my father's voice saying, as if he were standing over my shoulder as he did so many times, asking me questions to improve my line of thinking.

I know this based on the differing size of the crystals found below and above ground as well as the quantities of tin and other ores surrounding the site, as if the Earth's crust was stretched in order for the molten magma to push through.

"Excuse me, Miss Carne, but these letters come for ye this morning." Betty, my new maid, tried to find an empty place on the desk to set the letters, but there was none. She looked at me helplessly.

"I will take them. Thank you kindly, Betty." Betty did a polite curtsey and bustled out of my study. The wood floors made a lovely creaking sound as she walked out.

The first letter was from Caroline, my older sister, asking if I would like to donate funds to help buy the new bells that were now needed at St Mary's Chapel. *A grand idea for the Carne sisters! The need was mentioned two Sundays ago in their newsletter. I must see to the allocation of the funds tomorrow. I will stop by the house before I go to the bank. This is another pleasant diversion from my consternation about the stones.*

The second letter, which I opened quickly so that I could return to my writing, was from my other older sister, Mary, asking about the arrangements for the forthcoming Volunteers' Supper in Penzance for the First Cornwall Rifles, in which Archie, her son, was now Ensign. Captain Boase was going to be in the Chair. Caroline and I had agreed to help him with some of these arrangements. *Yes, yes, I have secured a suitable room to accommodate forty or fifty guests, as requested. I must write back to her about the number of guests, as the list seems to grow each time we discuss it, and items such as the table arrangements, the wine list, and so on.* I made a note on my list of pressing items to do this week.

The third letter was from my dear friend Caroline Fox, where she wrote that she remembered how overwhelming it was for me when we took in our five cousins, and she was now asking for my advice. She also said she had had a bout of bronchitis but was feeling better. *Dear me, that is a taxing job even without the constant coughing of bronchitis!* I had long admired Caroline Fox's antislavery meetings and also the donations she provided for stranded sailors. On top of all that, she was extremely well read and provided the best reviews of books. *I must write back to her about Boscawen Un. She will be positively sickened when she hears that and might have advice for me.* I put this additional item on my list.

The last letter was from Henry. A note to say that his job looking after the Penzance port finances was keeping him busier than he wished; and that he hoped that we could find time to go for a ride to Lamorna Cove very soon. *Perfect. We can have a look at how the cliffs there have eroded to form reds and blues, like the scales of a snake.*

I put the letters aside for the moment, and I returned to my writing. Father would have easily resumed the train of thought exactly where I left off.

"What leads you to this knowledge regarding the boiling granite and its emergence from underground?" Father would have said. He had such a fluid intellect and could navigate complex and ambiguous problems brilliantly.

I must refer to Dartmoor and Bodmin Moor, where the granite intrusion contains horizontal joints that can be clearly seen there. Perhaps I should revisit those sites and add a sketch of the joints in the paper. The similar joints at Lamorna Cove are not as pronounced; but Henry would enjoy going to Bodmin Moor as well. I will send him a note to ask if he would be available. And, out of courtesy, I will ask Mr Bodilly tomorrow if we can afford some time for me to finish this paper. I jotted down a few reminder notes.

The stones! Will all our beautiful experiences there now become only lasting memories? I could not stop thinking about the land. *What would Father say ... what would he do? Think rationally, Bess, not like a worried old woman. How can I think rationally in this situation? Consider only the facts.*

Steer Mr Richards towards other possibilities, even though the land is rightly ours, so that his interests are maintained, and he causes no further difficulty, I thought as I shuffled some papers into stacks on my desk. *Find another suitable piece of land for potato farming.* That thought came to me in conjunction with my farming friends, the Freethys. *Would their landlord be willing to sell any of his land to an eager buyer? Mr*

Freethy would now be in his late fifties, and I know that his son, William, is running the farm now, remembering my conversations with them over the years. What other land might be available that Richards could buy or lease for potato farming? Wait. Mr Richards, a potato farmer? That does not sound like it would be appealing to him. I laughed at myself at the little pun I made with "appealing." Then it hit me. *What if Richards knows of our family fondness for ancient sites and geology and is trying to strike back at the family to settle a score from years ago? It could not be. He has been married a long time and has children.* My mind kept turning the possibility of this over and over, and the more I thought, the more implausible it became. *I must discuss the available options with Mr Bodilly as soon as possible.*

The next morning, we sat in Mr Bodilly's office. I was more than eager to hear the news.

"The farmer who leases the land from us, by the name of Ernest Campbell, age sixty-three, has been notified via letter about the ownership of the land where the nineteen standing stones are located as well as the menhir, the solitary nine-foot stone that tapers at the top, which is located near Boscawen Un," Mr Bodilly said.

I asked, "What are your thoughts on the best approach?"

"First of all, I think that we need a better grasp on the facts," Mr Bodilly said, arms folded on his chest.

I nodded. "I would like to ride out to see Mr Campbell and ask him what he understands. It is a somewhat complicated arrangement. Then, perhaps you and I can discuss options to prevent further arguments over the land."

"I quite agree, Bess. I think you are the best person to meet with him. I hope you are able to find out what is going on and also smooth things over with him," Mr Bodilly said. "By the way, Bess, did you know that town council has started serious discussions on the new town hall? I know that is another project you have had your eye on."

"No, I did not. Have any plans been drawn yet?" I asked

"I am not certain, but I can find out by asking the council," he replied.

"Yes, please do. A project for another day. Meanwhile, I now have some idea of how to make the ownership of the standing stones clearer," I said, smiling.

I arranged to meet with Mr Campbell the next day. I rode out to his farm early so that I could see the stones beforehand. I had not been to visit them for some time. Sadly, three of them appeared to be falling down, or had been made to fall. A pile of earth, now covered with brambles, appeared to have been dumped in the middle of the stones. I went to the centre leaning stone and bent down so that I could more closely see the carvings of two axe heads on its posterior. Through the pale green lichen, I saw that the carvings were still there, of course, and I was as glad to see them as I would have been to see an old friend.

"Mr Richards was right about one thing. You are unkempt. You need a guardian, and that guardian will be me," I said aloud and determinedly to the stones.

I rode down the lane back to the farmhouse to meet with Mr Campbell. He was waiting for me, sitting on a wooden stool, in his work clothes and cap, his grey hair running down his back. He was of course leery of me at first as he had not met me, and it had been some time since he had spoken to Father. I told him about Father's death and that as his heir, I was the owner of the land now. Being a quiet man, it was difficult to engage him in conversation. We chatted about horses and then the stones.

"What were the stones fer, you think?" he asked, head turned to one side like that of a curious child.

"The people of the time made them into one of the main meeting places in Britain, over two thousand years ago," I tried to explain as simply as possible so as not to frustrate him on any specific point. I was not sure I wanted to go into possible funeral rites with him at this point.

"I see. What you want to do with them?" he asked, looking sideways at me.

"I want to keep up the property and keep this as a treasure of Britain for future generations so that they can see that people two thousand years ago wanted us to know they existed," I said slowly and with my heart in my throat.

"Mr Campbell, I understand a man by the name of Mr Richards offered to lease the land the stones are on from you. Is that correct?"

"Yes'm. 'E come to me door askin' how much. 'E say the land be needed for starvin' folk, for potatoes, 'e did."

"Other farmland is available for potato farming," I explained. "But there will never be another set of standing stones built by our greatest ancestors. Do you see that?" I asked, hopefully. "While we are glad you are here to lease the land from us, Mr Richards is not lawfully allowed to then lease it from you. Is that clear as well?"

"You not buildin' no circus 'ere, is ye?" he asked.

"No, sir! I would like to clean the middle out and plant a hedge around the stones to help protect them and perhaps some flowers – bluebells – along the entry path. That is all," I explained.

"Miss Carne, you go' a migh'y honest face. I did like your father."

"Mr Campbell, I would like you to stay here as our lessor and help me keep an eye on the stones here as well as the land close by to the east where the taller, nine-foot stone stands. And, since I am your banker as well as the landowner, as I explained earlier, I have access to your lease and all the terms. I hope you do trust me that I am explaining the lease correctly," I said, looking at him in earnest

"A lady banker," he said, quizzically. "Ye want to keep those stones bad, don't ye?"

"Yes, sir, I do," I told him. *No use pretending at this point.* I sat very still, holding my breath.

"I do, of course, want to keep my lease and we can discuss the terms when the lease runs out as I will want to renew it. You can keep yer stones!" He slapped his knee. "That Richards is gonna be surprised."

"Thank you. Thank you!" I hugged him and his cap fell off. We both laughed.

I got on my horse, possibly the happiest I had felt in a very long time. *We did it, Father. The stones are safe!*

"Feel free to tell Mr Richards when he returns that you know that the Carnes already own this land, Mr Campbell," I said as I started to turn my horse around.

"You can tell him yourself, if you like, miss. Here he comes down the lane." Mr Campbell pointed.

Blast. Here comes an unwelcome confrontation. Unavoidable. Might as well clear the issue personally with him. I sighed.

Mr Richards rode up to us at a canter on his black stallion, stopped abruptly, and tipped his shiny black top hat. He was dressed in a blue riding habit, with black boots and a black horsewhip. His white cravat was perfectly clean and tied. *How long must it take for him to dress in his finery?*

"Out for a morning ride, Mr Richards?" I asked, very politely.

"Why, yes. I am here to pay a visit to my land," he said grandly, with a sweeping gesture of his black-gloved hand.

"Not your land," Mr Campbell retorted, eyeing Mr Richards from his seat.

"All in good time, my good man. You see, Miss Carne, I have leased Boscawen Un. I will make this into a working asset, not merely an old plot of decaying and useless stones.

Why, may I ask, are you here, Miss Carne?"

"I came to see the stones and to pay a call on Mr Campbell, who is my tenant," I said, my eyes directly on his. "I think you know why I am here. You see, my aim is to keep the standing stones as a monument and tribute to our ancestors, who had the first meeting of the druids in Britain here in the year two thousand BC," I said, calmly.

"That will be quite impossible as I will be ploughing the land, starting within a day or two," Mr Richards gloated. He held his chin high and smiled.

"I can't lease to you 'cause she owns the land, Mr Richards," Mr Campbell shot out, getting up from his stool and standing at full height.

"What? Why, you filthy farm animal. I suspected as much. What did she pay you? I will double it!" he screamed, turning his horse around, harness jingling, to face Mr Campbell, sweat dripping from his brow.

"Have a care, Richards," Mr Campbell said, as he pulled his long black shotgun from behind his stool and laid it gently on his arm, barrel pointed directly at Mr Richards. "Get off the lady's land before I shoot you for trespassing."

Mr Richards' eyes widened, but he said nothing.

"I think we all understand each other here," I said quickly in an attempt to lower the tension. "I assume you received the letter from my bank advising that the land is owned by the Carne family. We best be on our way, Mr Richards. After you," I said, in a directive tone. I stared at Mr Richards, eyes unwavering. "I do know that the owner of Ednovean Farm next door has a plot of land that he may be willing to sell you for your potatoes, if you like," I said, with all the charm I could muster. I tried not to let him see how much I loathed him in his finery, trying to dupe and disrespect a hard-working farmer.

"Damn you, farmer," he seethed, wielding the reins, turning his fine black stallion with a rough jerk, its teeth flashing with the strain of the bit. "You do not own all of Penzance, Miss Carne," he said, his eyes glaring at me for several seconds. Finally, he slapped the reins against his stallion's neck. "Good day to you," he hissed as he kicked his horse sharply in the sides and galloped off.

***

I sat at my desk in my bank office reviewing our most recent mortgage requests, when there was a knock at my door.

"A Mr Robert Fox here to see you, Miss Carne," Mr Downing said.

"Mr Fox? Do show him in, please," I said in surprise.

"Good day to you, Miss Carne," he said with a huge smile. It was such a delightful surprise to see him.

"Hello, Mr Fox." I smiled in return. "This is a delightful surprise. I am so glad to see you. How is your family?"

"All is well," came his answer. "I know you did not expect me today, but I have some news you will be interested in, I am sure."

"I am intrigued, sir. What is this news, please?" I asked, confused.

"It is this. As president, I would like to inform you that you have been inducted into the Royal Geological Society of Cornwall for your esteemed geological work and papers. Congratulations," he said, proudly. "I would like to present you with this official written invitation as well."

I was dumbfounded. *Women are never admitted to such highly regarded societies as ours here in Cornwall. Being the oldest one of its kind, second only to the one in London, it has, over the years since its foundation, included eminent names such as Davies Gilbert, Sir Charles Lemon, and Augustus Smith, all of whom I regard as the top experts in the field of geology.*

"Well, Miss Carne? Are you pleased and do you accept our invitation?" he asked, looking amused.

"Why, yes! I do. Yes, of course. It would be my honour and privilege, sir," I stammered at last.

"Good. Then we will see you at St John's Hall to congratulate you in person at our next meeting in a fortnight. Do keep up the diligence on those papers," he said, as he tipped his hat and left my office.

The Royal Geological Society of Cornwall! I cannot believe it! Father would have been thrilled for me. I leaned on my desk with both palms down. I closed my eyes. *Thank you, Father, for all you taught me and all you helped me accomplish.* I said, picturing in my mind the two of us looking at the invitation and what he would have said.

***

"Wonderful to see you!" I said, excitedly, to Henry after we had embraced at what had become our usual meeting place on the slopes overlooking Castallack Moor and Lamorna Cove. It was springtime, and even though the ride to the cove was about six miles, we both loved to ride, so we made the trip on horseback, which was the best way to fully enjoy the scenery and air. We rode down the long lane in the wooded Lamorna Valley to the cove, which was lined with bluebells, our favourite flower.

We passed many trees with strange but lovely gnarled trunks and branches and saw several houses and outbuildings that were part of Higher Kemyel Farm on our left and Tregurnow Farm on our right. The most splendid things about the lane were the green ferns, trees, and flowering bushes surrounding us and the sound of the spring running towards the cliffs, like a child running with its arms open wide, celebrating, as it was about to fall into the open arms of its mother, the sea.

The smell of the water and the plants and the gurgling sounds of the rushing spring were so lovely, I asked Henry to stop several times just to listen to it. It soothed me to the core.

Once we reached the beach at Lamorna Cove, I jumped off my horse and said, excitedly, "I have news to tell."

"Do tell me then, please," he said as we walked down the rocky path to the water's edge. Both the cliffs and the path at Lamorna were steep.

"I am very happy to say that I have secured our land and the standing stones at Boscawen Un and saved it from becoming a potato farm," I said, giving his arm a squeeze.

He stopped abruptly and, with his strong hands, gently turned me to face him.

"I overheard Mr Richards saying he was leasing a farm, though I did not catch which one, at the beginning of the week. To settle an old score, he said. He was telling a group of men at the Fifteen Balls tavern on Market Jew Street. I was there with some of my friends from the boatyard."

"Well, later in the week I reminded the tenant farmer that we own the land and that he is not legally permitted to lease it," I said, simply.

"That will not sit well with Richards, Bess. Have a care. Be wary of going out without a manservant after this. You know what he is like," Henry warned.

"I plan on improving the site," I said, paying no heed to his warning. "I will plant a hedge around the stones, to protect them. And I will stand the three fallen stones back up again. Also, I think planting bluebells around the entrance would be a nice touch for the springtime, don't you agree? I would also like to engage a proper archaeologist to examine the site. I know it has more secrets to tell us."

"Such as?" Henry asked.

"Such as, was the leaning stone intended to lean like that, or has it very slowly fallen over through thousands of years?

A full examination by an expert will add to the historical writings on the stones by Camden, Stukeley, Borlase and Edmonds. I will include study on the Boscawen Un menhir as well."

"Yes, that would be a very worthwhile project, Bess. I agree. Congratulations. On behalf of Britons everywhere, we thank you." He took off his hat and bowed before me. "However, I still recommend that you be on your guard. Richards will most likely take offence to your actions."

I laughed. We continued walking, taking in the overwhelmingly beautiful blues, whites, greens, and golds of the scenery. I looked up at the striations on the cliffs and remembered Father's work regarding them in admiration. *Father published an article about them years ago.*

"I have also been invited to join the Royal Geological Society of Cornwall," I told him, excitedly.

"*The* Royal Geological Society? That is incredible, Bess! Congratulations and well done. Your papers impressed them, obviously," he said, kindly.

"I am so honoured and thrilled to be a part of that," I said, honestly.

"For a woman to be inducted is high praise, indeed," Henry said.

"We have also opened a new office of the bank in St Just. Did you know that?" I asked.

"Yes, I did. Well done and congratulations to you and your partners on the expansion. I am now even more glad that I moved my account to the Penzance Bank!" he added. I was pleased. As we walked further, we came upon the joints in the outcrops of rock.

"As I suspected, these joints are not so clearly in evidence as the ones on Bodmin Moor. Let us go down to the beach and take a good look at the erosion and see what insight we can glean, shall we?"

"Of all the coves in Cornwall, Lamorna is my favourite," Henry proclaimed.

"Why is that?" I wondered out loud.

"It has the most interesting crevices between the fallen rocks that create small tide pools and at low tide it is easy to walk amongst the water and sand and rocks, as if in an outdoor geological museum."

We walked through the very paths he mentioned and the water was a crystal blue, so blue and clear that it looked like a gem itself between the enormous, house-sized boulders. We admired the black and then red colours due to erosion. The dramatic edges to the cliffs where rock had fallen were beautiful and inspiring. *House-sized boulders. Houses, building projects, the new town hall! It is now under serious consideration, Mr Bodilly said. What might be built, and where? What about using Lamorna granite for building. Or, for ... I will have to think about these ideas later, or I will miss enjoying Lamorna now.*

The pools that Henry had described were deepening and turning a turquoise green in the changing sunlight. The ever-present wind pushed our backs and whipped our faces, as if to show us we were no match for its invisible force and enigmatic power. My hem and shoes were wet, but I paid no heed.

"Bess, I feel like you are leading the life you were meant to lead," he said, squeezing my hand.

"I am happy in leading a life governed by Methodist teachings and fulfilling the duties of my family legacy. I have no regrets in that," I said, gladly.

"I am very happy for you, given how diligently you have worked and how much you have sacrificed. Truly," he said sincerely.

"And I for you. You have come very far in your career and seem to enjoy your fishing trips!" We laughed.

"And I still enjoy seeing you at every opportunity. Perhaps

I will next see you at chapel this Sunday?"

"Yes. Can we dine together after chapel at my house? An informal dinner?" I asked. *I feel truly blessed in so many ways. Having Henry as a friend. The recent accolades. The successful business. My sisters. I feel happier than I have in a very long time.* Then I remembered what Father said about time. That we always thought we had more of it than we did. An unhappy thought on a most pleasant day.

"I would be delighted. I will escort you home now. It is late and your feet are soaking wet! You must be frozen solid!" We passed boulder beach and hiked back up the path, hand in hand, towards our horses, which neighed with excitement at the prospect of returning home.

***

"I believe the Queen herself would approve of the splendour of this dinner!" my sister Caroline said to me, surveying the long dinner table which seated forty officers and men at the annual Rifle Volunteers' dinner, chaired by Captain Boase, Archie's commanding officer, at a tavern near the Market House. The tavern, long-established, was known for its quite large rooms. *It smells of salt water and pine, as if the narrow-planked floor has just been washed.*

We, the aunts, had been invited to attend the celebration. Archie's mother, Mary, our sister, had to care for the younger children and remained at home. Caroline and I were quite proud of the genuine affection and regard Captain Boase and the other officers showed for Archie. The men commented on Archie's leadership and many talents, and we could not be prouder.

Captain Boase came to our table to greet us. He looked resplendent in his well-cut uniform. "We are very endeared to Archie, despite his only being with us a couple of years. He is an amiable lad with good sense."

"Thank you for your continued support of Archie," I said to Captain Boase. "He is an enormous asset to us at the bank, to our family, and to all of Penzance."

My other sister and Archie's mother, Mary, who was now a widow, and her younger children, along with Archie, had moved into our old home on Chapel Street. It was a perfect arrangement for all concerned. Mary and her family filled up the house and Archie was able to walk to the bank.

I for one am most grateful for Archie. He adapted very well to his new banking environment and is very diligent in his work. A fine student of the best banking practices. I enjoyed our tutoring sessions on the principles set out in the Practical Treatise of Banking *by James Gilbart. Father would have approved. Archie excelled and took on calculations and book-keeping with vigour. He seems to quite enjoy his work, and the fact that he does makes my life a joy. I can now fulfil the promises that I made to my father and grandfather about the family legacy to develop our business now that Archie is by my side. I hope now that I might eventually be able to take a step back, with the additional assistance of Mr Bodilly's son Thomas who would also become a partner in time. Our well-designed plans are in place and being fulfilled. There is no greater sense of satisfaction than family, and our family and our legacy are the greatest motivators.*

The captain continued down the table to greet the other guests prior to the commencement of the dinner.

"My, he is a charming and amiable host," Caroline said to me under her breath.

"I agree wholeheartedly." I could not help but reply.

We dined on several of Cornwall's most delicious fish dishes, including mackerel, cod, and fried Cornish hake. Wine flowed and so did many boisterous but good-hearted toasts. Sergeant Francis, a stout man with a barrel chest, who we aunts had just met this evening, said, "C'mon, good Ensign Carne, give us a toast then."

This was followed by Corporal Pascoe, a thin, pale, blonde man, who said, "Yes, sir. Give it a go!" Archie then stood up and the men's eyes followed him eagerly. Archie cleared his throat and at twenty-one years of age said,

"When a man has given so much of his time and energy to the volunteer cause as Captain Boase has, a vote of thanks on an occasion like this is the simplest mark of esteem we can show him. Let us not only drink to his health but give him a vote of thanks for his many kindnesses and do it by three hearty cheers!"

The men boomed out, "Hurrah for Captain Boase! Hurrah for Captain Boase! Hurrah for Captain Boase!"

I leaned into Caroline and shouted in her ear, "My ears are ringing from the loudness of all this!"

She could not hear me. The men were pounding on the tables for Captain Boase, and he responded by standing and giving a hearty salute to all the men.

As the cheering began to die down, Francis and Pascoe cried, "Three cheers for Ensign Carne!" and three booming cheers by all forty men at the table, and we two aunts, followed. To our great surprise, several of the men said, "And one more for his aunts!" and the crowd was wild with cheering for the Carne aunts, and we smiled and thanked them for their good wishes. *What camaraderie these men have. I have never seen or experienced anything like this! It is no wonder they love giving service to their country.* They then sang a volunteer song together, and I could see my sister wiping tears from her eyes, overwhelmed by the entire scene.

In the two weeks that followed the festive "volunteers' supper," life at the bank went on. Life with my geological papers went on. Life with our church donations went on. Spending small amounts of time with Henry went on. Life with the archaeological excavations at the Boscawen Un standing stones went on. In fact, the archaeologists discovered a burial mound near the stones and an ancient, two-thousand-year-old urn with an artistically decorative rim. I was delighted to no end with the finds. All was moving forward, and we were living the best possible life, it seemed.

Life then abruptly stopped the moment I received a letter from Mary on a bleak Monday morning. The letter was terse and to the point, saying that Archie was prostrate with fever and could not come into the bank this week. He had a very sore throat and high fever, with severe body aches and red rashes in between his arms and legs. Mary was extremely concerned at the alarming symptoms and had called in our family doctor, Dr Hennessey, who said Archie had scarlet fever. That was the end of the letter.

I sank to the floor, crushing the letter in my hand, and I started to groan and gasp.

"Miss Carne, whatever is the matter?" My maid, Betty, flew to my side and held my arm.

"It's our Archie. Oh, no. No! He has scarlet fever. I must go to Mary immediately and then to the bank." I gave her instructions, and I flew out of the house. I knew there was nothing that could be done by the sound of the letter and the symptoms Mary gave. Mary would be devastated. I tried to enter the Chapel Street house, but Dr Hennessey's assistant would give no admittance, stating the need for quarantine.

"Scarlet fever is highly, highly contagious, miss. You will likely contract it yourself. Pray for your sister and nephew, miss. That is all you can do now."

"But my sister, her children?" I cried out as I tried to push by him and into the house.

"Showing no symptoms yet," he said, pushing me back away from the door.

"Not poor, young, and dear Archie, Lord!" I prayed as I ran

down the street towards the bank office on Chapel Street.

I flung the doors open and rushed into Mr Bodilly's office, where he sat, head in his hands.

"You have heard then about our dear Archie," I said, voice trembling.

"Yes," he replied, looking up from his chair, red eyes watering. "So young and full of promise." A tear slid down his face.

"We do not want any open bank transactions that may have his name on them since he is now gone. Check any transactions made with his name appearing and endorse them with one of our names, please. We must avoid any uncertainty or conflict, as sad as we are. It is our responsibility to maintain continuity and trust here at the bank."

"Yes, of course," Mr Bodilly said, as he slowly got up from his chair.

I was already gone. I ran across the street to our chapel and looked around for our new minister. Mr Topham had been moved on many years before to another Circuit, and there had been several successors since.

"He has already gone to the Carne house, miss," the Deacon, who happened to be there, explained.

On Tuesday it was declared that there was no hope for Archie. By Thursday, he was dead. Our plans thrust aside by death once again. Back at my home on Coulson Terrace, I sat in my study and read the note announcing his death. *The song he and the men had sung at the dinner, and the speech he made, were the last words he publicly said to his comrades, and are now just a fond and revered memory. The brave, true hearted hope for me and for Penzance is gone.*

Chapter Fourteen

Capitalist

1865–1867

"Disturbing and concerning," I said to my partner, Thomas Bodilly, and our manager, Nicholas Downing, in our weekly meeting at our offices on Chapel Street. I always looked forward to my meetings with them, two people I admired and trusted, because we would settle down to business and discuss not only the running of the bank, but also any greater outside matters likely to affect us. We met each week in my office, which was modest but nicely adorned with pale blue walls and navy blue wing backed, velvet covered chairs with buttoned armrests. I had a pleasant fire going in the black iron fireplace. These men were, I felt, the closest I could get to my father himself, as they were very like him in intellect. The meetings gave me a sense of calm that I had ample support in operating the bank, even without Father.

"Yes, the amount of copper being mined more cheaply in other parts of the world, particularly in South America and other places, is turning the Swansea smelters away from our clients here in Cornwall. And then there is the cheap Malay tin. It is more than a passing thing, I am afraid," Mr Bodilly agreed.

"How much copper mining has shifted elsewhere, do we think?" asked Mr Downing.

"Difficult to say, but I would guess at least ten per cent, by the sound of it from our clients and what we read in the Times," Mr Bodilly answered.

"A key question to ask is whether the smelters will still need Cornish copper as well as that from other mines in the world? Will the Birmingham manufacturers and the ship-builders need more and more copper and brass?" I asked.

"That is something our agent in London can comment upon," Mr Bodilly suggested, and I nodded in agreement. "Let us keep an eye on how much ore the Cornish mines are raising, which is currently about 18,300 tons a year, and determine if it is declining at a rate similar to what our clients have said."

"We should think about how we lend to our clients in response to this," I stated.

"Agreed," said Mr Bodilly. "What do you have in mind? Tighten our belt, so to speak?"

"Yes. We need to shorten our lending terms to two years or less, as an example."

"Agreed," said Mr Downing, puffing on his white clay pipe carved with sea creatures, arms folded. "Let us ask our staff to keep an eye on accounts that might approach an overdraft and curtail advances until the market improves."

"Yes," I said. Mr Bodilly nodded his head.

"Any word on how our competitors are handling their lending terms?" I asked.

"I have heard word that Vivian, Grylls and Company, Mrs Vivian's bank in Helston, is losing money and lending too much," Mr Bodilly said, dryly. "It is a bad sign for us all when any bank is struggling. People lose confidence."

"Yes, that is certainly the case. I am sorry to hear that Mrs Vivian is struggling. I do have another idea for us, one which

may alarm you as it involves disposing of some of our assets,"
I said, slowly.

"We agree that more and cheaper supplies of copper ore
will come from overseas, undercutting prices for our clients.
Their incomes will be reduced, and probably more quickly
than anyone realizes." I paused. Both nodded. "This will mean
that the mines will be making calls on their investors for more
capital, which will bring them running to us for loans, even
though we have just decided to restrict our lending. I am
thinking we should have the foresight to sell some of_our
London investments while times are good and prices are
holding up, and before further collapse in the copper market,"
I continued, in a solemn and thoughtful manner. "By doing so,
we may be able to extend more loans and meet customers'
needs when other banks cannot."

Their eyes were intent on my face. "Our London investments, as you know, are of the kind that every country bank
like ours makes and maintains, as a source of steady income
from rock-solid institutions that are very unlikely to fail. We
have for example shares in the Bank of England and the
London and North Western Railway Company. They pay a
steady dividend year in and year out. We also have money in
the consols, of course – the National Debt, as it is called – Government bonds that pay a guaranteed if low interest until they
mature."

I paused. Mr Bodilly rubbed his hand across his whiskers.
Mr Downing sat very still.

"My father often told me during our tutoring sessions to
keep my eyes on the horizon, not at my feet; to consider the
winds of change and the wider context of our business, not
just the present conditions in and around Penzance. We need
to seriously consider selling some of these securities that are
the fundamental bedrock of our transactions, while that remains an option given the changing times, and provide ourselves with a capital reserve ready to hand that we may rely

on as things worsen, as they surely will do, to permit us to provide loans to those we trust who may be in critical need and can provide suitable collateral. That is my reasoning for making this sale, considering how things are changing so much before our very eyes. When times become better in future, we will easily be able to reinvest these funds in the London market." To me, this was a clear-cut opportunity to make the most of a developing situation in which men, and miners in particular, were starting to leave Cornwall in droves for overseas work, the price offered for Cornish copper had been dropping, and production was becoming less and less. I knew my partners were aware of all of this, and that this option would be good banking practice.

But I had more to say. "Some of this capital we will leave on deposit with our London agent, increasing our balance with them, which could then become the means of negotiating a larger overdraft arrangement for us in case of need."

"Miss Carne, you make sound and logical points here. Downing, if you agree, we can look over our London investments and decide which will realise the greatest value," Mr Bodilly said. "After all, we do not want to end up in some terrible situation where all our assets are tied up in mortgages and other long-lasting commitments which we will be unable to realise at short notice."

"I do agree of course," Mr Downing said. "In fact, I always follow and analyse the share prices and market reports in the papers, and I have formed a fair idea of the overall prospects."

"This leads us on to our next point of business. It sounds like we will need to go to London to make the necessary arrangements with our agent at Robarts, Lubbock & Company, Mr Thompson, and discuss market and industrial trade prospects in a bigger way and the likely effect on interest rates, if any," Mr Bodilly suggested.

"Quite right, Mr Bodilly. Perhaps you and I should travel

to London since Mr Downing has been there recently. I would like to speak with Mr Thompson directly as well as gain his insight on our shipping assets. Mr Childs has approached me about wanting a mortgage on a new venture."

"What is the nature of this new venture?" Mr Downing asked.

"He would like to purchase the *Constance,* a merchant ship of one hundred and thirty-three tons to trade in salt from the Turks and Caicos," I responded.

"How is the salt market these days?" Mr Downing asked.

I thought for a moment. Then I said, "I would say booming, but I would prefer to look into that. Would you be available to find out with certainty?"

"Yes," Mr Bodilly added. "Let us determine his likelihood of success and I assume he would have full insurance on the vessel? Will he have partners in the mortgage as well? Ask if he is agreeable to me being the 'ship's husband,' as we have always called them, given my previous experience with managing vessels. Remind him that a banker can be beneficial, in view of the trade credit which would be required to manage the paying of bills instead of waiting until the end of the voyage when the prospective cargo is sold and revenue is in hand."

"Of course," said Mr Downing, noting his actions to take.

"We need to know all of this. Mr Downing, please gather this information and we can discuss it and our London trip at our next meeting in a fortnight. We want to make sure that a total loss at sea would not affect us too badly or put the bank in jeopardy given the changing times. All in favour?" I asked, my eyes circulating the table.

"Aye!" my colleagues said, emphatically.

I was due that night for dinner with my oldest sister, Mary, at my former residence, now her residence, at 29 Chapel Street. It was to be just her and me so that we could discuss the now thorny matter of the next heir. We both dreaded having to have this discussion, since losing Archie was still so raw. Dressed in my mourning black, I knocked on the front door, politely.

"Miss Carne do come in, please," said Grace, who was now the new head maid of the house.

"There you are my dear sister. Please come into the dining room. Everything is ready." Mary was a wonderful hostess and a very busy person between her family and church. We rarely saw each other, so having a chance to speak openly one on one was much needed. I noticed that none of her other children were about and therefore apparently would not be joining us. She had spruced up Father's décor by adding some lovely wallpaper with maroon stripes, and pink flowers in the parlour. The house smelled of peppermint rather than pipe smoke, which was very refreshing. Several chairs had been replaced with maroon sitting chairs and tufted cushions.

"Your new décor is quite fetching, Mary," I said, hoping my compliment would set the right tone for the evening.

We sat down to monkfish in a light sauce with rice and mushrooms, which was a delight, but my stomach was ill at ease. I had a suspicion that we were about to have a difficult conversation. Mary was all grace, but I could tell she had undertones of tension in her demeanour. We chatted about our donation of the bells to St Mary's and how she was keeping up the Methodist library in our basement. We seemed to run out of pleasantries, so I dove into the subject at hand.

"What have you in mind about your next son in line for tutelage at the bank? I asked, hoping she would be pleased that another one of her sons would be handed a large opportunity that would rarely befall anyone else.

"That is precisely what we need to discuss. I imagine you are thinking John James, as he is the next oldest, would come to Penzance and learn banking and be your heir," she said, indicating that her plate could be taken away.

"Yes, he is the next oldest," I concurred.

"However, John is advancing his career in the military and has no interest in sitting inside a bank, you see," she said, with lowered eyes.

"No, I did not know that. However, could John return for a few years, until young Joseph finishes up with medicine? Then after those years, could Joseph join me at the bank?" I asked, pushing my food around on my plate. Without John or Joseph, it would be three years until young Charles would come of age to serve as heir.

"No, he cannot. Neither John nor Joseph is willing to part with their hard-earned careers for a job in banking, I am afraid," she replied, in somewhat of a short tone.

I was completely taken by surprise by her responses. *Surely she cannot mean that they have decided not to be involved in the bank.* I tried desperately to keep my composure.

"Are you concerned that I would try to force one of them to join me at the bank?" I asked, with a concerned but not heated tone.

"Yes, we all are, in fact," Mary huffed, shifting uneasily in her chair.

I sat and thought about my place in the family and the promises I had made. I stared at Mary. *How could she think I would do such a thing? But what choice do I have? Without either John or Joseph, I will be without an assistant or heir to train for three years. What if I die, or Charles for that matter, for some reason? What would happen to the family fortune then? It is difficult to think about.*

Finally, I said, "No, that has never been my intention. But without either John or Joseph to succeed, we have no continuity in our family business. We have no heir. You understand I am sure."

"Yes, yes, we all understand. We ask that you train Charles

when he is finished at Trinity College, when he can join you to learn what is necessary for his partnership," she said, somewhat defiantly. *Now I understand the tense aura around her that I felt earlier. A fine family situation in these changing times. Three years! Such a long time to wait. I will need to halt travel to protect my own health and security.*

"As I am sure you recall, I studied and worked with Father and his staff for six years after William died, and I had been working in the bank even prior to that for many years," I said, pleadingly. She was not about to change her position. She remained silent.

"What you are suggesting means that I would have no heir for three years and that he would come straight from college with no banking experience and start work in the bank. And you are expecting for him to be a partner in this capacity?" I asked, incredulously, leaning into the table.

"Yes. That is what we are suggesting." She pressed her hands down on the table.

"What if something happens to me prior to Charles beginning? You were in London when Father could barely breathe. His last words instructed me to keep the family legacy, keep the bank in the family." *I am in full disbelief at my family's lack of understanding of what skills banking requires. Maybe I should bring Gilbart's Practical Treatise of Banking over for their light reading pleasure.*

"We will determine that step if and when it comes to that," she said, flatly, waving a hand in the air, dismissively. She seemed to be trying to outrank me by seniority, being the older sister, in military fashion – instructed by her sons with their military training at Brighton College, no doubt. *I might be the current heir, but I will always be the youngest Carne to her.*

"I see that you have discussed this matter with your sons but have not included me, or considered the family legacy, in those discussions. I ask that you and the boys reconsider your thoughts and incorporate those of Father and Grandfather into their thinking as well. I thank you for a lovely dinner. I must depart. I am due in London later this week and I will see to it that we discuss this when I return," I said as I pushed back from the table and got up to leave.

"In that case, I daresay you should take care that you do return, and in good health, for the sake of the bank," Mary replied, cynically, as I walked towards the door.

***

Folios in hand, Mr Bodilly and I boarded the express train called the *Flying Dutchman*, which flew along the tracks to London at fifty miles per hour. *I continue to be astonished by the innovation of the railway system and happy that the trip no longer takes three long and bumpy days via stagecoach. No more horse changes. And the speed! It is hard to believe how fast the train runs! So fast the trees become a blur! It is truly a wonder of metal and steam, that remains difficult for me to comprehend. A man-made miracle of immense proportions!*

After we were comfortably seated and underway, we discussed several of the banking matters we now had in hand.

"We have carefully considered our investments," Mr Bodilly announced, lightly tapping his hands on his folio. "Mr Downing has drawn up a shortlist of what would be the best securities to sell, but we will have to check the prices at the Stock Exchange before we actually dispose of anything. Rather than doing it ourselves, it will be better for our agent's broker to do it for us. Mr Thompson will probably offer this anyway."

"Excellent. The funds we raise from this will be better used elsewhere," I responded, and Mr Bodilly nodded. "What were you able to find out about the progress with the new town hall?" I asked.

"Only that they lack funds, of course. The council is

reticent about its financial deliberations, but I would guess from what I do hear that, as yet, they only have some of the money they need," Mr Bodilly added. "In addition, I did find out that the architect's tentative plans require a large parcel of land. I believe they said half an acre. That will cost a pretty penny right in the middle of town," he cautioned.

"Am I right in then concluding that little or no progress will be made any time soon on the erection of a new town hall?" I asked.

"That looks to be the size of the situation, yes," Mr Bodilly responded.

"I see. And what of the mortgage on the *Constance* for John Childs. Has that been approved?" I asked.

"Yes, we have provided him with a mortgage to use the ship for the salt trade, as he proposed," replied Mr Bodilly.

"Good. What of our own shipping business? Are we in good stead to put an offer on a new vessel and do you have one selected?" I inquired.

"Yes. I have been on the *Nils Desperatum* and find it in good condition. She is larger than the *Constance* at one hundred and ninety-four tons and would therefore have a very large hold for our trade needs," Mr Bodilly offered. "Moreover, the price is favourable. Mr Downing seems keen on the deal as well."

I thought the size would offer better returns than a smaller vessel. *We do need to counter the dip in the copper market to offset any losses there,* I thought. I could hear Father's words echoing in my mind, "Look to the horizon, balance your assets."

"I trust your judgement on the quality of the ship. Shall we proceed with the purchase?"

"I will send the agent to make the arrangements," Mr Bodilly replied with a large smile.

As the countryside flashed by the window, I began to feel

excitement for London. I had always loved London in my youth. Father would rent a house for a month at a time, such as in the Georgian-terraced Great Ormond Street in Holburn, London, every winter while Joseph was attending school there. I had many long-term friends in and around London and knew the city quite well as a result of the escapades my sisters and I used to have along the Thames. We tried ice skating when the Serpentine froze, as it looked like such a lovely art. We were quite challenged by it. Often, we would push one another in a rented sleigh made for two on the ice. Many great family memories flooded back when I ventured to London, and I savoured them.

We were to spend a full week in London, which I relished. I had invited Mr Bodilly to stay with us but he said he needed to check on some property of his own in another part of London to the south of the Thames out in the new suburbs. We parted ways at Paddington Station, with its great arched roof, in the enormous bustle of people urgently coming and going and agreed to meet the next morning prior to our meeting with Mr Thompson at ten o'clock.

A hansom cab dropped me off at the house on Great Ormond Street, after passing through the noise and congestion of the busy streets, far busier and dirtier than Penzance. There were recognised crossing places for pedestrians, which were kept clear by the sweepers employed for the purpose. Horses and carriages of every description congested the roads, and delivery vans pushed their way through the traffic somehow to reach their next calls. Elegantly dressed people walked past the ragged flower sellers and news vendors that were ever-hopeful for custom. We passed the tobacconists that specialized in the kind of cigars that Mr Brunel the engineer had always seemed to be smoking when he visited Cornwall, and we passed many other kinds of shops that were unknown in Penzance. I saw the used furniture store on Church Street whose owners annexed the street for their shop as the contents, rocking chairs, tables, dressers, pot and pans, and the like spilled out into the street. There were also the ever-present omnibuses that I remembered around Holborn and in Skinner Street.

I hoped to visit a few of the ancient inns that remained, such as the Staple Inn, with its Tudor half-timbered exterior, so as to take in a bit of the history of the locality during my stay. I hoped I would have time to visit the British Museum as well to see what exhibitions were on and to spend time in their mineral collection, just for my instructive amusement. Perhaps I could check on Henry's Maltese Cross collection if it was on display and see it for myself.

My lodging was a four-storey red brick Georgian house, second to the end of the terrace, where I had stayed previously. The beautiful large ornate door knocker was exactly as I remembered. Once inside, I was glad to see Mrs New's gold satin curtains in the parlour. I remembered when they first arrived how we girls were impressed by them. Mrs Sarah New, a widow and her daughter, lived on the second floor and I would reside on the third floor, which had several bedrooms and a lovely sitting room with two plush green sofas with green cushions to match with the maroon fringe trim. I would enjoy sitting here and preparing for my discussions with Mr Thompson. There were several live-in servants to take care of our daily needs, which would be helpful, and I wanted to prepare several questions and thoughts for our meeting at Robarts & Lubbock's office on Lombard Street.

I was dismayed to hear that one of my favourite historical places in Holborn had been demolished, the Blue Tavern. Its galleried courtyard was said to have been infamous as a stopping point for soldiers on their way to the hangings at Tyburn. It was said that history had been made here when one of Cromwell's spies at the palace informed Cromwell that he had a death warrant served on his head. Cromwell then disguised himself as a soldier. He opened a letter from the King to the Queen, thinking it was his death warrant, but found out that the King was about to end the rebellion. In fact, it was the King who had been tried and executed in 1649. *If this story were true, how incredibly fortunate and surprised he would have been,* I thought to myself with a laugh. *Because the story is so fantastical, I know it was entirely fabricated by the locals to entertain their guests. It is endearing to me all the same.*

I rose early the next morning after a wonderful sleep in my canopied bed with down pillows. I rumbled through London in a cab to Lombard Street. Mr Bodilly was there to meet me, and we walked into the building to meet our host, Mr Thompson.

"Good day to you both. So wonderful to see you again. You have come at a time of good weather. Very fortunate," Mr Thompson chatted, as he set us at ease in his room, large enough to seat twenty. It was just the three of us and the room seemed huge, with its high ceiling and ornate chair railing trim, cornices and the beautiful crown moulding in the centre of the ceiling.

"We are indeed fortunate that you have made the time to discuss our country bank, sir," I said, giving him appropriate deference.

"You have done well with your Penzance bank. Your account balance has increased nicely. Perhaps you will share your secrets of success with me?" he asked, trying his best to be charming.

"We follow the precedents of Joseph Carne. That is our secret." Mr Bodilly laughed quietly.

"Ah, yes. A great businessman. I see he has passed down that ability to you, Miss Carne. I must say how sorry I am for the loss of your nephew. I understand he was talented and showing great promise in the bank," he added.

"Yes, he was. Thank you. Let us hope more of our family can make use of Father's knowledge for future success. Our concern today is exactly that, which is why we seek your counsel," I said, getting to the business at hand.

"Oh, how is that?" he asked, arching a brow.

"While we have enjoyed fair success to this point, our concern is about the business prospects in Cornwall, now that mining production is increasing elsewhere around the world. We anticipate that the changes we are seeing this year will have a serious effect on our clients, should the production in South America and other places continue to grow. We have come to present a proposal which will further increase our account balance with you. First of all, we intend to dispose of some of our investments, as shown on this list we have prepared."

Mr Thompson looked at the list. "Yes, these are good choices. The share prices are rising just at the moment. If you will allow our broker to handle the necessary transactions, he will ensure that the sales are made at the right time before they start falling again."

I looked at Mr Bodilly, who nodded in agreement, and we assented readily to this suggestion, aware that there would be a brokerage fee for the service. It was a task that would be much better performed by a specialist with experience.

"Thank you," said Mr Thompson. "The proceeds of the sales will appear on your weekly statement in due course. But may I ask what you intend to do with this increase in your capital?"

"We intend to draw some of it immediately to increase our cash at hand in the bank," I replied, "but the remainder we intend to leave on deposit with you. We would like to enquire whether you would consider increasing our overdraft facility in consequence, to give us more money at call should the need arise? We think it prudent to be sufficiently prepared for such contingencies." I named the amount we had in mind.

He considered this for a moment, and then told us that he would have to refer our request to one of his bank's partners as a matter of procedure; but that he did not anticipate any difficulty. He would inform us of the outcome.

"We thank you for your generous assistance with this," I said. "Now, to return to the subject of world copper production, we would now like to ask your opinion about how much you anticipate this production growing in the short and long term given the ongoing demand from manufacturing industry." I hoped I was clear in conveying our questions and that he would be equally clear in his response. Bankers in London, I noticed, could drone on and on about this or that banking technicality, and neglect to fully answer the question, which would be bothersome given our limited time for the discussion.

"Yes, just so," he began. He described each incremental development in what must have been ten or twelve different countries. His discourse continued to talk about fluctuations in rates and the causes of each fluctuation, and the possibilities arising from each. He continued to talk about various aspects of industrial progress, from the 1862 World's Fair innovations to the current state of steam engine design to the developments in water pumping in the mining field.

"Your discourse is quite fascinating and complete, Mr Thompson. Could you please summarise your conclusions on any growth in the demand for copper relative to the supply, and how that affects Cornwall's mining in particular?" asked Mr Bodilly, trying to bring him back on course to answer our question.

"Of course, sir. It is simply this." For the next forty-five minutes, he provided us with a tutorial on political economy and factors that affect supply and demand, including the weather and how commodity prices changed with movements in the financial markets. I tried not to yawn or fidget, but while his thoughts were all interesting, I began to think Mr Thompson thought us country banker bumpkins. *Perhaps I should have asked the question a different way. One that would give a more succinct answer.*

"What say you, Mr Thompson, about South Australian production?" I knew that this was a place where many Cornish miners, with their families, were now going. The Yorke Peninsula there was becoming known as "Australia's Little Cornwall." Perhaps keeping the questions simpler would produce the result I needed. At this point, my frustration was surely showing as I attempted to get what we came for.

"Yes. Industrial needs are growing fast, it is true. In past decades, the United Kingdom contributed more than half of the world's output of copper, the bulk coming from Cornwall. The large tonnages that will be meeting the increased demands will be coming from South Australia and Chile. As Cornish mines are becoming depleted and their costs rise, customers will turn more to these countries and others where mining costs are lower, despite Cornwall's more advantageous location, perhaps. Even though shipping costs are much higher, their selling prices will be lower," Mr Thompson said, succinctly.

Finally, a straightforward answer. I cheered silently to myself. I was afraid of this dour forecast but was glad to have my suspicions confirmed early on before things became much worse, rather than stumbling around in the dark, which is what I had felt we had been doing.

"That seems an ominous situation, sir," Mr Bodilly said. "Given this, what guidance can you provide to us as a small country bank?"

"Shipping! Ship building! Diversify! Look to tin as a possibility! Conserve capital! Be moderate with loans!" Mr Thompson rattled.

Now he has staccato answers for us? What a peculiar fellow. And I notice he is checking his pocket watch repeatedly.

"You are right to think about the wider situation. If you will excuse me, I do have another engagement shortly. It was a pleasure to see you again. Please call again soon for any help you may need. I remain your humble servant," he said, standing and giving us a slight bow.

"I will see you out now," he added, moving towards the door.

"Yes, thank you for your time and help," I added as I was whisked out the door.

"Always a pleasure, sir, and thank you," added Mr Bodilly, as Mr Thompson's back had already turned, and he went back through the door.

"That went well!" Mr Bodilly laughed, sarcastically. "Although it looks like we have achieved what we have come to London to do."

We were standing outside the front entrance of the bank and suddenly, my mind was overcome with memories from the 1847 miners' riots in Penzance. *How similar that situation was to the current situation! It was a hot day in May. A large, angry group of ragged miners with pickaxes hurried up Chapel Street, past the bank. One of our employees pointed out the window. Bodies swarming past, most in brown trousers, as I recall. I rushed to the window. We all held our breath, fearing broken shop windows or worse. I remember hearing their shouts and demands for fair prices for corn and flour. The whites of their eyes flashing. Their grimy faces. They were in a frenzy and headed up the hill to Market House ... That could happen again.*

"He said our market will plunge," I said quickly, recalling the riot. "Thousands will be out of work, leave the country as they are already doing. Women and children will starve, even more than they are now. You remember the riot of '47, do you not? Mr Bodilly, It could happen again! I have an idea. I will now be able to draw some of my capital from the bank, and I can buy the land for the new town hall. It would put hundreds to work, at least."

"You want to buy the land for the town hall? That would be an enormous property," Mr Bodilly said, pondering the idea.

"Yes. Boulders as big as buildings, Mr Bodilly," I said, as he hailed a cab.

Chapter Fifteen

Philanthropist and Political Scientist

1867–1871

"I've heard that it is the largest granite building in the country, Bess. You simply must come to the grand opening of our new town hall," my sister, Caroline, pleaded. "I walked here to your house from Chapel Street to try to convince you in person."

"Yes," I replied. "The top step is the largest piece of granite ever quarried. Lamorna granite, if I am not mistaken. I am, of course, impressed with the splendour of it – its sheer size and all the work of the masons. The giant portico is impressive, and the Tuscan columns have vastly improved our civic grandeur."

"The ceremonial hall inside is said to be enormous. Please come on the tour the town council is giving," she asked again.

"No, I prefer to stay out of the crowds and avoid any publicity. You know that if I attend, it will be as if I am seeking applause for my part in donating the site, and that would be garish. No, I am most comfortable touring it on my own at my own pace, thank you," I retorted. "Sadly, it has only provided a temporary supply of work for the community. The decline in mining has hit Penwith badly," I reminded Caroline.

"I will congratulate you, then, on the improvement made to the town hall and the Market House by putting that statue of Sir Humphrey Davy in front," she said, smiling – because she knew what I thought of that statue, I concluded.

"Yes, but I do still think the funds for the statue would have been better used for an almshouse for the poor, as I am sure you have guessed."

"Always the ever practical one, sister," she said, tying her bonnet ribbons in the entrance hall mirror. "As you wish. I will pass along your regards to our civic leaders," Caroline said as she strode out my front door with her usual flourish.

***

Sitting in my study overlooking the gardens across Coulson Terrace, an overwhelming compulsion came to fruition. I felt a compelling need to compile what I had been learning and thinking over the last year. As a result of my many trips from Cornwall to London and back again, social, political, religious, and environmental themes and ideas had built up in my mind. These themes had become constant and pressing, and I could not stop thinking of the impact of each on the others. I could plainly see dire implications when, for example, "country" was wise and "city" had become foolish, or vice versa. So pressing were these thoughts that I decided to write these themes down as hypotheses. It was as if my mind had become a library and my ideas had become books, overstacked and crowding tall shelves lining the walls of my inner thoughts.

I started by pulling the first idea down from the shelf in my mind.

"Society is healthy when the country pours its calm, strong

life blood of young men into the city, and the city sends back the fruits of its quickened life to the country. Each in its weakness borrows strength from the other."

I had found no similar hypotheses written down in the economic, political, religious, or social literature, of which I had read and studied many of the principal works. So pressing indeed were these thoughts and their implications that, as I wrote them down, I decided that they could, if published, become worthwhile contributions to that literature. *I would like to write them up in proper form as I do think they offer guidance and reflection on how to live in a better society and lead better lives. I am going to begin a book, writing when I can, and organize these ideas and implications into chapters.* I continued to review my hypotheses and revise them for better clarity. I reached into the shelves in my mind for more ideas.

"National greatness is achieved when country boys and men are offered up to the grinding stones of the cities. The cities want good raw material ten thousand times more than they have the means of giving this raw material a high finish through education and training. Schools must be improved to do so."

"The three dangers of civilization are 1: Variety undermining liberty; 2: Variety undermining itself; and 3: Liberty undermining itself."

Mr Treffry would have been pleased to know that I remembered these tenets from his sermon of so long ago, I thought, remembering him fondly.

"Prosperity drives additional stimulation, and too much stimulation, as in the city, is the destruction of civilization."

"Factories and machines take the skill and satisfaction out of our hands and thus out of our work."

Finally, my most important hypothesis that would most likely have the greatest impact for a better civilization and which would form the most prominent part of the book would be: *"The differences in classes create isolation and monotony of thought and feeling, and then prejudice and class differences separate us from justice." I will look to how much I have learned from Henry, the Freethy family – and yes, even Mr Richards – and also the perceptions of my friend Betsy the baker, the miners and the bal maidens, to enrich my book here and I am all the better for knowing these people and their abilities and perspectives. I see how others in the world could also benefit.*

After reviewing my list, I said to myself, *"Surely smaller towns like Penzance, and their communities, are the places where these things might be better fulfilled. I shall turn these hypotheses into principles and illustrate them with examples from my own experience with my missions, solving problems for working people directly, and my discourses with my father's luminaries over the years, as well as my own schooling and reading. I will blend these together as examples for my book. I will entitle it, Country Towns and the Place they fill In Modern Civilization." I will solicit reactions from Bell and Daldy, publishers in London, and ask them to publish it, if they are favourable. I believe these were the publishers my cousins, the Brontës, used, but I will confirm.*

As this is one of my most original works, I will publish it with my own name on the cover, I told myself, boldly. *"I feel like the book will spill out of me on to my paper almost in one piece. I have thought about the structure of the work so thoroughly beforehand that I estimate it will be a labour of love and that I will write it with pleasure and ease."*

I sat for a while, soaking in the reality of what I just agreed with myself to do. *I am writing a philosophical and political book that society will likely condemn, look down on, and say I have no right to publish. But it may also begin to change society for the better, here in the United Kingdom and abroad.* I placed a hand on each side of my desk and held on to it tightly. *I have come into my own strength. And no one will prevent me from spreading the power of good via this book. No misgivings.*

***

As I had hoped and prayed, our strategy of judicious lending to our established clients, supported by the very favourable terms that had been given us in London, was a good one. We were now in the midst of continual falls in the price of copper, and the miners were leaving in the hundreds for overseas work as one by one the mines were becoming too expensive to continue. We were doing well notwithstanding; and Mr Bodilly and I had planned to visit our new schooner, the *Nils Desperatum*, now moored in the harbour. Mr Bodilly had done a complete inspection of the schooner prior to our purchase, but he wanted to ensure that a problem with worn running rigging had been corrected properly and to check that a new suit of sails we had ordered followed the sail plan correctly. Our intention for the schooner was to use her ourselves in trade, carrying pilchards and potatoes to Italy and Spain. When we felt we had achieved a modest success with that, we would consider further, more ambitious ideas, such as carrying china clay out of Charlestown to other parts of Europe.

We walked from our office to the deep side of the harbour where our vessel lay docked. Along the way, we saw only a few women buying fish, when in better times, many would be haggling for mackerel and monkfish for their suppers.

Mr Bodilly sighed as he tossed a coin to a boy begging on the pier at an empty stall, which he snatched from midair with delight.

"I have heard that, though most do so, many men are not able or willing to send money back to support their families here because they are making only enough to support themselves overseas," I added, sadly.

"Yes, this is quite often the case. Have you heard about the five-pound divorces in the United States?" Mr Bodilly asked.

"No. What are you referring to?" I asked.

"For five pounds, a husband may make a legal deposition stating that he can no longer support his wife and family. Then he is free of his obligations. It is a pity," Mr Bodilly lamented. "Not only that, but for some here, I have heard, the move overseas has become a convenient way out of a marriage."

"I agree. Often women are deserted by their husbands overseas, and become in effect 'Married Widows,' not knowing if they are still married or not,'" I added. "For many, the poverty cycle appears to be worsening. Look around us. It has reached a point where the downward spiral may be impossible to stop." *My book speaks to these issues and while it may not solve everything, articulating the problem with my voice, my writing, is a huge step forward. I can and I will make change happen.*

"Yes, it seems so," Mr Bodilly replied.

We arrived at the *Nils Desperatum*, but my mind suddenly went back to a discussion I had had long ago with Henry about breaking this cycle of poverty, about lasting solutions to the problem.

I had long wanted to start new schools in Penzance and the surrounding villages. *"What better time than now to begin that work? If not now, when?"* I asked myself.

White gulls with black faces landed on the docks, looking for scraps of fish. The water lapped the sides of the *Nils Desperatum* in a constant rhythm. Several hands were aboard, some of them old sailors now home for good from the sea, working on sail and rigging repairs. The patched sails would be supplementary to the new suit we had ordered.

As they worked, they sang and whistled. *If offered the ability to read and write over being a sailor, which would they prefer?* I wondered, as I watched them from the quayside.

Sadly, these men most likely never had, nor will ever have, such a choice.

"There is no better time than now, I say, to invest in schooling for children. They need hope for a better life than mining or fishing can now provide. That alone will break the cycle for good," I said to Mr Bodilly with conviction.

"Where would you begin?" Mr Bodilly asked, shrugging his shoulders.

"I know from speaking with my friend Emily Bolitho, who is at St Paul's every moment that it is open, it appears that the former Reverend Batten – who married my young cousin Anna Marie – was highly disposed to talking with me about a new school. He has very recently moved on to another parish and has been replaced by a young Mr Aitken. I will visit Mr Aitken, the new vicar of St Paul's in Madron, to see if he might help me to instigate and support as many schools as might be needed to provide education freely for young children, without making them a burden on the ratepayers. It would also avoid the imposition of one of Mr Forster's new School Boards on us to dictate what we should and should not do. Will you support me, Mr Bodilly?"

"Yes, of course. But first, the ship," he said, as we ascended the gangway to board the vessel.

***

Riding in my carriage on my way to meet with Mr Aitken at his residence in Madron, I refused to let any misgivings about the schools creep into my thoughts. *I have made up my mind to fund the schools, regardless of any unfavourable circumstances that might arise. Time is of the essence, for I know that if sufficient schools can be established around Penzance, a School Board would be unnecessary, and no contribution would be required from the ratepayers, who were paying* enough already through the local taxes that we householders had to contribute to make Penzance and its environs a better place in which to live.

Dismiss them as I might, I could not help but reflect on the difficulties that might await me, as I swayed back and forth on the journey. I tried to focus on the rhythm of the horses' hooves instead. *Times are tumultuous and the financial world uncertain. It is now 1870 and just four years ago, in May 1866, in London, the firm of Overend and Gurney failed. Everyone had thought it to be the most solid and dependable institution in the city after the Bank of England itself. The Bankers' Magazine had been full of it. The general panic! I feel a chill down my spine just thinking about it. And, here in Cornwall, Hawkey and Whitford's bank in St. Columb and Falmouth also went under. Some said that Agra and Masterman's attracted depositors with high interest rates which they could not afford to pay; and that too much of the partners' money had been tied up in iron mining in north Cornwall. What an uncertain business that always is! I feel a throbbing in my head, considering that those failures could happen to our bank. The Agra failure had happened just after Mr Whitford had died; and his two executrices, Mrs Burridge and Miss Moyse, had joined the business without much knowledge or experience. That scenario sounded all too familiar, given my own problems with an adequate heir. What if Penzance Bank went the same way? We would be ruined! And it is still hard to believe that the London and Southwestern Bank so impertinently opened a branch right here next to us in Chapel Street! Still, no one seemed to take to them very much, although Mr Brewer, whom they brought in as manager, seemed reasonable enough to me. Thank goodness he has moved away, back to London, and the bank quit Cornwall altogether.*

Even more banks than those have failed, but Bolitho's banks seem set as always to go on forever in their Mount's Bay

Bank. Mrs Vivian in Helston seems to have survived the panic and carries on even though she is getting on in years. I heard that her son might be coming from London to join her. So, still competition from many angles!

I cannot stop thinking about all the things stacked up against me. *Mr Bodilly had told me that on May 3 of this year (of 1870), the Constance, Mr Child's ship financed by our bank's mortgage, had been wrecked on the west reef of Providence in the Caicos Islands in the Caribbean and was a total loss. We still do not know what happened to the captain and crew. I refuse to think of the competitors' successes and the wreck as bad omens,* I scolded myself. *All shocks to be sure, but these tragedies are all too common. Who knows what uncertainties lie in the future for banking; and as for the loss of the ship, we will have the insurance to cover it, at least. I am determined to get those schools open despite any crisis that tries to tell me otherwise,* I told myself with conviction.

I strode to Mr Aitken's front door undaunted and feeling full of vinegar. I rang the bell without hesitation. *I am glad that Mr Aitken accepted my invitation to meet to discuss the funding to support the opening of schools in our district. I aim to get to know him and develop him as an ally. Perhaps Emily Bolitho put a word in his ear about my earnest reputation. Still, I do not know what to expect of our discussion.*

I was greeted by a maid who let me in and directed me down the hall to another door with black metal trim. The assistant pushed the door open so that I could step into the room where I saw a man in his mid-thirties, who I presumed was Mr Aitken, seated at his desk in his study with an empty chair next to him. As I moved to sit in the empty chair and the door widened, I saw an elegantly dressed late middle-aged man and woman seated in chairs by the wall, behind the door. *Who are these people? Am I in the correct room? There must be some mistake.*

"Miss Carne, I presume? I am Robert Aitken," the mid-thirties man said. He was slim with thin, wispy hair and dressed in a rather wrinkled brown linen suit.

"Yes, Mr Aitken. Very nice to meet you, but have I caught you at an inopportune time?" I glanced over at the man and woman, who seemed to be evaluating my appearance. They sat silently with their eyes moving over me from top to bottom. *How rude. I wonder what their purpose here is.*

"Oh no, Miss Carne. This is Mr and Mrs Shackelworth," he said, gesturing his hand towards them. "They asked if they could join our meeting, and I agreed. They have a rather distinct point of view on the subject."

"Pleased to meet you," I said, giving a slight curtsey. Both of them stood up and gave respectful but cold acknowledgements.

"Pleased to make your acquaintance, I am sure," said Mr Shackelworth, in a very baritone voice. Mrs Shackelworth simply cocked her head to one side and nodded. *A rather cold and odd greeting, I must say. My, they are dressed impeccably well. Her blue silk fitted jacket and skirt suit her well, given her black hair. And his green linen suit and crisp white cravat are striking. But why are they quite overdressed for this occasion?*

We sat in his comfortable study, a bit awkwardly, not exactly knowing where to begin.

"Mr Aitken, thank you for sparing the time to see me today," I began.

"It is I who must thank you, Miss Carne. I am very glad to meet you in person, as I am new to St Paul's, as you know. It is not every day that I have visitors who come to offer assistance of such magnitude," he replied, a little overanxious and with a nervous laugh. *He is young and a bit awkward but full of energy. I hope I can gain some share of his mind as he is most likely working quite hard and spread very thinly. But I am getting an odd feeling about those two in the corner.*

The Shackelworths remained quiet. "Of course," I said, eyeing the Shackelworths. "You see, my family and I have made donations for those in need and to instigate new works where they will be of benefit," I continued.

"Yes, yes, Miss Carne. We are familiar with your family's generosity," Mr Shackelworth said, with a hint of sarcasm, his deep, manly voice reverberating against the walls of the small room.

"And for that the entire community is most grateful," Mr Aitken stuttered, interrupting Mr Shackelworth, who scowled at Reverend Aitken. Mr Aitken shrank down in his chair.

I gave the vicar a questioning look. *I wonder how they all seem to know about that since my family attends the Methodist Church in Penzance?*

"Your friend, Miss Bolitho, kindly told us all about it at the reception the Shackelworths were kind enough to have for me at their home here in Madron. She is here at St Paul's most days and, well, she seems well informed." At this point, he was clearly cowering in his seat. *Emily Bolitho? Reception at their home? A most nervous vicar? I wonder why?*

"It's true, Emily is something of a wren, flitting around St Paul's and St Mary's supporting those who follow the church-es. She has taken on service to the church as her life mission, it seems to me," Mrs Shackelworth explained. *What a high pitched, very feminine voice. Almost girlish.*

Mr Shackelworth made a sweeping motion with his hand across his lap, as if his wife's comments were crumbs on a table to be wiped away. He said, in a very serious tone, "Miss Carne, let us get right to the point." He took a breath.

"Yes, let us please do that as I was unaware that I would be accompanied in this discussion with Mr Aitken," I said, very clearly, standing my ground. *Calm but clear and direct. Stay calm.*

Mr Shackelworth looked taken aback by my interruption and he briefly pressed his lips together as if holding back his words. "Miss Carne, as I was about to say, we heard about your interests in generously providing funds for schools about the area. However, we suggest pausing your plans to avoid any potential social discord."

"I am not taking your meaning, Mr Shackelworth," I replied very smoothly.

"My meaning is this, Miss Carne. Many here in this parish believe that providing schooling outside the gentry creates false expectations. That is to say, once a child from the lower order is educated, what would he do with that education? I ask you, where would he take a position? At your bank?" He let out a sarcastic scoff at the suggestion. Mrs Shackelworth gave a girlish giggle.

"Perhaps, he or she may apply themselves in the railway or positions that have yet to be imagined," I replied with no hesitation. I smiled and tilted my head, waiting for his response.

Mr Aitken gave a nervous laugh, his eyes flicking between us.

"We would hate for these pupils to be left with no current employment, with no future employment, and we all know how limited higher-level positions are at the mines," he replied, knowingly. "And for those reasons, we ask that you not disrupt social order with schools that will only build empty dreams for the vulgars, Miss Carne."

"I see," I replied. I paused briefly. *He is getting impatient and angry now. I can see his teeth clenching and his face becoming red. I cannot believe what I am hearing. Certainly, Emily would not endorse these thoughts. She must have innocently relayed my interests. I must dissuade them from their point of view. But how? And it does not seem that Mr Atiken is at his strongest here. I will not be put off or dissuaded by anyone.*

"Yes, I think I understand. You think that by building children's ability to read, write, and solve problems, it will create a group of adults with false hope, with no clear path forward," I said, jumping in. "And that false hope could lead in any number of discontented directions. I ask you; did *you* know what your path forward would be when you were in school? Are there not jobs now that did not exist then? Did you and your friends stay out of trouble more because you had more favourable diversions, such as reading? How do we break the cycle of poverty that comes with the ups and downs of mining and fishing, that you clearly mention, for those without a proper education?"

"That is best left to the social and governmental leaders, Miss Carne."

"What if by doing so, by leaving these challenges up to leaders who are often without resources, years slip by? In the future, will you have talented tailors to make your fine suits? A tailor who cannot read or multiply will have difficulty with your measurements. What about your estate manager and staff? I imagine you have at least one and that he can read. Builders? Shoemakers? Bakers? Clerks for banks, as you suggest? What if we have a shortage of all the people you need to make your life as comfortable as it is now? What if in the future, because of a lack of tradespeople, you had to provide the reading and solve the problems yourself?"

The room was silent.

"Mr and Mrs Shackelworth, my endeavour is to offer education as a means of giving children better prospects in life. And in the Lord's eyes, no child is vulgar. We have heard your concerns. Now, I suggest you depart and let us move forward before it is much too little, too late."

Again, silence. Mr Shackelworth opened his mouth to respond, but nothing came out. He snapped his wide-open mouth shut like a mackerel, caught in a net, gulping to breathe. Mr

and Mrs Shackelworth looked at each other. Mr Shackelworth stood up and lifted his wife's hand, indicating that she
should stand as well. With that, they snatched up their coats
off the coat stand. Mr Shackelworth grabbed the doorknob and
abruptly pulled the door open. His wife passed through the
doorway.

"You should expect to hear more on this from me and
others," he snapped as he loudly closed the door behind him.

Mr Aitken looked like a limp silk scarf that would slide
from his seat down to the floor at any second.

"Now then. Without further delay, I came here today to
say that I would like to work with you and your parishioners
to open a new school to serve the villages around Penzance,
fully funded and which will incur no cost to the ratepayers."

"How extraordinary!" Mr Aitken said, shaking his head. "I
am delighted to hear this, despite what the Shackelworths
said. Miss Carne, you are a blessing. We would welcome an
opportunity to work with you," he said, straightening up in his
chair. "However, I fear that finding a suitable location would
create feelings of discontent in the community," he said, shaking his head.

"What do you mean?" I asked in surprise. *Oh please. Not
more reasons why we cannot create schools.*

"We have several places which are in need of a school; and
I fear that there will be some who will clamour for the school
to be built near them, rather than in a place more convenient
for the district as a whole. We have many children, for example, in Wesley Rock, near Heamoor. Then there is Carfury near
Madron. Also, many children come from Bosullow, near
Morvah. How could we possibly choose one over the other?"
he asked, nervously, his hand rubbing his forehead.

"Not to worry. If we have enough children in these three
areas, we will fund schools for all three. Would that ease your
mind?" *If each school could help fifty students, then one*

hundred and fifty children a year could be taught to read and write, and perhaps more the following year. In ten years, as many as two thousand students could be literate. Only a drop in the sea, but at least it is a start. Perhaps it will lean the voters towards free mandatory education for all children, as I saw in Pau on my French holiday many years before.

He stood up, now full of energy and excitement and asked, "Are you sure this would be possible? I do not think we have anyone who is qualified to start a school. But I could make inquiries. What ages would we serve? What would they learn, and who would teach them?" he asked, as if he was anticipating anxious questions from his parish. *I can tell my ideas appeal to him, but he is anxious about the reactions of his parishioners, which is reasonable, given he is new here and he has people like the Shackelworths to deal with. He is intelligent and energetic even if he does lack confidence. I like that. I think he will be an asset to St Paul's and to my mission.*

"What if we were to begin with the prior necessity of proper and suitable buildings, fully able or adaptable to provide for the children's needs. I imagine there could be several adaptable large houses or public halls which might be acquired or made available for the purpose. After that, we will define the curriculum and find the teachers. I will help and perhaps we can find volunteers from within the parishes or Penzance itself. I can engage architects to inspect any vacant buildings we can find and assess their suitability. Does that sound reasonable?"

"Miss Carne, I can tell that you are a bright light. A brilliant, shining light," he beamed.

***

I sat in my office with my solicitor and thought, *I have made it. Thankfully, I now have an heir of legal age. The family business will continue as Grandfather, Father, and I had always hoped.*

Having lost both Archie and the argument for one of Mary's older boys, I was more than happy to have at least one male relation who was college-educated, of age, and willing to accept the mantle bestowed upon him. With one stroke of a pen, I named Charles Campbell Ross, my sister Mary's youngest boy, as my heir. He was already twenty-one and would shortly join me at the bank and begin his training.

I considered Charles as I finished signing my name, leaving my bank partnership and many assets, including property, ships, the mineral collection, and more to him. I was having an argument with myself as I put down each letter of my name, knowing I had no other alternative. *Three years to reach this point has seemed an eternity.*

He is consumed with politics and with courting Isabella Carne, my late cousin John's wife. I do suppose he will marry her, and she will be glad of the fortune, I imagine. What influence will she have on his ability to maintain the legacy? It appears they prefer to live chasing after high fashion rather than with a more seeming modesty. They are already looking at an expensive house in the gardens across the street from my house. Quite lavish. In reality, what time will he devote to learning banking as Archie did? Will he cherish the mineral collection as I do? After the Royal Geological Society of Cornwall turned down my request to display the mineral collection at St John's town hall and not wanting to sell the collection to a university, I just erected a building to display the collection for public viewing on Queen Street, near my home. Will he put forward that amount of effort to safeguard the collection for the public benefit? Still, he has proven his academic prowess and is amenable to the work. Endless worrying will not enable you to control the situation any more, I scolded myself as I set the pen down. *I can build within him the skills he needs. Or can I?*

***

"Your post, miss," Betsy said, appearing out of the entry hall where she typically sorted the post that laid on a thin table against the wall under a mirror.

"Thank you, Betsy," I said, rifling through them as I sat in in the parlour, enjoying a ray of sunshine that beamed in through the garden door. I shuffled through the stack. A letter from Caroline Fox leapt to my eyes and I tore it open. It read,

Penjerrick, January 5, 1871

And now, dear, thank thee so much for that earnest pamphlet. Thank thee for so bravely speaking out the conviction, which was doubtless given thee for the good of others as well as thy own, that nothing short of communion with our present Lord can satisfy the immense need of man. How true that we are so often fed with phrases, and even try sometimes to satisfy ourselves with phrases, while our patient Master is still knocking at the door. I trust that the seed thou hast been faithfully sowing may lodge in fitting soil and bring forth flowers and fruits, to the praise of the Lord of the garden, and to the joy of some poor little human creature with whom He deems to converse. In hopes of a happy meeting whenever the fitting time may come, and with very loving wishes for the new-born year,

Ever Thine very lovingly, Caroline Fox.

How kind it was of her to read and respond so favourably to my recently published spiritual pamphlet, *England's Three Wants*! Not wanting undue attention or flattery, I had published the pamphlet anonymously. The key topics, arising from the hidden poverty in rural communities, which we had both not only seen for many years, but tried as individual families to relieve, sounded like they resonated with her, of which I was most glad, as her keen intellect would be one I would want to capture and arouse with my writing. She and I agreed on the premise in my lecture and pamphlet that the churches as a whole must do more to fill in the depths of poverty surrounding individual families, but often we find church and chapel alike uncommitted, and parishes and communities unprepared to meet such needs. That she agreed that addressing my three premises – the lack of the thirst for the "water of life", the lack of education and curiosity, and the ineptitude and unwillingness of the church to minister to the poor properly – would also solve a multitude of other social problems meant that my premises stood in good stead with the most devout and committed. I always revelled in her letters. Her intellectual reviews of anything from gossip to religion were a joy. Little did I know that this would be her last letter to me.

***

The following week, I received a letter from Penjerrick, the Fox family home. I sat in the garden at the back of my house, expecting some welcome news from Caroline or an invitation to an event. It read,

> *Our dearest Bess, it is with heavy hearts that we must convey that our beloved Caroline has succumbed to bronchitis and has joined our Lord this day, January 12, 1871. The Fox family.*

I ran up up the main staircase to my bed chamber and closed my door. Shock and disbelief ran through me like ice water. *My loving friend from childhood was gone? She had bronchitis, but it must have gotten worse. Much worse. The suffering she must have endured over these last weeks! The fear she must have known in those last hours. If only I could have been there with her,* I thought, sobbing. *How cruel death is,* I thought in anguish, as I cried alone in my bed chamber.

"Why?" I asked aloud. "Why, God, did you take her? She was doing your work as well as any human possibly could. She was pure and generous. She loved people. Lord, why take her?" I seemed to answer my own question. *You must have taken her because of her goodness, to be part of a great company of angels, which would look over us from above.*

"Lord, I must thank you for the time you gave me with her. She was so precious to me. Thank you for creating such a beautiful friend as her to be my companion through as much of my life as we did have together," I said aloud, kneeling on my bedroom floor.

I looked out my window to St Mary's across the street. The sight gave me no relief. I went to my nightstand and pulled out a little leather-bound book Caroline had given me years ago. It was about two inches wide and three inches long and was referred to as "a friendship book". The red cover with a bouquet of gold flowers embossed on it always cheered me. I looked at the book's title through my tears. It was called "The Lady's Token Gift of Friendship". These small books had become popular, and I remember Caroline writing to me that I must have one to remind me of her. I opened the little book and the poem that appeared randomly was called, "Old Friends Together". I took out a handkerchief, wiped my eyes, and started to read it.

> *Oh, time is sweet, when roses meet,*
> *With Spring's sweet breath around them;*
> *And sweet the time when hearts are lost,*

If those who love have found them.
And sweet the mind that still may find
A star in darkest weather-
But naught can be so sweet to see
As old friends meet together.

I will see you again in heaven, but not on this earth, I thought painfully. "Death is not final. But I will be lost without your wit, your humour, your most kind heart. Going on without you is unthinkable," I whispered aloud. *But somehow, I must,* I thought, gritting my teeth together as I sat on my bed and cried in a deep sorrow. *I must go on with only your memory now. I will raise those schools and see them function in your honour, Caroline,* I promised.

Chapter Sixteen

The Bravest

July 16, 1872, On Board the
Earl of Arran

It was a beautiful day, and I was engaged in conversation about education aboard the *Earl of Arran*, a paddle steamer on the way to one of my favourite quiet holiday places: St Mary's in the Isles of Scilly. It had been quite a while since I had been to the Scillies, with all my commitments at the bank and my efforts to get the new schools up and running. Just two months ago, my partner and dear friend, Mr Bodilly, had died unexpectedly, though he was full of years. *What a tragedy! I miss him terribly. Without his diligence, Mr Downing and I have had to manage the bank shorthanded; but since Mr Bodilly's partnership passed on to his son, Thomas, we are both keen to build his knowledge of banking practices more quickly.*

It has been a sad and hectic couple of months. I had taken the ticket on this voyage to the Scillies prior to Mr Bodilly's untimely death. I had decided to continue with this holiday, which would be a short interval of rest and recuperation. I needed time alone to consider the business consequences of Mr Bodilly's sad demise and think clearly and strategically about the future of the bank now that he was no longer with us to impart his wisdom and guidance. I would do as much sketching as I could and take in the warmth of the sun now that summer was well advanced. I had decided that the best way to make the sea crossing would be on the *Earl of Arran*, new to our waters.

Built in 1860, she was an older vessel and had been in a few previous scrapes during her previous service on the Clyde between Glasgow and the Isle of Arran; but she had recently been refitted for her new owners and was large enough to accommodate one hundred passengers. I also wanted to travel between St Mary's and St Agnes to visit various rock formations, so I had hired a small lugger for myself in the harbour at St Mary's. I would take with me only my personal maid, Betty, who had been in service with me now for over ten years.

Once on board, we found ourselves sitting next to an Earl, no less, and his companions. *Their fancy fishing attire must designate the purpose of their trip. At least they are not wearing black tie so typical of their station. The Earl is quite friendly, probably because of the anticipation of the trip.* We soon became acquainted. The sea was relatively calm compared to what it can often become, although there was quite a breeze; and we fell into conversation that quickly turned to a discussion on the 1870 Education Act, one of my favourite topics.

"I believe the Education Act of 1870 is an ideal piece of legislation to deal with the educational needs of children in Britain," said the Earl. "Furthermore, it demonstrates a commitment to education on a national scale." He tightened his hat down on his head in the strengthening wind.

I tried to hold my tongue back from the lashing it wanted to give the right honourable gentleman. "It allows voluntary schools to carry on basically unchanged, sir. If we want to improve Britain's chances of future greatness, we must make schooling mandatory for all children," I retorted.

"If so, Miss Carne, then many farmers will be left with no one to work their fields," he smugly replied, crossing his legs and lighting his pipe, the smoke blowing away towards the stern of the ship.

"Precisely. Do we want a civilization of farmers? Or do we achieve national greatness best when the lower orders are equally educated, with less isolation and prejudice?" I asked.

"Now you are changing the subject from education to class distinctions, Miss Carne. Two very different matters." *Clearly, I have touched a nerve with involving class distinctions, so I will follow his interests back to education itself as soon as I can respond back to him.*

"Excuse me for the interruption. I am the captain, Stephen Deason." Captain Deason was in early middle age, I thought, with a full beard and quite respectable in his captain's uniform.

He continued. "I wanted to apologize for the late departure. We were waiting for the mails."

He winced very subtly.

I noticed the wince and debated whether or not to acknowledge it. "Are you quite well, Captain Deason?" I asked.

"Yes, quite. Thank you. I must inform the other passengers if you will excuse me." He attempted to stride away.

The Earl gently raised his leather-gloved hand and spoke quickly. "Oh, Captain, I was hoping to show my companions here some of the more interesting rock formations en route that I have heard so much about. Would it be possible to arrive any sooner, given the delay caused by the mail? I simply must have more time on my excursion, as I had originally planned. Is this possible? Perhaps we could increase our rate of speed to make up time?" the Earl demanded. *Clearly, he thinks he has provided an alternative the captain will not be able to refuse.*

241

"It is possible, in fact, given the low swell, sir. We could change course, and instead of entering through St Mary's Sound or Crow Sound, we could go through St Martin's Neck. That course would enable us to arrive, oh ... about thirty minutes earlier. Would that suffice?"

I offered, "There are several fascinating formations along that way, but the tide might be an issue ..." I was cut off before I had a chance to finish my sentence.

"If you agree, sirs, then we will change course." Sweat was beginning to run down Captain Deason's white face at this point. He shifted from one leg to the other. *Very odd*, I thought.

"Sounds agreeable." The men nodded confirmation of the decision.

Captain Deason swiftly left our seating area and went below – in the direction of the privy, I assumed.

"The good captain did not look well at all to me. I think he is quite ill," I said.

"Maybe it was something he ate at the Turk's Head," suggested one man.

"Or drank!" laughed another.

"Yes, bad water can be very damaging to the digestive system," I replied, trying to show some sympathy for the captain.

"Now, where were we? Ah yes. The 1870 Education Act. Many children do work during and outside school hours. It is precisely this child labour that we want to infuse with better knowledge, and place children in free compulsory education between the ages of five and ten. Attendance in these years at our present schools is only eighty-two per cent. What kind of future will we all have if our children are insufficiently educated?" I directed the question at my critic.

"Miss Carne, you may be more erudite on this topic than I, but it seems to me that ..." He continued, but my attention was drawn to Captain Deason talking to a passenger at the top of the stairs going down to the lower deck. Captain Deason was clutching his stomach and indicating with his head that he needed to go below again.

Poor man! The gentleman passenger nodded his head and gesticulated with his hands to indicate what I thought to be the new course for our voyage, the shortcut past St Martin's that the captain had mentioned to us. Odd, I thought. The passenger walked away in the direction of the helm. *Perhaps the captain is seeking advice about this shortcut from a passenger who happens to also be a captain who happens to be familiar with these waters.* I shrugged inwardly.

I turned my attention back to the Education Act of 1870. "Given that, Miss Carne, do you not then agree that the Act drafted by Mr Forster – which was quickly passed in Parliament, I might add – provides for many of our educational needs?" the Earl asked with arched eyebrows.

"Many but not all. It is a move forward, to be sure, but to improve our nation's ability to compete with the rising manufacturing capabilities of mainland Europe, we need free, compulsory, and non-religious education for all children."

The group stared at me, blankly. *Either they think me unusually bold, or I am not influencing them as I had hoped.* I could not tell which. I continued.

"In fact, I myself have funded the construction of three schools in rural areas in an attempt to further, rather than merely discuss, the cause of better education in Cornwall."

"Quite commendable, Miss Carne," the Earl conceded with a bit of a sigh. *Is he rolling his eyes at me sarcastically?*

"I see we are just passing a large rock formation called Hanjaque Rock." I pointed to the formation and the gentlemen turned to view it and seemed quite impressed. I was just opening my mouth to describe the configuration of the rock itself when I was cut short.

A shockingly loud BANG and violent shudder halted our conversation immediately.

"What the devil was that?" asked the Earl, loudly, clearly alarmed.

The engines stopped. Everyone was quiet. Terror filled the eyes of every passenger. The engines reversed again and then again, without any motion. Someone yelled, "She's sinking, fast." *Oh Lord, protect us!*

"Betty, run forward and ask immediately what the problem is," I said, trying to be as calm and normal as I could be, as if we were on terra firma, perfectly safe, and that the problem was merely as simple as if our luncheon was late. Betty nodded and sprinted down the deck to the helm. Betty was still quite young and was quite capable in her physical strength and reflexes.

Pandemonium broke out in an instant. Men were shouting, "We've struck Irishman's Ledge." And "The engine room filled in the first five minutes." Women were screaming and crying.

Male passengers ran to the sides of the ship and tried to release the thick ropes tied to the lifeboats with their bare hands. Steam hissed. The ship shuddered again and men's faces blanched and quivered.

Captain Deason appeared without his jacket and his shirt was untucked. He shouted, "Women and children first!" as men and women alike made a mad stampede for the lifeboats.

"The saloon is now filled with water!" someone screamed.

"We are two miles offshore!" one of the crew yelled.

Betty came back with another terrifying report. "There is a sizeable hole in the port bilge, miss!"

The Earl, fist in the air, boomed, "Deason, I will have you strung up for this!"

I did not move from my seat. I shut the parasol I was holding over the Earl's prostrate friend. "Stay calm, ladies," I called out loudly.

The captain shouted through a megaphone, "Stay calm. The engineer says the fires are out, but the steam pressure is still high. She is well done at the bow, but we have enough steam to reach Nornour in only a few minutes."

I said in a loud voice to try to calm anyone within hearing distance, "I trust we shall. Certainly, no good can come of being alarmed or from rushing about. Betty, go forward again and ask if our hired vessel can be summoned in any way to come immediately to aid the passengers."

She nodded and sprinted off again.

Within a minute more of absolute dread, with tears flowing and insults of every nature as well as curses being hurled at the captain and crew, as well as from the crew to the captain, we ran aground.

I asked Betty to help me usher the women into lines by the lifeboats to ensure no one was trampled. Forming queues like this is part of our British heritage, so it seemed to calm the ladies down to have order amongst the chaos. Other boats were already on the scene and were taking passengers, and it appeared we were out of imminent danger, even though the steamer was still in deep water. Betty and I ensured that every woman was off the ship before we departed ourselves. We then climbed aboard our lugger, which had come anyway when the alarm was raised, and then we continued to help the men aboard until every last space seemed to be occupied.

"Permission to make for St Mary's, miss?" the master of our vessel asked.

"No, do not quit the steamer's side until we are quite certain we can hold no more," I said sternly.

As our vessel finally pulled away, I heard one of the crew still on the steamer's deck say, "There goes as brave a heart as ever beat."

I started to shake, but I felt firm in myself and our good

fortune. All one hundred passengers, crew, mail, and cargo were safe.

"God has blessed us this day," I said to my fellow passengers as we made way for St Mary's.

Chapter Seventeen

Futurist

August 20 – September 7, 1873

After feeling that I had fallen out of the pages of some novel, following the wreck of the *Earl of Arran*, I found that, over the coming year, many of my family and friends wanted a good story to be told, and I received several invitations. One of them intrigued me. My dear niece Fanny, married to the erudite landowner and magistrate Thomas Roxburgh Polwhele, invited me to their estate near Truro for a few days to tell my brave story, show her my sketches of St Mary's that I had made after the watery ordeal; and best of all, to see their new baby born the previous year.

I would also be interested to hear Thomas discuss his surveying of the Bagshot series and other sites on the borders of Hampshire and Surrey. While these geological findings were not new – they dated from the year 1858 – I had several questions I wanted to discuss. I wanted him to enlighten me about the relation of geology to other sciences. That is, how geology can affect the biology of living species and how geology, specifically in relation to ancient sites, such as stone circles, can affect humans living in that environment. I excitedly accepted the invitation and sent my response that I would arrive on the twentieth day of August. They offered to send their carriage to the railway station in Truro to take me to the Polwhele estate.

Since my father had been an investor in the West Cornwall Railway almost from its inception in 1846, I decided to buy my ticket in his memory. Five passenger trains ran on weekdays and two on Sundays.

Packed and ready to go, I sent word to Caroline, my sister, to let her know where I was going and what I would be doing. I also sent a note to Henry to say that I would be back in two weeks after some much needed and stimulating geological conversation with Thomas Polwhele and our lovely Fanny. Caroline replied that she was intending to visit the Fox family in Falmouth while I was away. Henry replied that he had planned to go out deep sea fishing from Mousehole with some friends from the shipping office. I then sent a brief note to Mr Downing, my partner and bank manager, to say I would be back in two weeks and to please hold any significant lending or business decisions until my return. Away I went.

I carefully packed the brown portfolio that held over twenty-five sketches from my recent Scillies holiday, which had been very enjoyable despite the debacle. I had made several of the ruins of Cromwell's Castle, some scenes in Hugh Town, scenes of boulders with water and seagulls overhead and the landscape that had always appealed to me in such a special way. Even a nearly fatal shipwreck could not make me ill-disposed to the Scilly Isles! I planned to use the train journey to continue working on my piece, *The Realm of Truth*, also neatly tucked in my leather portfolio, in which I was emphasizing the prime responsibility of the churches in the alleviation of poverty. Perhaps I would ask Thomas and Fanny for their opinions of the treatise.

The platform at Penzance Station seemed cramped as it was very crowded with late summer travellers, for what looked like both business and pleasure from their attire. I wore my light wool, light grey day skirt and bodice with a ruffled white shirt that buttoned at the top of the neck and my black satin bonnet with the white ruffles. I regretted my bonnet choice while on the platform as it seemed a bit drab compared to some of the finery other women were wearing, but I reminded myself that a modest appearance better suited my moral compass. I preferred the train to the changing of horses required every hour on the slow journey it would have been if travelling by carriage on the turnpike roads. The train journey, which according to the timetable took an hour and twenty minutes, would give me an ideal time to work on my paper in some peace. I had with me a small supply of water and a small pack of cheese and bread to tide me over until I arrived at the Polwhele estate. After a few moments of jostling to get a seat and my bags properly stowed in second class, we were off and hoping for a most pleasant journey.

Immediately after departure, however, a mother and her three children created a boisterous disturbance after the youngest child, maybe four years old, dressed in a very smart navy blue and white trimmed sailor travelling suit, lost hold of his cup, the contents of which spilled everywhere. He sounded like what I thought a baby pterodactyl would sound, screeching and cawing. I wordlessly held up my jug and looked at the mother, suggesting I offer some to the child. The mother, holding tight to one child and the belongs of the other, agreed with a nod and tilt of her head. I pulled out the cork and refilled his cup. It was, after all, a very hot day. Soon the contents of my small jug were gone, given to the other thirsty children, but there were smiles all around after that and I set upon my writing to the sway and hum of the train, and completely forgot about the children. I was so engrossed in diligently completing my paper.

By the time we arrived at Truro station, the smoky railway

atmosphere seemed to have made my throat very dry and taut. While waiting for my baggage and for the arrival of the carriage the Polwheles were sending for me, I thought that it would be good to have a cup of tea. The station refreshment room was unaccountably closed, so I went down the road towards the town in search of something; if not tea, then perhaps some water. Eventually I reached a little shop with a sign in the window which said, "Thy Sweetness".

The shop was a poor affair, with a very small offering of cakes and pies that looked like they had been baked a few days ago, since their centres were sunken in, with liquid accumulating.

There seemed to be no tea on offer; but I did not have enough time to venture further into the town.

The plump matron appeared from the back of the shop in a grimy white apron and cap. Her face was sweating.

"G'day to you, ma'am. Can I help ye?" she asked.

"Yes, please. I wondered if you have any fresh water, or perhaps water that has been boiled, that I could drink," I asked in my parched voice.

"Let me ask in t' back." She smiled and scurried off through a door at the back of the shop.

"Thomas, a fine lady be askin' fer fine fresh water," she said with a laugh.

"We got stream water," a man answered her. "Give 'er dat and if she ain't buying no cakes, be off wi' 'er." He swore under his breath. *How rude!* I thought, wanting to get out of the shop quickly. Then I heard what sounded like dishes clanking in the back and the sound of someone spitting. *No matter. Probably the rude man just spitting on the floor. Disgusting.* I said to myself, sorry that I had picked this establishment.

"Here ye be," she said, handing me a wooden tankard of water.

"Thank you kindly," I said. The tankard looked clean, so I

took many gulps of the water thirstily and placed a halfpenny and the empty tankard on the counter. I swung open the small wooden door, left the shop, and found the porter with my bags, and the carriage, waiting for me just outside the station. The journey and the arrangements I had made had gone as well as I had hoped so far.

However, the Polwhele estate was a distance to go still, and I could not wait to see its magnificence. The earliest parts of the estate were built in the seventeenth century, with granite arches said to date back to this period. Thomas had renovated the house, adding a tower and more arches where his and Fanny's initials were carved.

Upon arrival, I saw that each room was sumptuously furnished with historic paintings, candles, and velvet uphol-stery. The main hall had vaulted ceilings with large iron chan-deliers. Centuries old tapestries lined the walls, each more beautiful than the last. *The roast goose with baked apples, potatoes in butter, slender green beans, and fine wine are all spectacular. But, given their new baby is sleeping, I will not get a chance to meet him this evening.* After dinner, we began our discussions in their large sitting room filled with antique objects from former times, further reminders of the history of the house and its estate. *I am looking forward to investigating them more closely during the coming days of my stay.*

"It has been much, much too long since I have seen you, Thomas and Fanny," I cajoled and they agreed. We discussed our mutual geological interests heartily. I described the pro-gress that Caroline and I had made with sorting and housing the mineral collection my father had left me and our dream of eventually exhibiting it at Cambridge University.

"Please, Elizabeth, give us an account of your narrow escape on the *Earl of Arran*. How close was the ship to actually sinking? How did you manage!" she asked in a fervour. When I told them about the Earl shaking his fist at the captain, telling him how he would string him up and other dastardly acts of vengeance while others were trying to save their lives and not go down with the ship, Thomas and Fanny laughed at my impression of the Earl and his misguided priorities.

"Imagine! An Earl in fishing gear swearing and pumping his fist in the air at the ill captain. Hilarious!" Thomas claimed he had not heard anything quite that humorous in years.

What of your book, *Country Town*? Have you had much call to discuss it?" Thomas asked when he at last regained his composure. "I must say I found it a very logical and forward thinking read and have recommended it through the years to a good many of my colleagues."

"Why yes, I have spoken about the book to several groups, some ladies' organisations, some church social functions, and some lectures this summer as part of a garden series. Most find it favourable. I will admit there are others, both men and women, who find many premises in the book disagreeable."

"Oh, on what grounds, may I ask?" asked Fanny, somewhat taken aback.

"Mostly, I find people are reluctant to think about engaging others from different classes, as if they are another breed, and cannot be educated," I responded. "It is understandable how some people dislike change, but change for the betterment of the whole must be undertaken if we are to compete globally."

"Here, here! I say!" said Thomas, in solidarity. "We need to harness all the intellect and skill our people can muster here in the United Kingdom! Be gone with these ultra conservatives who ignore the masses."

I wondered about the veracity of his statement, given his luxurious surroundings, so I decided to change the subject and draw on my sketches for conversation. I gave them a quick presentation of my Scilly drawings of the town of St Mary's, the boulders surrounding the beaches, a few harbour scenes, each with a quick colourful narrative. They offered very kind words about my work.

"What talent you have!" Fanny exclaimed. "We have been to the Scillies, and you have captured the rock formations perfectly. How you have achieved the correct scale in your work is extraordinary. Your work is truly worthy of any gallery in London," she added, examining the sketches one by one again. "We would be most pleased to hang one in our own gallery."

"Thank you most kindly," I replied.

"Yes," said Thomas, "most impressive work. I too would like to see them exhibited for others to admire."

It was a very relaxing and enjoyable time at Polwhele. I completed my writing and made it ready for submission to the publishers. I was freely able to explore the estate and absorb the house and garden; but most pleasurable of all was the company and stimulating conversation of my hosts. We continued to tell the most amusing stories and my sides were hurting from so much laughter. I was sorry to leave at the end of my ten-day stay. The carriage took me back to Truro station, where I was in good time to board the train for Penzance.

Having settled down in my compartment, this time alone, I realized that I had left my portfolio behind at Polwhele. *Never mind,* I thought. *It is in safe hands.*

As I sat on the train, the strangest feeling started to come over me, as if I was becoming ill. My throat hurt and my body ached a bit. "I must have caught a cold," I scolded myself, always having been impatient with my own illnesses. The train passed through Hayle, past Copperhouse and Carnsew where Father had had so much trouble in the bitter conflict with Harvey. Phillack too was in the distance, and Riviere House where I had been born, but which I had been far too young to remember, before we moved to Penzance. While living there, I noted, my father had use of a laboratory in the basement, visited by Sir Humphrey Davey himself, I thought ironically, thinking how much Father had contributed to science without a statue erected in his honour. The train rumbled on, and I became more and more dizzy and ill at ease.

We reached Penzance, the end of the line, on time, and I was glad to be near home as I was feeling very hot, realizing I had a fever. *I feel so weak, like I am having trouble walking home. I am out of breath. This is so unusual for me.* My luggage I left to be collected later. I had to stop on the steps in my garden going up to my front door and I struggled up the staircase to my bedroom, using the spindles on the staircase like a ladder. The effort to climb the stairs and undress to my nightclothes had caused me to be out of breath. I lay on my bed, barely moving. *What has come over me?* I worried. *Whatever it is, it has hit me with a force I have not felt before.*

At about seven in the evening, I said to myself, *I feel pain in my neck and back, as if an illness is taking hold of me. But perhaps I will feel relief in the morning.* I could not sleep all night because the fever had taken a terrible turn for the worse. I soaked my white cotton nightdress and my soft cotton bed-clothes with sweat. I was trembling and shaking. My spine ached badly. Using the chamber pot had become impossible. I had very little strength left.

The next morning, I was feeling no better. *I feel even more tired than last night, if that is possible. I feel like I cannot get out of bed, in any timely way anyway. I feel very feeble and very weakened. I have to do something.*

When Betty, who had been with me on the *Earl of Arran*, appeared to enquire if I wanted breakfast, I told her that I had come down with an illness. She brought back water, toast and some ham. It sat on my side table untouched.

I am behaving very unlike myself. I must call for Dr Hennessey to be summoned to come and examine me. Typically, I would have waited to see how the illness progressed and would have used my own bodily resources to cure myself. But, I am beginning to worry because I have never felt this ill before. Nothing can be done. I am very sick, no doubt about it.

Within about three hours, Dr Hennessey arrived. He had been our family physician for years, and we had come to rely on him. He had a very stately manner but would fall into joviality when appropriate to ease tension with his patients.

"Now, Miss Carne, what seems to be the trouble?"

Before I could speak, he took one look at me and shook his head. "Proceed," he said.

Sitting up with some difficulty in the bed, I told him my symptoms and his expression grew even more grave.

"What have you had to eat or drink out of the ordinary during the last ten days or so?" he asked. "Who have you been in close contact with? What time, approximately, did your fever begin? In particular, have you been drinking water in a strange place?" His questions were to the point. I told him as best I could about my holiday, about my crowded train journey, about the horrid shop in Truro. My throat ached and strained as I spoke.

"Miss Carne, I am very sorry to tell you that you have typhoid fever. You probably drank water that contained human waste, either at the small shop, or came into contact on the train or platform with someone who is contagious. I have heard from my colleague Dr John Waddle in Truro – who has been studying medicine since 1833, by the way – that farther up the stream from that shop, residents dump waste in it, so I believe that is the most probable source of the infection." He paused. His eyes scanned mine to determine my level of comprehension. I knew what typhoid could do to its victims, and I became fearful for my life.

"What can be done?" I asked, stoically. I did not want to endanger Betty or anyone else. *And what about the Polwheles? I will have to alert Fanny immediately.*

"Drink as much water as you can. You will have a few days of abdominal pain and your stool will become liquid. You may have blood in your stool. You will likely get a high fever and in that case, hallucinations are common," came the solemn reply.

"How long do I have before the onset of these symptoms?" I asked directly.

"Maybe a few hours, by the look of you. I can give you laudanum for the pain, which is taken only a few drops at a time. It will relieve the spinal pain and some of the intestinal pain," he offered. "But I must tell you, as you may already know, typhoid is fatal in one out of five cases."

"Do you think I am one of those cases?" I asked, feebly, trying my best to be brave.

"Possibly. If you can make it past five days, I think you will survive."

"Thank you for your evaluation." I was so tired. I laid back down in the bed, my mind in a racing panic. *Five days! I possibly only have five more days to live?* I asked myself in disbelief.

"I will tell your servants about your condition and advise them on how to keep things hygienic and safe." With that, he tipped his hat solemnly and left the room.

I heard Dr Hennessey advise Betty, "Keep a basket of face coverings outside the door and use one every time you go in the room. Boil or burn these masks and anything she has come into contact with. The bedding. Dishes. Disinfect every privy, every drain, with lye or your strongest disinfectant. Make it mandatory that everyone in the house washes their hands frequently and wears a face covering. Let no one, and I mean no one, come into contact with her. Leave a pitcher of water at her bedside." Through the door, which was slightly ajar, I saw that he drew several small bottles out of his medical case. "I am giving you laudanum for her pain. Tell her only a few drops at a time or this will kill her by overdose. I will also leave these vials of quinine and turpentine. Good luck." I heard his slow footsteps going down the hall.

"Betty?" I asked.

"Yes, miss. I am here," she said, voice scared and hesitant, through the door.

"I will have you write several notes for me to send out. Come back with writing tools and paper, and I will dictate the letters."

We wrote the letters. I explained that I had seen Dr Hennessey and my resulting diagnosis. In the letters, I urged each recipient to stay away. *"... nothing can be done so please do not come near as I am very contagious, and the last thing we need is for you to become ill as well. I wish you all of God's blessings."* In my note to Mr Downing, I asked him to sell the *Nils Desperatum* to create some ready capital given the continuing uncertainties. *I deeply regret the pain they will all feel upon reading these letters. I know they will be upsetting, and I, in turn, am worried about each one of them. What will happen to them? To our assets? Thomas Bodilly only just passed away the previous year. What a demise! Mr Downing will be given added grief and responsibility and I am very upset and saddened for him.*

I was in equal parts terribly ill physically and emotionally. *Will I last past five days? My head hurts so badly I think it will explode.* I tried to drink sips of water as the doctor instructed, but each time I did, all I could think about was that it could be infected with human waste and was disgusted. *What a dreadful state of being.* I laid on my bed and my mind wandered. Hours passed. *Dr Hennessey was absolutely correct. My insides have turned to liquid and gush out of me with a fury. The cramps and spasms are excruciating.* I took the medications and began to feel some relief.

From the replies I had received prior to my trip, Caroline and Henry would be difficult for my new letters to reach. All that night, no one came, which is just as I asked, but I still longed for someone to come to help me. I tossed and turned. I was in a burning fever. I dropped the medicine next to the bed but was too weak to retrieve it. I was soaked in sweat and my own bodily fluids. My hair was matted down to my face and neck. My lips were cracked and felt very sore. *I am dying,* I cried to myself. *I am not going to make it past this night.* I prayed through my cracked lips, but no sound came out. *God, please take me. Take me to your side as I am now a hideous waste. Please take me.* Even if someone were to come, there would be nothing anyone could do.

"Please, God, if I have done anything to serve you, please take me now and end my suffering," I cried out, but no tears formed. I ached so badly in my spine, the sides of my lower back, and my belly. The smell was beyond hideous. "Oh Lord, please save me," I whispered.

It seemed far into the next morning before Betty reappeared. *She is so young, twenty-five, and energetic, but not knowledgeable about nursing someone as badly off as I am,* I thought, desperately.

"Oh, dear God. Miss Elizabeth! Look at you! Tell me what to do. I can help you," she stated nervously. She quickly lit several candles on my mantle.

"Water," I croaked.

"Yes, miss." She poured water into a cup and tried to help me drink it.

"You cover your face," I demanded. She wrapped a handkerchief around her nose and mouth and tied it tightly.

"Remove and bring new pot," I pointed weakly to the chamber pot. "Wash hands."

We worked together, me giving her instructions on how to roll me over and remove the bedding. She found a clean nightdress, and I painfully put it on. "Burn these outside," I said, pointing to the soiled pile of clothes and linens. I was glad to be in a clean bed with a clean nightdress at least. "Vials," I said, with great difficulty in making myself understood. Only a few drops remained in each of the three vials. She gave me what was left and set them on the polished wooden washstand where she washed her hands vigorously. "Fresh water." I croaked. She came in and out of my room, wringing her hands.

At this point, I had very little fluid left. *Is this how my father felt when he was dying? I should have been more sympathetic,* I said to myself, crossly. My head was swimming with memories of him and my mother. *My arms feel like they are floating. I must have a high fever. I am so tired. So exhausted. I cannot move my head. My spine hurts so much I want to cry, but I have no energy to do so. Betty must have left for the night.*

The next morning, I think it was, she came in with her face covered in a white handkerchief, took one look at me and said, "I am getting on a horse to find Dr Hennessey again and no mistake." I heard her ride down the lane. *Betty, it will not do any good, and I imagine Dr Hennessey will agree with me. He likely will not come.* I could not remember what day it was. Or what time of day it was. I could hear birds singing. *Is it day or night? It seems like hours have passed. Be calm. Try to stay calm.*

I heard a female voice downstairs. "Bess!" she screamed. She ran up the stairs. A hand flew up to the lace handkerchief over her mouth at the sight of me. It was Caroline. I could barely swallow. My body pain was excruciating to the point of not caring what she was saying. I let out a whimper.

"Oh, Bess! I came as fast as I could. Betty is trying to find Dr Hennessey. What can I do for you, my lamb?" she asked, frantically, looking around for some magical solution to this horrific, impossible scene.

"Bess, you must fight. You are a strong woman. You have climbed mountains, remember?" She bent down to see if I was still breathing and to briefly feel my forehead. I could not answer her. I tried to move my eyes back and forth so that she would know I was still alive. My body was shaking uncontrollably.

"You have lost weight, Bess. Can you drink anything? Bess, can you hear me? Bess, you are on fire; you are so hot with fever. Oh, my poor dear. Fight Bess, fight it!"

I tried my best to fight it. I was glad to see her, my beautiful, cheeky sister. *We worked well together when we had to, and she was my faithful travelling partner. So different, the two of us, but cut from the same cloth. Family.* She patted my hand for a few seconds and then backed up to keep her distance. *Typhoid is highly contagious. Apparently, she knows that.*

It was so difficult for me to respond. My thoughts were scattered, and I had difficulty focusing my mind on any one thing. I pointed my finger to the dresser against the wall where earlier I had laid two notes. With each note, I had placed a flower from my writing box earlier. Caroline looked in the direction of the notes, but quickly turned back to me with a panic-stricken look on her face.

"Bess, keep breathing. Help is on the way," she whined, her voice very strained as she tried not to cry. "Please do not let your light burn out! Keep breathing!"

One of the notes was for her, the other was for Henry. In Henry's note, I had torn a small hole and placed in the hole the stem of his favourite flower, a dried bluebell, which I had saved for years from one of our mission trips together. On the paper, over the flower, I wrote in very faint handwriting,

> *Henry, I kept my promise, for this world and the next. Please do not be angry, as I am with our Lord now. Stay on His path. I have loved you well. Bess.*

I placed the incredibly blue vivianite mineral he had given me so long ago next to the note. Some amount of time passed. Caroline stood in the far corner of the room, only her eyes showing out of the face covering, as she watched my every breath grow more and more faint.

Bang! I vaguely heard the front door open and crash against the wall. "Bess!" someone yelled.

It was Henry. He came! I heard running up the stairs. Strong hands lifted me up.

"Henry, you must cover your face!" Caroline shrieked.

"Let the illness take me, too," Henry said, defiantly.

I felt his lips on mine, delivering a soft pang of joy as it washed over my body. I was enveloped in a warm happiness but was very confused. My mind was muddled, swirling, and slow, and even though I tried, I could not regain my speed or clarity of thought. *Confused. What? Think. Try again. Not sure. Who?*

"Bess, stay. Please, stay," someone whispered close to my face, crying. "I came as fast as I could. Help is on the way, my love. But if the pain is too much, then go to Him and I will follow. Go to Him if you must, my solid beauty. I will find you. I will see you again, Bess? Bess! Bess!"

Is it Father? Is Father calling me? It is Father! And he is with Mother! We are at the opening of the Boscawen Un Standing Stones. Mother! Father! I am so happy to see you both! Look, it is our favourite Quartz Stone. It shines so brilliantly in the sunlight! Can you see how it shines?

"You will be remembered ... for your many gifts. For educating children, building lives, and for tearing down class barriers and allowing everyone to play a part," Father said, as we walked through the stones, hand in hand. "You are a luminary, a light who brought people together and showed us there is more light among us when we come together. You have served God well, and He is here, Bess."

I smiled faintly. Then I was free.

"Civilizations ... demand for improved work throws the workers into separate departments of industry and intellect, and raises up classes in the place of tribes. We have our own terrible monotony of class thoughts, feelings, and prejudices; our own terrible isolation of class employments, sympathies, and interests ... how great must be the evil, which, like strongly marked class distinctions, is both a monotony and a slavery; which binds us to one set of ideas, to one bond of fellowship, to one aspect of life. The danger which threatens us is very great, and we ought to prize and cultivate any phase of English life which brings different classes nearer together."

- Elizabeth Carne, *Country Towns*, *1868*, p.39–40.

Epilogue

The events following Elizabeth's unexpected death were quite interesting. Mr Nicolas Downing resigned from the bank a year later, either to retire or to escape what might have been differences between him and Charles Ross and the younger Thomas Bodilly. Even though Charles Ross managed the bank for over twenty years in what appeared to be a reasonable fashion for local customers, his political ambitions and activities became a preoccupation and may have compromised his banking responsibilities. He became a big man in Penzance, served as mayor several times, and represented the local St Ives constituency in Parliament. He had ambitions for the bank too.

Elizabeth had opened a branch in St Just, and he added another in St Ives and – surprisingly – one in faraway Plymouth. In 1890, the bank was converted from the private partnership it had always been into a limited liability joint-stock company, with the title of Batten, Carne, and Carne Banking Company Limited. There was a large number of shareholders, most of them local; and the directors were Charles Campbell Ross (managing), Thomas Bodilly, Major John James Ross (Elizabeth's nephew, whom she hoped might have joined in the 1860s), Thomas Bodilly's younger brother, Ralph, and a Colonel Innes. Still bent on expansion, a further share issue was floated in 1895, but hardly anyone took it up. To withdraw the issue would start damaging rumours that the bank was in trouble, so was out of the question. But the bank really was in trouble; and liquidation was the only answer. In

1896 the business, with all the customer accounts, was transferred seamlessly to Bolitho's Consolidated Bank of Cornwall Limited. This company had been formed in 1890 by the amalgamation of most of the independent banks trading in Cornwall at that time. The customers were happy, maybe even glad to have avoided the impending collapse of the once solid Penzance Bank. It was a different story for the shareholders, who were faced with heavy losses in meeting the outstanding debts of their former business.

It was then, in the series of shareholders' meetings that continued until 1903, that the true nature of Ross' shady dealings came to light, and the extent of his malfeasance. The reputation of the Carne family, so carefully nurtured by Elizabeth, was totally ruined. In need of funds, Ross ended up selling the Carne estate, including the house on Chapel Street and its contents, by auction. That was the end of the Carne legacy. A rather ugly article appeared in the press about the auction and the Carne family's comeuppance. The mineral collection was also auctioned and was only saved at the last moment by the University of Cambridge, where it still is today, in the Sedgwick Museum of Earth Sciences. Charles then left Cornwall for London and became the director of the Whitechapel Gallery. He died in 1920. His brother, the Major, became the custodian of the standing stones at Boscawen Un and did oversee the upkeep.

The house at 29 Chapel Street is still there and is now called "Chapel House". It has been completely restored by a loving hand to become a luxury boutique hotel where I personally stayed as part of my research for this project. It was the closest to time travel I think I have ever come, and the service was excellent. Chapel Street continues to bustle with shops and studios, pubs, shops, and eateries as a highlight of Penzance.

After Elizabeth's death, it appears that Fanny and Thomas

Polwhele gathered up her sketches and papers and donated the sketches to what is now the Morrab Library in Penzance, where they rest today. In addition, her paper, "The Realm of Truth" was published posthumously in 1873. We have much to thank the Polwheles for in preserving her sketches and words.

Elizabeth's schools were started and, in 1876, the new elementary schools in the United Kingdom opened to provide mandatory free education, just like she was hoping would happen. It is very sad that she missed this event by three years.

Caroline Carne seemed to live a quiet but very long life, outliving all her relatives and living until 1900 in the old family home on Chapel Street. The sisters' famous cousins and novelists were the Brontë sisters, whose grandmother and grandfather also lived up the hill on Chapel Street when the Carne girls would have been infants. These homes are still there, receiving visits from curious admirers.

Anna Maria Fox asked for and received the letters her sister, Caroline Fox, wrote to Elizabeth, and they were published, although first heavily edited by their family friend and attorney, in a book called, *Memories of Old Friends*, which was a Victorian bestseller. The person whose correspondence is featured the most is our friend Elizabeth Carne. The book includes Caroline's letters to friends describing her adventures helping shipwrecked sailors. One particular story seems to describe Caroline in enough detail as to begin to really know her as a person. She takes up writing letters to the family of a sailor who cannot read or write and winds up reuniting them, much to their joy, before the sailor passes away. It is interesting to note that Caroline Fox had a long-term love for John Sterling, despite his marriage and children. When his wife passed away, Sterling proposed to Caroline, but she could not accept, even though she would have liked to, given his lack of commitment to Quakerism. She was devastated for a period of ten years or so. I imagine the unedited versions of the letters would have included kind words from Elizabeth about this heartbreak.

It is important to note that the Methodist Chapel remains today on Chapel Street, and two granite plaques that resemble scrolls commemorating William and his son, Joseph, for their substantial support and leadership. In addition, at least one of Elizabeth's schools is still functioning and teaching children, which was her passion. With approximately fifty children per year attending this school in recent times, this would mean that over the last one hundred and fifty years, over seven thousand children have been educated in that one school alone. Imagine how different many of those lives must have been after the children had learned to read, write, and perform mathematics. And certainly, their children, in turn, would also have been educated throughout those years. And so on. Bess played her part in changing the course of history and positively impacted thousands of lives in the region by changing education. Incredible.

As Elizabeth hoped, the stone circle Boscawen Un still stands today and is a sanctuary for peaceful reflection, as mentioned throughout the novel. There is some disagreement about the drawings on the centre leaning stone. Some say the drawings are two axes – others say they are two feet standing or perhaps laying down. According to discussions with Peter Herring (2022), a professional heritage and historical landscape consultant who has assessed the stones and published his findings, he leans toward axes rather than feet. However, Tom Goskar, an archeaologist (2022), refers to his assessment of the center stone compared with similar stone carvings in Brittany and his view is that the drawings are clearly feet. I hope that one day someone will be able to figure this message out, either axes or feet, and explain it to the world. In addition, and as of this writing, we are still hoping to locate the burial urns from the burial chamber next to the entry path to the stones. If we locate them, I will inform everyone via social media.

Elizabeth's books *Three Months in Pau* and *Country Towns* are still sold today and are easy to read, interesting, and relevant to our current diversity issues. If you feel like you want to spend time with a luminary, read her books and enjoy her light and a bit of time-travelling.

List of Characters by Chapter

Plus, further notes on people, institutions and some other matters mentioned in the text

Shown in order of appearance. Fictional characters are shown in _underlined italics_.

Preface

Hypatia Trust: https://hypatia-trust.org.uk

"The Hypatia Trust was formed to collect, and make available, published and personal documentation about the achievements of women in every aspect of their lives."

Hypatia (350 or 370–415) was a Neoplatonic philosopher, mathematician, and astronomer in Alexandria in the late Roman period, when it was a cosmopolitan cultural hub in the eastern Mediterranean, a crossroads and intersection of cultures. She met a tragic and violent end at the hands of a sectarian mob during a riot. In Elizabeth's time, Charles Kingsley wrote about her in his novel _Hypatia_ (1853).

Chapter One: Discovery

<u>Elizabeth Catherine Thomas Carne (Bess)</u> (1817–1873): The main character of this novel and a change maker through her philanthropic efforts and publications in geology, political science, travel and Methodist values. She was brilliant in mathematics and languages and was much loved by her family, friends, and community. She was elected to membership of the Royal Geological Society of Cornwall in 1865. She was noted for her philanthropy in Penzance, particularly in regard to education and the provision of new schools. She never married but was greatly loved by the public. Upon her father's death, she inherited £22,000 and became the senior partner in the family bank. She died unexpectedly of typhoid fever in September 1873. She used the pseudonym of "John Altrayd Wittitterly", a comical character from Charles Dickens' novel *Nicholas Nickleby*, for some of her first publications, including *Three Months' Rest at Pau in the winter and spring of 1859*.

<u>Joseph Carne</u> (1782–1858): Husband to Mary Thomas and father to Elizabeth Carne and seven other children. He was a partner in the Cornish Copper Company at Hayle from 1802 to 1844, and their general manager from 1807 to 1819, living in the Company's house "Riviere" in Phillack, where Elizabeth was born. He moved the family to Penzance in 1819, becoming a partner in the Penzance Bank; but continued his involvement in the Copper Company, now as partner and trustee, increasing his shareholding in 1834. His interest in geology led him to become a founder member of the Royal Geological Society of Cornwall; and, although self-taught, he published several authoritative papers in this field. Later he became a vice president of the Royal Cornwall Polytechnic Society in Falmouth, and president of the Penzance Natural History

Society. He also became elected a Fellow of the Royal Society in London, the premier learned society of its kind.

Mary Thomas Carne of Kidwelly (South Wales): Joseph Carne's wife and mother of eight children, including Elizabeth Carne, the youngest. Not much is known about Mary Carne other than that she was busy raising their eight children and was considered an invalid for what appears to be a long time. She was born in 1777, and married Joseph in 1808.

John Stuart Mill (1806–1873): Famous English philosopher, political economist, and Member of Parliament. A very influential thinker and writer in liberal politics, he was dubbed the most influential English-speaking philosopher of the nineteenth century and was an advocate for women's suffrage. He was a friend of the Carne and Fox families. His "walking tours" in different parts of Britain were an annual event. He adored his wife, who fell ill and died on a vacation trip to Provence in the south of France. He was so distraught that he bought a house there so he could be close to her. He died shortly after her in 1873, the same year as Elizabeth Carne. Elizabeth likely saw some of his articles that had been published in the journals and newspapers of the time, notably the *Morning Chronicle*, the *Westminster Review*, and the *Monthly Repository*. His major works include *The System of Logic* (1843), *Principles of Political Economy* (1848), *On Liberty* (1859), *Considerations on Representative Government* (1861), and *The Subjection of Women* (1869).

William John Carne (1754–1836): Elizabeth's grandfather and father to Joseph. He was a leader in the foundation of Wesleyan Methodism in Cornwall and a friend of John Wesley himself. He owned ships, was an adventurer (investor) in copper mines and then became a prosperous banker, opening

271

the Penzance Bank in 1795 with his partners John Batten and Richard Oxnam. He was said to be quite friendly and generous, having given away £10,000 in his lifetime, which was considered a huge sum at the time.

Joseph Thomas Carne (1809 –1831): Elizabeth Carne's older brother who died of tuberculosis in Madeira, a Portuguese island in the Atlantic.

Chapter Two: Mockery

Cornish Copper Company: A partnership in Hayle harbour which began in 1758 and was successively renewed until it ceased trading in 1870. Its original purpose was the smelting of copper; but it diversified into mine merchanting and shipbuilding, and eventually became a successful iron foundry and important engineering works. The largest surviving Cornish beam engine, preserved in working order at Kew Bridge in west London, was designed, built and installed by them. The Company's residual assets were sold to their great and bitter rivals and neighbours, Harveys of Hayle, who operated in the same lines of business. Both William and Joseph Carne were partners in the Copper Company, with Joseph continuing as a Trustee. In later years it traded under its trustees' names as "Sandys, Carne & Vivian". The negotiation described here is fictitious; but it is possible, given the diverse nature of their business, that they might have traded in arsenic; and they and their partners were certainly very influential in the management of mines, more so as the industry became rationalized as it declined.

Mary Carne (1811–1890): Elizabeth's oldest sister; married to Dr Archibald Colquhoun Ross of Lanark in Scotland, who was a surgeon in Madeira. They lived there for several years when they were first married. As a widow, she returned to live in Penzance.

Anna Carne (1813–1887): Another older sister, who married Dr David Johnson of Edinburgh and Bath. They had no children.

Henry Pearce (1814–?): Henry is a fictitious, everyman type of character. He represents the common man struggling to overcome obstacles and achieve prosperity. His intelligence and character are things Elizabeth admires, as she also admires them in common people. Elizabeth most likely did have a real Henry or several Henry's in her life that led to her understanding of different classes, what binds them together, and the benefits of breaking down those class barriers. Henry represents the love the public had for Bess.

Mine purser: The financial officer or treasurer.

Captain Richard Rowe: A Captain, Richard Rowe did exist and became a writer about mining activities, but this character here is complete fiction.

Delen and Carenza: Fictional girls, pretentious peers to Elizabeth who mock her background and intellect.

Caroline Fox (1819–1871): Elizabeth's best friend and a great intellect who wrote diaries from teenage to adult years. In her diaries, she wrote anecdotes about the prominent people she met and the places she travelled. Caroline and her family, who lived in Falmouth, were staunch Quakers and were advocates of many causes, including the abolition of slavery. Caroline also aided lost sailors. Her diaries, heavily edited for publication, became a Victorian best seller. In them, probably the person to whom she wrote and who returned her correspondence the most was Elizabeth Carne.

Emily Bolitho (1817–1886): A childhood friend to Elizabeth Carne and Caroline Fox, apparently not a frequent letter writer, but she kept a diary. Her letters contained much in the way of spiritual encouragement. Some of her correspondence and diary entries, including two transcriptions of letters from Elizabeth Carne, were published in Penzance by Beare & Son as *Letters and Reminiscences of Emily Borlase Bolitho* (1889).

Charity Hosking (1806 –?): A resident servant to the Carnes in Chapel Street and listed in the 1841 census. Because her name is listed at the end of the list of staff, we know she was not the cook and more than a maid.

Mr Richards: A slippery and shady businessman in the employ of the Cornish Copper Company, where Joseph Carne had previously been a partner and general manager until 1819. This character is fiction, but there were men named Richards who worked at the Copper Company.

Mr Alexander: Fictional character who works with Mr Richards for the Copper Company.

Mining sett: The area specified in a mine's lease within which it was to work, below ground as well as above.

Caroline Carne (1815–1900): Elizabeth's older sister by two years. She became the woman of the house and ran the household after her mother's death. Caroline was interested in antiquities and was active in the Penzance Antiquities Society, as noted in an actual roster currently held at the Chapel House, Penzance. Caroline also was involved in philanthropic work with St Mary's and with local Penzance residents and did help Elizabeth with the management of the mineral collection and likely with the foundation of schools.

James and Charlotte Carne: Joseph's younger brother and sister-in-law. James was a minister in a Church of England parish in Plymouth. They both died in a cholera outbreak there. Their five children came to live with Joseph Carne in the Chapel Street home.

Ann Bodinner (1811–?): Resident servant in the Carne household, in this story presumed, given the order of her name in several censuses, to be the parlour maid who also assists Elizabeth.

Ann Morris (1801–?): Cook in the Carne household, and most likely the cook, given her name is at the top of the staff list in the census

Chapter Three: Remedy

John Wesley (1703–1791): The founder of Methodism, whose evangelistic and pastoral journeyings around England, which often took him also into Cornwall, occupied much of his lifetime. In Penzance he was hosted by his friend William Carne, who in turn became the reputed "Father of Cornish Methodism".

William Lock (Jacka) (1816–?): Known resident servant in the Carne household, taken in this story to be their coachman. His nickname here is fictitious.

Charles Brown: A chemist on Chapel Street, Penzance. He and other traders mentioned here are described by G.C. Boase in his *Reminiscences of Penzance*.

James Tonkin: A grocer and flour merchant on Chapel Street; also painted miniatures of people and the town as noted by Boase.

Captain Trepen: The promoter of Wheal Penzance, a local mine which failed at first but did eventually yield results as described. The ruined shopkeeper was Henry Molyneux as noted by Boase.

A baby brother: George Thomas Carne (1821–1822).

William and his wife Fanny: William Thomas Carne (1816–1852) and Frances Cornish.

Chapter Four: Treachery

John Pixley: A real smuggler in the 1700s. Here Elizabeth encounters his fictitious descendant of the same name, and his fictitious accomplice *Jake*.

Reverend Richard Treffry: Minister of the Penzance Wesleyan Methodist Church in Chapel Street. He would have been well known to the Carne family. He was one of several ministers and preachers of the Penzance Methodist Circuit. He died in January 1838.

James William Gilbart: Author of *A Practical Treatise on Banking*, the standard and authoritative textbook on banking practice in the nineteenth century, going through several editions in Britain and America. From 1834, he was general manager of the London & Westminster Bank.

Philip Marrack had been an employee of the Penzance Bank since at least 1810 and had been the manager for a long time before becoming a partner in 1844. He died, or retired, in 1855 or 1856. He lived in nearby Newlyn.

Freethy family: Based on a real tenant farming family of Ednovean Farm, near the Boscawen Un Stones. The farm dates from the seventeenth century and has now been fully restored to offer luxury bed and breakfast accommodation. The head of the family, William Freethy, also serves as an everyman character in Elizabeth's life as she comes to understand the problems of common people.

Patrick Hewitt: Fictitious tailor and father-in-law to Henry Pearce. This is not the real-life Richard Hewitt, who had a tailor's shop on Chapel Street.

Elizabeth's cousins: Edward Turner Carne; Francis Frederick Carne; Catherine Charlotte Carne; Anna Maria Carne; Charles Thicknesse Carne. These were the cousins of Elizabeth who came to live with them in Penzance after the deaths of their parents, Charles and Charlotte, from cholera in Plymouth. Anna Maria later married the Revd. Henry Batten of Penzance and lived until 1913; Charles became a mariner who died in Hull, Yorkshire, in 1852.

Mary Pearce: Henry's fictitious older sister.

Chapter Five: Country

<u>John "Eyebrows" Thomas</u>: A person buried in Gulval churchyard, with a skull and crossbones on the gravestone with eyebrows included. The story about this character is a combination of legend and fiction.

<u>The King</u>: The reigning monarch at this time was King William IV (1830–1837). Victoria, his niece, was Queen of the United Kingdom of Great Britain and Ireland from June 20, 1837, to her death in 1901. Her reign became known afterwards as the Victorian Era and was longer at sixty-three years and seven months than that of any previous British monarch. It was a time of great industrial, political, and scientific change, which makes it a very intriguing and fascinating period for historical study. The king in whose reign John Thomas lived would have been an earlier eighteenth-century monarch – George II reigned from 1727 to 1760.

Chapter Six: Poverty

<u>Talwyn Hewitt</u>: Fictitious daughter of Patrick Hewitt, who becomes Henry Pearce's wife.

<u>Botallack Mine</u>: one of the larger mines in Penwith, literally on the clifftops overlooking the ocean. Its underground workings went far out under the sea, so that the miners could hear the ocean's roar – over their heads. It suspended work for a time during 1835.

<u>Mrs John</u>: Fictitious bal maiden and mother whose miner husband has gone overseas to find work.

Levant Mine: Another clifftop mine along the coast from Botallack and Cape Cornwall. It is now a working museum and part of the World Heritage Site.

Ladder roads: The access shafts with ladders are known in Cornwall as ladder roads. The climb up them could be several hundred feet.

Chapter Seven: Empathy

Barclay Fox (1817–1855): Brother to Elizabeth's friend Caroline Fox, and also a diarist. He was the son of Robert Were Fox (1789–1877) who, like Joseph Carne, was a Fellow of the Royal Society in London. A Quaker along with the rest of his family, Barclay Fox's diary has been published in more recent times as *Barclay Fox's Journal, 1832–1854* and is useful as a detailed historical reference for life in Cornwall during this period. Barclay suffered from respiratory ailments and ultimately went to Egypt for a warmer, drier climate but died there in the company of friends in his camp by the Pyramids.

Charles Dickens (1812–1870): An English writer and social critic. He created some of the world's best known fictional characters and is perhaps the greatest novelist of the Victorian era. His novels include *Oliver Twist* (1838), *A Christmas Carol* (1843), *David Copperfield* (1850) and *A Tale of Two Cities* (1859). They were commonly serialised in magazines before being published as books, which was where Caroline was reading *Sketches by Boz*. (It appeared in book form in 1836.)

Anna Maria Fox (1816–1897): The older sister of Caroline and Barclay Fox, who at the age of seventeen originated the idea for a Falmouth Polytechnic, which later became the Royal

Cornwall Polytechnic Society, for the purpose of developing art, science and culture.

The Mermaid of Zennor: Henry relates one version of the local legend.

Charles Hutchins: Architect for the reconstruction of St Mary's Chapel in Penzance, which began in 1832. The work took three years, during which time a temporary wooden chapel was used on the edge of town at Alverton (G.C. Boase, *Reminiscences of Penzance*).

The Bolitho Family: A prominent and wealthy family who had been friends and business associates of the Carnes since Elizabeth's childhood. From 1828 to 1838, Joseph Carne was a partner with William and Thomas Bolitho in a tin smelting house at Angarrack near Hayle. The Bolithos were also bankers in Penzance and Liskeard, eventually with their Robins and Foster partners becoming dominant in Cornish banking at the end of the century.

Chapter Eight: Journey

Boase and Branwell families: These large families were prominent in Penzance and cousins of the Carnes. Their literary Brontë cousins, Charlotte, Anne, and Emily, who lived in Haworth in Yorkshire, were contemporaries of Elizabeth and are very well known as novelists. Charlotte is the author of *Jane Eyre,* Anne of *The Tenant of Wildfell Hall,* and Emily of *Wuthering Heights.* These family connections are explored by Melissa Hardie in her *Brontë Territories: Cornwall and the unexplored maternal legacy, 1760–1860* (2019), which also has much information on the Carne family.

John Sterling (1806–1844): An author and a poet from London who travelled to Cornwall and met the Carnes and the Fox family. He struggled with tuberculosis and moved to various places to improve his health. In 1841, Sterling moved to Falmouth and lectured at the Royal Cornwall Polytechnic Society originated by Anna Maria and Caroline Fox. He and Caroline fell in love and became engaged after Sterling's wife died, but he could not convert to Quakerism and so the engagement ended, sadly for both John and Caroline. He is frequently mentioned by Barclay Fox in his Journal.

Rev. John Carne (1789–1844): Travelled widely in the eastern Mediterranean, Egypt and Palestine and published accounts of his travels. Brother to Joseph Carne and uncle to Elizabeth Carne. He was said to tell amazing stories that would draw crowds at parties. Ordained as a deacon in the Church of England, he never officiated as such, except for a brief period in Switzerland.

Davies Giddy Gilbert (1767–1839): A prominent personality in Cornwall, and one of the instigators of the Royal Geological Society of Cornwall. He was President of the Royal Society in London from 1827 to 1830. His family owned Ednovean Farm, where the Freethys were tenants.

Chapter Nine: Promissory

Charles Fox (1797–1878): Uncle of Anna Maria, Barclay and Caroline Fox, with an especial interest in geology.

Betsy Allen: A popular pastry cook in Penzance who was a favourite of John Carne. Her story about him is shaped from G.C. Boase, *Reminiscences of Penzance*.

Sir Charles Lyell (1797–1875): One of the leading geologists of the time; published his *Principles of Geology* in many volumes, 1830–1833.

Lord George Gordon Byron (1788–1824): Famous Romantic poet, best known for *Childe Harold* and *Don Juan*.

Chapter Ten: Integrity

Reverend J.J. Topham: A Wesleyan Methodist minister in the Penzance Circuit.

Chapter Eleven: Successor: The Youngest

Mr Bodilly: Thomas Hacker Bodilly, a prominent Methodist in Penzance, with a family grocery business at 36 Market Place alongside his involvement in the bank in which he became a partner with Elizabeth in 1859.

Nicolas Berriman Downing: A clerk in the Penzance Bank from 1848, he became manager in 1861 and then a partner in 1872. He retired in 1874. He was a real person in these roles but his dialogue in this story is fictional.

Archibald Ross Carne (Archie) (1844–1864): The oldest son of Elizabeth's oldest sister, Mary Carne Ross, and born in Madeira. His mother returned to Britain after the death of her husband, living at first in Sussex before moving back to Penzance. Archie, who had been educated at Brighton College in Sussex and been in the military cadets there, also came to Penzance and joined the bank, also adopting the Carne name.

Well-liked in the community, he died at the age of twenty from scarlet fever. Elizabeth had high hopes for him as her possible successor at the bank.

Charles Campbell Ross (1849–1920): A younger son of Mary Carne Ross who, after his brother's death, became the heir apparent to Elizabeth at the bank, succeeding her as senior partner. He also attended Brighton College, and went on to Trinity College, Cambridge. His subsequent career is summarized in the Epilogue above. His spouse was Isabella Emily Carne. The Ross Bridge in Penzance harbour is named after him.

Mary: Elizabeth's fictitious servant at Coulson's Terrace.

Visit to Pau: This part of the story is based on Elizabeth's account of it in *Three Months Rest at Pau in the winter and spring of 1859,* which was a combination travel, geological, weather, and moral living guide. She made several trips to Europe during her life: another, recorded in an article for the Royal Geological Society of Cornwall in 1865, was to Menton and the French Maritime Alps.

Geodes are rounded hollow stones containing crystals, typically quartz.

Chapter Twelve: Modernist

Mr Alexander: Fictitious customer of the bank.

Mr John Childs: An actual shipowner and mortgagor of the Penzance Bank, who traded in the Caribbean. He did eventually acquire the *Constance,* using a mortgage from the bank.

Chapter Thirteen: Geologist and Preservationist

<u>William Camden</u> (1551–1623): Antiquary and pioneering student of British history.

<u>Thomas Bodilly, Jr.</u>: Son of Thomas Hacker Bodilly ~~senior~~ who took over his father's partnership at the Penzance Bank after his father died.

Betty: A fictitious maid at the Coulson Terrace house.

<u>Captain Boase, Sergeant Francis and Corporal Pascoe</u>: Volunteers serving with Ensign Archibald Carne in the First Cornwall Rifles (a company of a militia regiment), and present at their annual dinner as recounted in Archie's newspaper obituary.

Ernest Campbell: Fictitious farmer who rents the land at Boscawen Un from the Carnes.

<u>The Town Hall, a.k.a. St John's Hall</u> also incorporated a geological museum. Originally in 1861, when the Royal Geological Society of Cornwall decided to build a new museum and offices, Elizabeth had given £200 in memory of her father for the land on which the new building would stand.

<u>Sir Charles Lemon</u> (1784–1868): Member of Parliament and Fellow of the Royal Society in London; president of the Royal Cornwall Polytechnic Society, 1841–1846; contributed articles to the Transactions of the Royal Geological Society of Cornwall.

<u>Augustus Smith</u> (1804–1872): An educational pioneer, philanthropist and Member of Parliament for Truro from 1857 to

1865. He lived at Tresco Abbey in the Isles of Scilly, which he leased from the Duchy of Cornwall. President of the Royal Geological Society of Cornwall, 1857–1862.

William Stukeley (1687–1765): Antiquary who wrote about Stonehenge and Avebury, and the supposed connections of these and other standing stone formations with the Druids.

Reverend William Borlase (1696–1772): Ordained in the Church of England: the rector of Ludgvan and vicar of St Just in Penwith. A noted antiquary and archaeologist elected a Fellow of the Royal Society in London in 1750.

Richard Edmonds (1801–1886): Antiquary and geologist, born in Penzance.

Menhirs: Individual standing stones from the Megalithic epoch; in this case one standing apart from but associated with the stone circle at Boscawen Un.

Dr Hennessey: Fictitious family doctor treating Archie for scarlet fever.

Chapter Fourteen: Capitalist

Mrs Vivian's bank: This was the Helston Union Bank, at this time being run by Cordelia Vivian, daughter of its founder Thomas Grylls. It eventually failed in 1879. Her late husband John Vivian had been a partner and trustee in the Cornish Copper Company with Joseph Carne.

Mr Thompson: A fictitious employee at Robarts, Lubbock & Company at 15 Lombard Street in the City of London. This bank acted as the London agent for the Penzance Bank as well as two other banks in Cornwall – the Miners' Bank in Truro and the South Cornwall Bank in St Austell.

Grace Piper (1801–?): Mary Ross' parlour maid at the 47 Chapel Street house.

John James Ross: Mary's son with a military career, eventually attaining the rank of major. He succeeded Elizabeth as custodian of Boscawen Un. He was a church warden at St Mary's Chapel, and a Freemason in Penzance and London. He became a director of the bank in 1890 when it was reconstituted as a limited joint-stock company.

Joseph Ross: Mary's son who became a medical practitioner.

Mr Brunel, the engineer: Isambard Kingdom Brunel (1806–1859): He was well known in Cornwall. He was designer of the railway bridge over the Tamar at Saltash, which includes components made by the Cornish Copper Company. He was a heavy smoker.

Mrs Sarah New: The actual owner of the home on Great Ormond Street in London that Elizabeth rented.

Chapter Fifteen: Philanthropist and Political Scientist

Nils Desperatum: This vessel did come into the ownership of the bank around this time, but the intentions here are fictitious.

"Married Widows": The whole subject of the wives and families left behind in Cornwall by emigrant miners is addressed by Lesley Trotter in *The Married Widows of Cornwall* (2018).

Reverend Henry Batten: Curate of Madron and instigator of St Paul's in Penzance, a new Anglican church built in the 1840s to supplement St Mary's Chapel. Born in 1813, he married Anna Maria Carne, one of Elizabeth's young cousins. In 1867, St Paul's and St Mary's became separated as parishes in their own right from Madron.

Mr Robert W. Aitken (born in 1836 in the Isle of Man): Vicar of St Paul's from 1869 until 1877. St Mary's and St Paul's were combined into one parish in 1973; but St Paul's Church was closed on 30th April 2000. It has come to ruin and was put up for sale by Prince Charles. It is sadly currently filled with pigeons.

Mr Forster: William Forster (1818–1886): Quaker industrialist and Liberal Member of Parliament for Bradford in Yorkshire, and instigator of the 1870 Education Act, which set up an elementary school system. It left existing provisions alone (though subject to regulation); but where there was little or none, School Boards were to be set up to carry it out. It was not popular with those like Elizabeth who believed that local church and chapel initiatives, funded by them, were superior to any state system.

Overend and Gurney: This solid London bank failed in 1866 after a new management team took reckless chances in what was becoming a speculative money market.

Hawkey and Whitford: A Cornish bank in 1866 which had become over-dependent on its failed London agent (Agra &

Masterman) to stay afloat. Elizabeth Burridge and Frances Moyse probably lacked the experience to be aware of its true condition, which was worsened by its poor accounting practice.

Iron mining in north Cornwall: At this period, the industrial demand for iron was high, and prompted much speculation all over Britain in marginal and unproven deposits of iron ore. While some Cornish iron mines were moderately successful, none lasted very long.

London & South Western Bank Ltd: A London bank incorporated in 1862 with the objective of bringing financial services to the "underbanked" South West of England and Cornwall. They opened several branches in west Cornwall but all had closed before 1870. They were always outsiders everywhere they went. Eventually the bank focused on the expanding London suburbs, where there was a real need for banking development.

Mr Brewer: William Brewer was brought in to be the manager of the London & South Western Bank's Penzance branch, and was a stranger to Cornwall, having previously worked for another bank in Sussex. He made his later career with the bank in London.

Isabella Carne: The widow of Elizabeth's cousin John Carne (1824–1860), the son of Joseph's youngest brother William (1797–1861).

Mr and Mrs Shackelworth: Landed gentry who represent the point of view that education disrupted the social order.

Chapter Sixteen: Bravest

This chapter relates to the shipwreck of the Earl of Arran *in July 1872, and is closely based on newspaper accounts, obituaries, and the official report of the government inquiry into the incident.*

The Earl and his companions were passengers on the ship and did survive, but their names have not been included as their dialogues here were fictitious.

Captain Stephen Deason: The licensed captain of the *Earl of Arran* who allowed an unlicensed passenger (Wood Alexander) to steer the ship in an attempt to run the shorter and more dangerous passage into the Isles of Scilly. He ultimately took responsibility at the official_inquiry into the wreck and was suspended for four months. No one knows exactly why Captain Deason allowed this; the story here suggests that he was trying to make up lost time to satisfy an important passenger.

Chapter Seventeen: Futurist

Mr Thomas Roxburgh Polwhele and Mrs Fanny Carne Polwhele: Fanny is Elizabeth's niece and daughter of Elizabeth's brother, William. Thomas is Fanny's husband and a geologist. They lived in and renovated the Polwhele estate near Truro.

"Thy Sweetness" is a completely fictitious business.

Dr John Waddle: A very experienced physician from Truro who was a real person but whose role in this novel is fictitious.

Reading Group Questions

1. Why is the book titled the way it is? Is there more than one reason?

2. Henry represents the common man in this novel. What did the last scene with him and Bess mean, given Henry's representation?

3. One of the themes in the novel is freedom. How and where is this used, and how would you describe the differences of this theme in today's world?

4. Elizabeth experiences resistance to her new role in the bank. How is this different or the same as experiences today, and what can you take away from Elizabeth's approach to it?

5. Another theme in the book is purpose and meaning. How did Elizabeth derive this in her life? How did it impact her? What can you do in your own life to create more purpose and meaning?

6. How is the title of the book related to diversity and inclusion? How does Bess experience problems with diversity first-hand? Where have you had success with diversity and inclusion, and what outcomes did that success lead to?

7. If messages like Elizabeth's on diversity have been public since the 1860s, why are we not further along in inclusion?

8. How are the many types of love used in this novel? How many different types of love do you have in your life and are any key types missing? How do the missing types impact your life?

Acknowledgements

One of the strangest and most incredible things of the 2020 and 2021 pandemic for me has been that I had not met some of my best, most supportive friends, and colleagues for this novel when I began. It is remarkable to me that four total strangers, three from anotherl country, would care enough about their history to help me with a tribute to Elizabeth Carne, never having met me. That, in itself, is a testament to Elizabeth Carne. Thankfully, I was able to meet them in Penzance to discuss the Carne family, stay in the Carne family home on Chapel Street, now called Chapel House, and soak up the history first-hand. Together, we meticulously embedded as much history as we could into this novel.

To that end, everyone I met in Cornwall was extremely helpful, friendly, and kind. Cab drivers offered stories to add to my novel. Hotel staff were intrigued and asked questions. People on the street explained this and that. Their help gave me faith in humanity that collaborative, kind-hearted people do exist in the world, especially in Cornwall.

First, thanks to my initial readers, Jennifer Lemler, who was one of the first passengers from way back in the time machine, and Gwenn and Alitta Boechler, who give the best feedback and support.

Next, my fine arts mentor, who has been one of the key people to get me through the pandemic with some sanity – Di Ann Pitts Hand. She read through my first jumbled draft and encouraged me to go on and "research the crap out of it." So, I did. Her tenacity and never-ending drive for high quality, polish, and uniqueness is a daily inspiration.

Also, my first editor, Linda Cleary, who read my sloppy mess, turned me around (which is not easy to do), and helped me gain the polish needed to hopefully give Elizabeth justice in this work. She is a beautiful writer herself and has the superhero power to use her expertise to make others better.

I would like to also thank my new friend and Carne family historian, Susan Stuart, who now owns the Chapel House and has turned it into a gourmet B & B. She answered so many questions about the footprint of the house and showed me her historical findings from her renovations. Fabulous!

Also, I was very lucky to work with B.E. Alatt, my last editor, who is a fabulous editor and an unsinkable person. A true inspiration.

In addition, my mentor and expert on Elizabeth Carne, the historian and author decorated by Queen Elizabeth, Melissa Hardie, Director of the Hypatia Trust, Cornwall. Her article "Take Thy New Existence" inspired me to learn more about Elizabeth, and Melissa's unending support and her ten plus years of research of the historical facts were treasures. Without her work, Elizabeth might have been lost entirely. Melissa is a treasure and a true friend, and I was so lucky to spend a wonderful time with her in her offices in Penzance discussing this novel.

Finally, I would like to thank John Dirring, Ph.D., historian, Victorian banking expert, author, and editor whose depth of knowledge is endless. John is the Swiss Army knife of editing. John not only elaborated on his dissertation on banking in Cornwall in Victorian times, but also went out of his way to offer me several of Elizabeth's life experiences that were unknown to me and would have continued that way if not for his wonderful collaboration and weekly correspondence. He has truly kept history alive with his support of this novel and is an ideal collaborator and writer in his own right. He went so far as to tromp through four inches of mud and hike miles with me to find the stone circles, graves and more in London and Penzance. An incredible person and adventurer!

I also wish to thank my husband, my three teenage children with their high praise ("Cool, Mom") and especially my energetic and driven mother, Janet, who has always believed in my dreams and held up the sky, for their unending support which made this project possible.

Thank you all for making this an incredible experience.

About Atmosphere Press

Atmosphere Press is an independent, full-service publisher for excellent books in all genres and for all audiences. Learn more about what we do at atmospherepress.com.

We encourage you to check out some of Atmosphere's latest releases, which are available at Amazon.com and via order from your local bookstore:

Dancing with David, a novel by Siegfried Johnson

The Friendship Quilts, a novel by June Calender

My Significant Nobody, a novel by Stevie D. Parker

Nine Days, a novel by Judy Lannon

Shining New Testament: The Cloning of Jay Christ, a novel by Cliff Williamson

Shadows of Robyst, a novel by K. E. Maroudas

Home Within a Landscape, a novel by Alexey L. Kovalev

Motherhood, a novel by Siamak Vakili

Death, The Pharmacist, a novel by D. Ike Horst

Mystery of the Lost Years, a novel by Bobby J. Bixler

Bone Deep Bonds, a novel by B. G. Arnold

Terriers in the Jungle, a novel by Georja Umano

Into the Emerald Dream, a novel by Autumn Allen

His Name Was Ellis, a novel by Joseph Libonati

The Cup, a novel by D. P. Hardwick

The Empathy Academy, a novel by Dustin Grinnell

Tholocco's Wake, a novel by W. W. VanOverbeke

Dying to Live, a novel by Barbara Macpherson Reyelts

About The Authors

Jill George, Ph.D., is an industrial psychologist who has worked in the organizational and leadership consulting space for thirty years. As part of this work, she has travelled the world extensively and met with thousands of leaders. She has published several books and many articles on leadership in engaging work cultures. She employs her competency and assessment skills to build deep and intriguing profiles for her characters. Jill has been a lifelong history enthusiast and lover of all things Victorian. She has been thrilled to partner with true historian, John Dirring, Ph.D., of Devon, UK, on this project. Her next novel is called *Illuminating Darwin: Arabella Buckley's Story* about the only woman who was a close friend to and discussant with Charles Darwin. Jill lives in Pittsburgh, Pennsylvania, with her husband and three teenage children, whom she adores. You can find many photos and videos from her research for this novel and her next novel on her website www.JillGeorgeAuthor.com, Instagram @jillgeorgeauthor, and on twitter @jillgeorgeauth1.

John Dirring has had a wide-ranging commercial and academic career. His doctoral thesis at the Institute of Cornish Studies at the University of Exeter in 2015 embodied considerable and still ongoing research into the history of banking in Cornwall and its methods, and is titled, "The Organization and Practice of Banking in Cornwall, 1771–1922," and it was here that he first encountered Elizabeth Carne and the Penzance Bank. He resides in Devon, UK, where he continues to write about the origins of Cornish banking. He has expertise in a wide range of Victorian topics, such as railways in Britain and railroads in America, sailing vessels, and farming as well.

CPSIA information can be obtained
at www.ICGtesting.com
Printed in the USA
BVHW040101220922
R14055300001B/R140553PG647658BVX00001B/1